JACOB
OF CANAAN

HELEN WOOD

Selah House Publishing
South Plainfield, NJ

Scripture quotations are from the King James Version of the Bible.

Jacob of Canaan by Helen Wood
ISBN 1-887065-00-8
Library of Congress Catalog Card Number #95-68643
Copyright ©1995 by Helen Wood

Published by:
Selah House Publishing
P.O. Box 257
South Plainfield, NJ 07080

Printed in the United States of America.

*To my children, David Wood and Cathy Wood Herring,
and the memory of their beloved father, my husband
Nolan Wood.*

Contents

Author's Note: It is not my intention to add to or detract from the Bible. This story is biblical fiction, based on the lives of Jacob and his sons in Canaan. (See Genesis 37-46)

Preface

Once I had completed the book titled *Prince of God* (the story of Jacob's early life and loves, and the births of his twelve sons—who become the Twelve Tribes of Israel, from which came the modern Israeli nation), it seemed only right to continue Jacob's story into his later years, "fleshing out" the meager facts provided by the Scriptures.

I began the task soon after an early retirement from teaching. I did not hurry with the manuscript, and did other writing along with it, so it took some three years to complete. It then remained unpublished for years, until after *Prince of God* and another book, *A Brief Summary of the Bible,* had been published.

I am pleased to see the book, *Jacob of Canaan,* finally come into being. I sincerely hope it will be of help and enjoyment to many readers.

1

Jacob Loses His
Favorite Son

. . . And Joseph went after his brethren, and found them in
Dothan. . . . And they said one to another, Behold, this dreamer
cometh. Come now therefore, and let us slay him, and cast him
into some pit, and we will say, Some evil beast hath devoured him:
and we shall see what will become of his dreams.

(Genesis 37:17-20)

The mid-afternoon Palestinian sun sifted through the
branches of the twisted old tamarind tree onto the stone
terrace in front of the spacious, sprawling house. Jacob
shaded his anxious eyes as he gazed questioningly toward
the sound of swiftly approaching hoofbeats.

Moments later, ten weary camels halted before him as
ten dusty men dismounted and bowed to him.

"Is it well, my sons?" Jacob asked, the lines in his sun-
browned forehead deepening. He searched the group for
Joseph, his favorite son.

Simeon winked slyly at Levi as the men began to remove
their sweaty turbans. The tallest, Judah, a bronzed giant with
an arrogant face and heavy black hair, approached his father,
slowly unfolding a blood-stained garment. He spoke in a low
voice, "I fear it is not well, my father. Do you know this coat,
whether it is Joseph's or not?"

Jacob took the torn, multi-colored coat into trembling hands. Alarm appeared on his lined face and in his voice.

"Yes, it is my son's coat. Where did you get it? Where is Joseph? What has happened?" The atmosphere was charged with a sense of panic.

The other men gathered around their father. They looked at each other with knowing glances as Judah answered, "We do not know. We found this by a path near Dothan, where we took the flocks when the grass gave out at Shechem."

Jacob cried out and began to show his distress by pulling at his hair and garments. "O Jehovah, some wild beast has torn my son in pieces! Why did I send him out alone? Oh, my beloved Joseph! My beautiful Rachel! Both gone! Jehovah, how harshly you have dealt with me! I have nothing left!"

He crumpled upon the ground, sobbing. He was still pulling at his robe as he began to beat his head upon the hard ground.

His sons looked on in consternation; they had never seen their father in such a state. Only Reuben, the eldest, could remember his father's anguish, during Rachel's travail while giving birth to Joseph. They all could remember that their father had been calm when his beloved Rachel died soon after the birth of her second son, Benjamin.

The scene of anguish and grief was too much for Reuben, who whispered fiercely, "See what you have done to our father? He is old; he will die. I shall at least tell him that you have sold Joseph as a slave. It will not be as hard for him as thinking he was killed will be!" Reuben's eyes flooded with angry tears.

Judah and Levi immediately drew daggers from their long, dusty robes. "You will tell him nothing!" Judah hissed, "He would have us go back and search. We are rid of this dreamer Joseph; we shall stay rid of him!"

"But how can you stand by and watch our father suffer so? It will kill him, I tell you!" Reuben placed his hand on his own dagger.

Levi went on, "Has he not done worse to our mother all

these years? Have we not heard her weeping many nights when he was with his beloved Rachel? He has never cared about hurting her, and he cares little for us, her children—only for Rachel's Benjamin and this dreamer!"

The bitterness in Levi's voice stayed Reuben's hand. He turned away and sank to the ground with Jacob, trying in vain to still his father's wild, flailing movements and his agonized wailing.

By now their mother, Leah, had rushed out. She was accompanied by her daughter, Dinah, and several servants, all clamoring to know what was wrong. Small Benjamin, in a short, brown robe, followed by more servants, came around the side of the house. The brothers, all babbling at once, explained that Joseph had been undoubtedly torn in pieces. Had not his blood-stained coat been torn to shreds?

Leah dropped to her knees beside Reuben and her husband, Jacob, trying to comfort him, talking softly as if to a child, tenderly stroking his hair. Dinah stood silently near her, with her dark head bowed as tears coursed down her pale, heart-shaped face.

Benjamin stood under the tamarind tree, watching his father. Bewilderment registered on his cherubic face. His dark eyes were clouded by tears.

The older brothers still stood around uneasily, looking expectantly at Judah. Finally, at his beckoning, they knotted on the far side of the old tamarind, and in coarse whispers and many oaths, sealed each other to secrecy. They vowed to kill Reuben if he ever told what had really happened to Joseph.

Satisfied, Judah left the group, went around the tree and roughly lifted his distraught father, leading him to the stone steps. "My father," he said impatiently, "it is not good that you should weep so. Calm yourself and let me help you into the house."

Jacob stared at him blankly, as if unaware of being addressed or touched, then his head sagged upon his knees and his moaning resumed.

Immediately, Judah dropped before him and shook him

3

roughly by the shoulders, while Reuben stared in shocked silence. The older man at last ceased moaning and raised his face. He looked confused as he turned toward Judah.

Judah shook him again, more gently this time. "Come, I will help you into the house."

There was no response in Jacob's eyes. He wailed more loudly and lowered his head once more. Judah raised his father's head quickly and forced him to look up.

"Stop it!" he commanded sharply. "Will this bring Joseph back?"

Awareness returned suddenly to Jacob's dazed eyes. He pushed his son away roughly and stood up.

"Eleazar!" he called. A tall servant with a leathery face rushed forward and bowed before him.

"Bring my swiftest camels. You and Zabor shall ride with me to Dothan. Someone there may know about Joseph."

"No, Father," said Judah quickly. "We talked with the men there. They know nothing and it is a long journey."

"I shall go," Jacob stated with finality. Judah was silent. His father might be old, but he was still head of the family.

Reuben, looking defiantly at Judah, said, "I will go with you, my father. We came by a shorter way, which I can show you."

Judah returned Reuben's look with a menacing one, his hand going to his dagger, but he said nothing. The faces of the others were tense.

"No, my son," Jacob said to Reuben. "You are tired from riding already. You can tell me the way you came." Judah's handsome face relaxed, and the other brothers breathed a sigh of relief as Reuben began to give his father directions.

Eleazar hurried toward the camel corral beyond the house. Leah and Dinah rose from the steps and went inside, followed by Jacob who was weeping again as he beheld Benjamin's troubled face.

After a few moments, Eleazar led three huge, fresh camels—two brown, one white—toward the front door of Jacob's house. Grizzled old Zabor hurried from the back, carrying food that Leah and the maids had hastily packed in a heavy goatskin bag.

4

After he fastened the bag securely to his camel's harnesses, Eleazar took three large, full water-skins from another servant and placed one on each camel. Then he stood holding the reins of the big white beast as Jacob prepared to mount.

Dinah ran to her father and hugged him, weeping. "Jehovah give you a safe and fruitful journey, my father," she said softly and then turned away. Small Benjamin clung to his father. "May Jehovah be with you and help you find my brother," he said.

"Bless you, my son. And, you also, my daughter," returned Jacob with a quivering voice, weeping afresh as he mounted and took the reins from Eleazar. He bowed toward Leah and her two handmaids as they stood on the steps. Then he turned his mount and rode swiftly away, followed by two of his servants, yellow dust rising like a cloud behind them.

Reuben stood a little apart from the other brothers with his arm around Benjamin, who was still weeping. He spoke soothingly, "Do not weep, Benji. It will be well with our father."

"But will he find Joseph?" the child earnestly questioned. Reuben turned away and did not answer; Benjamin returned to the house with Leah and Dinah.

Once the brothers were alone, Judah smirked. "So you did not go to show him the way! You would have told him all. I warn you again, tell him nothing—ever!" Judah's hand went for his dagger again, but Reuben had already drawn his. Reuben spoke quietly, looking deep into Judah's flashing black eyes, almost on level with his own. "Perhaps it is better our father does not know the truth after all, for he would worry about Joseph being in a strange place. I shall not tell him. But hear this: I am my father's first son; you are his fourth. I shall take no more from you!"

His huge brown hand had caught Judah's arm before he could reach his weapon, and Reuben held his own at Judah's throat. Shoving him roughly aside Reuben stood facing his other brothers defiantly. They shrank before his gaze.

Disgusted, he sheathed his dagger slowly and went into the house.

Judah, recovering from his surprise, looked around at his brothers. "All of you remember: Never tell our father anything," he warned. They all went quietly into the house.

In the morning, after breakfast, they all gathered on the porch. Levi, who was just a bit older than Judah, sat next to his mother, who was again weeping.

"Dry your tears, my mother. With this dreamer Joseph gone, our father may turn to you. Anyway, we shall see what becomes of his mighty dreams!"

Leah brushed a full yellow sleeve across her eyes, then she looked at her son curiously. She thought, *Why, he is glad Joseph is gone!* She looked from one son to the next, at the faces of the handmaids' sons, as well as those of her own flesh and blood. Neither grief, nor worry showed on any face except Reuben's. *They're all glad! Only Reuben really cares. The others do not even mind Jacob's anguish.*

She said nothing, but realized that all of them were avoiding her searching eyes. *I wonder what really happened to Joseph.*

There was a long silence. Finally, Leah asked, "What about the animals you were tending at Dothan?"

"We left the herdsmen with them," Judah answered. "We will return to get them when our father comes back."

A sense of foreboding filled the air. Soon the sons rose and went about their morning's work.

Dinah, dressed in a white robe, her eyes red from weeping, came out of the house with Benjamin. She sat beside her mother on a stone bench, while the child continued on to the old tamarind tree. Benjamin stood staring in the direction his father had taken, kicking idly at a knot of parched grass. Dinah noticed tears streaming down his face, onto his coarse garment. Her own eyes filled with tears again as she moved to comfort him. He freed himself from her arms and ran to the clump of oak trees on the left side of the house, a private spot he sought out often when he was troubled.

Dinah returned slowly to where she had been seated at her mother's side. They talked about the tragedy for awhile, and of their worry for Jacob. Would he be safe, and what would he be like later if he came back without Joseph? They both remembered the state he remained in for months after Rachel's death. Dinah and Leah held each other close as they wept again.

Dinah kissed her mother, murmuring words of comfort, then returned to the house.

Leah, left alone, pondered the strange actions of Levi. She recalled Levi's words to her. Her sense of uneasiness increased as she recognized the jealousy and animosity his words had revealed.

"If only Jacob could turn to me!" she whispered wistfully. "But there is yet Benji left—he is a part of Rachel, too, so Jacob will give all to him now." There was no bitterness in her voice. She merely sighed and went into the house, softly uttering a prayer to Jehovah for Jacob's safety.

In the late evening, well-fed and arrayed in clean garments, the brothers sat on the low porch as a full moon rose over the old tamarind tree, casting eerie shadows. Crickets chirped their age-old song and in the distance, wolves howled hungrily. Benjamin's muffled sobs and Dinah's gentle voice could be heard from inside the house.

The men were silent; each appeared to be engrossed in his own thoughts. Judah jumped to his feet and began to pace the length of the stone terrace. Reuben gathered his garment about him against the chill, and walked away into the night, weeping again at the thought of his father's anguish.

Simeon and Levi sat apart from the others and began to whisper. Levi worried aloud, "Suppose some man of Dothan tells our father about the caravan passing through there a few days ago? He may connect Joseph's disappearance to that. We shouldn't have let him go!"

"How could we stop him?" asked Simeon. "All the same, nobody in Dothan saw us selling Joseph to the Midianites."

"How do we know? I can't help worrying," returned

Levi. In an even lower whisper, he asked, "Did you see how Judah gave in to Reuben? Do you think he fears him?"

"Yes. Judah will tread more softly now. Perhaps it is best. Why should we let Judah always lead? We're both older than he is."

Dan and Naphtali, Zilpah's sons, sat silently side by side. Gad and Asher rose and walked into the night, just as Reuben had. Zebulun and Issachar sprawled upon the stone floor, their heads against the wall. They were mumbling to each other.

"Jehovah, I wish Joseph's cries would stop ringing in my ears and that I could stop seeing his pleading eyes!" Asher said with a shudder.

"Are you a piteous old woman?" asked Gad contemptuously. "Anyway, it was more profitable than killing him and bringing his blood upon our heads, for he is of our flesh. And our father will get over it in time, when he knows Joseph is gone forever."

Asher was silenced, but his thoughts would not stop. After a while he asked his brother, "When do you think our father will return? Sometime tomorrow?"

"Yes," Gad answered. "Or the day after, at most." But it was a week before Jacob returned, defeated, sorrowful, in utter despair.

The whole tribe was plunged into a month of mourning. For Jacob himself, the mourning would never cease.

2

Jacob Moves to Shechem

And Jacob came to Shalem, a city of Shechem, which is in the Land of Canaan, and pitched his tent before the city.

(Genesis 33:18)

It had been two months since Jacob's sons had brought him Joseph's bloodied coat. "Leah," Jacob said, "I have found little peace in this place. With Joseph gone, I can no longer bear it."

His voice shook and his eyes filled with tears as Leah looked up at him from the stone step. He turned away as he continued, "Jehovah has dealt harshly with me here. He surely will not be displeased if we leave. How soon can we go?"

Leah was neither surprised nor unhappy. She had known they would move sooner or later. Her heart leaped as she thought, *We can now find a place that will not remind him of Rachel or Joseph. I will finally have a house of my own and Jacob will at last love me.*

The lines around her darkly beautiful, though weak, eyes deepened in the fading light as she answered, "We can leave within a week, when the moon is full."

Jacob turned back to her. "It is well," he said, glad that she seemed pleased, though he did not understand why. He had thought she would resent the change, though he knew she would not resist his decision. He turned and walked across the stone terrace, sat on a low stone under the tamarind tree, and stared into the gathering darkness.

Leah knew he was thinking over the time they had spent here. She sat still, as she also reflected on the past five years: *It seems so long since that awful night. Yet I still remember Rachel's suffering, and the baby's cry when it was over, Jacob's relief and pride at having another son.*

Their caravan had been returning from worshiping Jehovah at Bethel when Rachel's time of delivery came, just outside the small settlement of Bethlehem. Remembering, Leah could still hear Jacob's glad cry, "Another son—Benjamin!" and Rachel's voice, hardly more than a whisper, "Benoni, son of my sorrow."

Jacob had gathered her in his arms to comfort her, and minutes later, she died. Jacob had become as one who was living in a dream then, and he continued in this state for many, many months. Leah and the servants had taken care of the burial arrangements—Leah herself had sent to Bethlehem and bargained for a burying place. Jacob still held Rachel's body, unable to believe she was dead.

Hours later, at Leah's insistence, they had carried Rachel's lifeless body to the shallow grave the servants had dug. Leah and the weeping Joseph had led Jacob away while the servants covered the grave with earth and placed stones over it. Weeping and mourning filled the household. Leah also grieved, for she had loved her beautiful younger sister even though she felt jealous of Jacob's deep love for her. As the sun set that day, Jacob had taken Joseph with him and they had set up a great stone at the head of the grave, with the help of the faithful servant, Eleazar. While they were gone, Leah, Jacob's sons and the servants had prepared the caravan for leaving.

At dusk, Jacob, at the head of the caravan, still as if in a daze, had not led it on to Bethlehem, but turned instead toward the northwest. Leah could not understand this because Jacob had told them before they went up to Bethel to worship, that Jehovah had commanded him to live in Bethlehem.

They had traveled all that night and for many nights thereafter, mourning still for Rachel. Finally they had reached this place and Jacob had said they would settle here. Those were the first words he had spoken to any but Joseph since Rachel's death.

Young as he was, it was Joseph who had comforted his father and made sure the baby Benjamin was cared for. It seemed to ease his own grief to help these two who were closest to him.

Week after lonely week, Leah had watched as she was shut completely out of Jacob's life. *Will he never forget?* she had thought over and over, *will he never wake from this dream and live again?* She, the sons, and servants took care of the animals and the business of everyday living—food, water, cooking, washing—as best they could from the tents they used continuously now. The herdsmen had taken many animals to distant pastures, carrying their light tents with them, hoping to buy food wherever they stopped.

Leah supervised the care of the infant Benjamin by a servant woman who had a child close to his age. She took him to Jacob when he sent Joseph for him, but Jacob never spoke to her, never seemed aware of her presence. She took food to his tent regularly, but it was often untouched. She noticed how thin he was growing, how gray his hair was becoming at the temples and how unkept he often was.

My heart broke a thousand times during those months, she thought now as she sat on the steps, looking at Jacob's bent figure, as he watched, without seeing, as night fell and the stars came out. *But what could I do? I prayed to Jehovah day and night—but nothing changed.*

After many weeks, she had known that they must have better shelter for themselves and the servants, as well as for the animals. This place was much farther north than they were accustomed to, and winter would soon come. Finally, she sent Reuben, the firstborn—who had once been very close to Jacob, Rachel, and Joseph, and to Dinah, also a favorite of her father, to try to get through to him. They had carried small Benjamin, and somehow the two of them, along with Joseph, had made Jacob see that he must return to reality and take up his life again.

That afternoon, Jacob came to Leah's tent and talked with her about what kind of dwelling place could be built in the short time before winter, and what type of stalls and sheepfolds could be erected for the animals.

Oh, it was so good, Leah thought now, still sitting in the friendly dark, *to have Jacob back again, even in a small way! I remember thanking Jehovah and praying, Please give me back more of him, more than I have ever had. Oh, if he only would stay and let me care for him tonight!*

Now she could smile ruefully at her long-ago impatience! Actually it was many more weeks before he stayed with her, but she had watched him grow strong and well again. She continued to take his favorite dishes to the tent that he had once shared with Rachel, and now he ate them hungrily.

Soon Jacob and a few servants began to build the modest dwelling that had been home to them for almost five years. The sun turned his skin to a glowing bronze color and his graying hair only added to his attractiveness. Leah was happier and stayed very busy, praying still that Jacob would come to her soon, that he would be all hers. She realized, of course, that a part of him would always cling to Rachel's memory. Joseph still slept in his father's tent, and now took the tiny Benjamin for his father to play with before the household retired for the night. Leah never went with them, but she often heard sounds of laughter and joyful chatter. Though she was lonely, she was glad that Jacob could find some joy even in Rachel's children.

Later, Jacob used as many servants as could be spared from caring for the animals to help with the building of the house and shelters. At Leah's suggestion, servants were sent to instruct the distant herdsmen to bring the animals home again. The nights were becoming colder, the days shorter, and food had to be found for people and animals for the winter. Jacob sent out servants with pack animals to buy provisions from nearby towns and villages. Leah had earlier planted vegetables and she and the other women had dried all the surplus. They had also scavenged in fields and woods for native fruits, berries, and nuts. Even so, there were many foods they still needed, as well as warmer clothes for the colder climate.

Somehow they had managed that first winter, and by the next year, had grown all they needed. Little by little, the place had become home for them. Jacob himself finally come back to Leah; that is, all of him that would ever be able to come, as she well knew. Joseph had grown to young manhood; Benjamin was now a five-year-old lad; Dinah had become a beautiful young woman; Leah's sons, and the sons of the handmaids, had grown into big, bearded men, sometimes rough and defiant. Leah had known they were beginning to hate Joseph, partly because Jacob showed favoritism toward the boy, partly because Joseph was so different from them—a sensitive dreamer, and given to telling his father when he knew his older brothers had done wrong.

Leah's thoughts went again to that terrible day two months ago when the brothers brought Joseph's bloodied coat to Jacob, who had concluded that some wild animal had attacked and devoured him. Leah wondered again, for the hundredth time, if the boys were deceiving their father and if they had destroyed Joseph. *Oh, if only Jacob had not sent Joseph to find them! Surely he knew they had no love for Joseph, and had despised him even more when he had told them of his dream of the sun and moon and stars bowing down to him. Of course, they had interpreted the dream to mean that both their parents and they should bow to him someday. How could Jacob have been so trusting of these angry brothers? Why had he sent Joseph, of all people, to find them?* She loved all of Jacob's sons but she also <u>knew</u> them well. If she listened long enough, she knew she would learn the truth about Joseph, but she wasn't sure she wanted to know!

Jacob came back across the terrace, took Leah by the

hand and led her into the house. As she lit the lamps in their room, she heard coarse laughter and loud voices coming from the back of the house, and she wondered what kind of crude conversation her sons were carrying on. They were so much like her father, Laban, and her brothers. She thought, *Jacob should have brought them away from my father's influence long before he did. Perhaps a new place and their father's sorrow will help to change them. If only Jacob had spent more time with them long ago!*

Jacob was silent as they prepared for bed. Then as he sat on the bed, he spoke softly, with the familiar grief in his voice that made Leah's heart ache.

"Remember when the lad told us his dream of our sheaves bowing down to his sheaf, and the sun, moon, and stars making obeisance to him? We thought those dreams were from Jehovah, but now they will never be fulfilled." Tears coursed down his lined, brown cheeks. Leah sat beside him, as he sobbed, his massive shoulders heaving. "If only I had not sent Joseph to find them!"

O Jehovah, wondered Leah, *how many times has he said this in the past two months? How many times to me, how many times in his heart?* She held Jacob's graying head tenderly to her chest as he wept, stroking his hair and cheeks, wet with his bitter tears.

"Jacob," she said softly, "do not blame yourself. Do not think of it. You cannot change things and thinking about it constantly will only cause you even more grief." Her own tears fell at the anguish of this man she adored, this man who had never really loved her, though she had borne him six sons. She wondered again how her own love had failed to engender some response in him, why a little of his overflowing adoration for Rachel would not spill over onto her, especially now that both Rachel and her beloved firstborn son were gone. Once again, hope rose up within her, the hope that had kept her going and made life bearable through the long, lonely years. *Perhaps someday!*

She lifted Jacob's face and dried his tears with her nightdress, caressed his shaking shoulders as he calmed himself, putting away his grief for the night. She blew out the lamp and asked Joseph about their up-coming journey.

"Where are we going?"

Jacob hesitated, then answered, "Toward the south. Do you recall the great grassy plains we passed through near the place called Shechem, when we first came from Haran? We stopped and asked Prince Hamor, the Hivite, for permission to cross."

"Yes," answered Leah, "I remember it well."

Jacob continued, "Prince Hamor seemed peaceable and the land is good. Perhaps we can buy land for a dwelling, and the grasslands will bear our animals well. It is not too far away from where I thought my sons were when I sent Joseph to find them."

"The city was called Shechem, after the man's son," Leah recalled. "Dinah went out to see the prince's daughters, though she was only seven or eight years old. She said they spoke of their brother who was away on some journey at the time."

"Yes," Jacob responded. "I had forgotten."

"Do you think Jehovah approves of this move?" Leah asked hesitantly, remembering some of the groves and heathen gods they had seen near Shechem.

"I have inquired much of Him," Jacob answered, "but I have not felt the closeness of Jehovah since Joseph has been gone." His voice broke again. Leah pressed his hand and waited. Jacob continued, "I must go from here, and it is a good land. Surely Jehovah approves. At least He has not said no."

Leah's heart was troubled. Suppose Jehovah would not have them go to Shechem? Would not evil come of it? Her first enthusiasm for the move had cooled, but she said nothing else. It was long before either could sleep, though they knew that the morning, indeed the week, would be busy.

It was an impressive caravan, stretching for miles, that began its journey a week later, sometime after nightfall when the moon had risen. They traveled mostly by night, then they rested while the animals grazed by day. There would be no hurry, so they would not be overdriven. Scouts had already gone ahead to select the best route for grass and water.

Jacob, on his great white camel, rode up and down the line, calling instructions to drovers, urging stray animals back into line, making sure the family belongings were in order, seeing that Leah, the handmaids, Dinah, and Benjamin were comfortably seated on their animals.

Some ten days later, about mid-morning, the caravan, now weary, reached a huge clump of trees, perhaps ten miles from the city of Shechem, which was plainly visible now in the bright sun. Jacob gave the welcomed command to halt, and word passed swiftly to the farthest droves. All began to gather around the trees, through which a small stream ran. It was fed by a large spring on the west. The animals, smelling water, were no trouble to herd, and almost within the hour, the men and animals had slaked their thirst and were resting in the cool shade.

Jacob questioned his sons about this land, but they told him they had grazed animals farther to the northeast and had not come in sight of the city.

By mid-afternoon, Jacob, Simeon, and Levi, along with three herdsmen, were racing their camels toward Shechem. Jacob was in command of his emotions now; he had managed to cover his grief. He looked every bit the part of Prince Israel, with his head held high, his long hair flying. He was certainly an imposing figure of a man on his magnificent beast.

In less than an hour they were passing through the city's massive gates. After satisfying the two gatekeepers that they were peaceable and wanted only to speak to Prince Hamor, they soon drew rein in front of the prince's large, sprawling house at the center of the city. The prince came down the steps to meet them. He immediately noticed their fine attire, their handsome beasts with expensively jeweled trappings, and he greeted them graciously.

"Ah, is it not Prince Israel from Haran? Welcome! I remember when you passed our gates and pitched your tents there." He pointed to a slight hill to the northwest. "How long ago? Some six or seven years?"

"Ten years by the next new moon," answered Jacob.

"It doesn't seem that long ago," rejoined Hamor. "But I keep you waiting. Come down from your beasts and enter my humble dwelling." He gestured toward the wide, massive door above them.

"You are kind, ruler of Shechem, but we want only to pitch our tents near the terebinth grove for the night. Tomorrow, I would like to speak with you about buying land. These are my sons and servants. I have nine other sons, many servants, and much cattle back there by the stream."

Hamor acknowledged the sons with a bow. Jacob had noticed how Prince Hamor's eyes had gleamed as he had taken in all of their clothing and other trappings. He no doubt thought of the gold he would receive for his land.

How like Uncle Laban the man is! Jacob thought. *I must beware.*

"The land is yours," declared Hamor. "Pitch your tents as you will. My servants will help and we can provide food."

"You are gracious," returned Jacob, bowing, "but we will need only water and land for our tents. Thank you for your kindness. We will go now for there is much to do. I shall return in the morning. Perhaps, then, we can bargain."

As Jacob talked, Prince Hamor's memory stirred. He asked, "You had a small daughter who visited my daughters before. Is she well?"

"She is well," answered Jacob, smiling. "Small no longer, but grown into a young woman."

"Ah, yes," laughed Hamor. "So she would be after ten years. Perhaps she will come with you tomorrow. Certainly my daughters and my wives would welcome a visit from her."

"Thank you," returned Jacob. "I shall tell her. Now we must go."

"Then I shall look forward to your visit tomorrow. Peace, and may your God give you rest and joy in our land tonight." He bowed to Jacob and his sons, and they returned the gesture. Then they mounted and clattered away with heavy dust rising behind them.

Hamor watched them, his eyes glinting shrewdly. He smacked his thick lips greedily while he rubbed his hands together.

Leah and Dinah were eagerly awaiting Jacob's return, and as soon as he dismounted, Leah asked, "Is it well? Was the prince willing to sell?"

"All is well," Jacob answered, tossing the reins of his beast to a servant. "He was willing—too willing, I fear. But we did not bargain today. I must search out the land first."

By now all his sons had gathered, and Jacob spoke to them. "Mount and ride in all directions. Try to be back at dusk, and we will consider what you have found. Benjamin, you shall ride with me."

Pleasure brightened Benjamin's childish face as he bowed. "Thank you, my father." He hurried off to fetch his mount, his older brothers following at their own pace. Jacob instructed Leah, "Have our tents raised under the great oak near the water, and the others round about them. The drovers may pitch with the animals, as they choose. I shall return soon and erect an altar to Jehovah." He mounted and rode, with Benjamin at his side, toward the west, while his older sons turned their mounts away in several directions.

Before dusk fell, Leah and the servants had the camp in order. She had bathed, brushed and coiled her long, dark hair, and changed her journey-soiled coarse garment for a flowing robe of deep blue decorated with silver ornaments. She stood at the edge of the grove. A look of anticipation lighted her eyes when she spotted Jacob's big white camel and Benjamin's smaller one returning.

As Jacob dismounted, his eyes surveyed her briefly. She thought she caught a fleeting light of pleasure in them, but he merely said, "You look much rested from the journey. Come, we will gather stones and build an altar before nightfall." Her heart leaped at the invitation.

"Shall I gather too, Father?" asked Benjamin.

No sooner had Jacob answered than the child was off to a distant outcropping of rock. "Bring large ones, my son," Jacob called after him.

As Jacob and Leah carried smaller stones to a place he selected north of the trees, he told her something of the land he and Benjamin had ridden over. "It is rich, grassy land, with few stones, but there is no spring or stream. I hope our sons will have more success in finding a good site for us."

"Why not this land with its spring and stream?" asked Leah timidly.

"Much too close to the city," Jacob responded. "I have no wish for my sons to have much to do with city life. Anyway, its not likely the prince would sell land so close by, since he has animals to graze also."

When the sons returned, they all went for the evening meal the servants had placed on a long table near the stream. Night was beginning to fall, a few stars were coming out, and late birds were flitting about under the trees. The birds, crickets and frogs began their nightly songs. Leah and Dinah remarked how quiet and lovely it all was. Jacob recalled silently and sadly that this had always been his and Rachel's favorite hour of the day, and that Joseph had enjoyed it with them as well. A sharp pang of bitterness sprang up within his chest. *Rachel, wife of my heart, and Joseph, my beloved son, I miss you both.*

As they ate, each son described the territory he had covered. Only Judah had found land with springs and a large stream. He described it enthusiastically, "One spring is larger than this one here; it is the beginning of a wider, slow-flowing stream. Another smaller spring runs into the stream some two miles below the first. There is a great rock outcrop on the north that would shield a house and give the animals shelter from the cold winds. The land is dark and rich and almost free of stones. The large spring is some seven or eight miles from here, in the opposite direction from Shechem." He turned, and with a wide sweep of his brawny arm, indicated the location. "You must ride to see it in the morning before you go to bargain with the prince. He will surely want a great price for it, if he knows how good it is."

Jacob spoke with interest, "We shall indeed see the land tomorrow. And now let us go and burn our offerings on the altar we built and worship Jehovah on our first night in this land."

3

Dinah

And Dinah the daughter of Leah, which she bare unto Jacob,
went out to see the daughters of the land. And when Shechem the
son of Hamor the Hivite, prince of the country, saw her, he took
her, and lay with her, and defiled her.

(Genesis 34:1-2)

Prince Hamor sat alone on a stone ledge outside the city
gates, gazing toward the sun as it set in red glory, but he
was not conscious of its beauty. He searched the horizon for
some sign of his son Shechem's return from a trip toward
the Great Sea.

Hamor loved his bronzed and handsome son as much
as he was able to love anyone or anything, other than wealth.
He was impatient for his return so he could tell him of Prince
Israel's offer to buy some land from them. He wanted his
son's opinion as to what land to sell and at what price. He
licked his dry lips and his eyes glinted again as he thought
of the hard bargain he could make with Israel. Several times
he shaded his squinting eyes, looking for some movement
in the distance. Then, growing restless, he returned to the
gate where the guards were standing watch. They bowed
slightly and one asked, "Are you expecting Prince Shechem
this night?"

"Yes," Hamor answered absently. "He has had plenty of time to complete his business. I pray that no harm has befallen him." Pointing toward Israel's camp, he continued, "Watch well and bring me word if any of his men come in view. They likely will be searching out the land. See that you are especially gracious to any who would enter our gates. We may well use them." He smiled slyly, and the guards smirked and bowed once more.

"As you wish, Prince Hamor," said the larger man. As Hamor went back toward the ledge, the sentinels winked at each other and whispered knowingly.

Very little light remained on the horizon now. Hamor watched awhile longer. Just as he was about to return home, disappointed, he suddenly detected faint movement. Before long he could make out what he knew was the dark mass of his son's camel, silhouetted against the last fading light.

When the tired and dusty men on camelback reached him, Shechem dismounted, bowed and kissed his father on both cheeks. "My father, it is good to see you. Are you well?"

"Yes, my son," Hamor answered. "It is good to have you home again."

Hamor turned to the servants who had accompanied Shechem. "Isnor, let me have your camel. You can ride with Mison." The servants bowed. "Come, you shall soon have food and rest." The servant hastened to obey.

He and Shechem mounted and rode side by side. Hamor said, "I have good news, my son."

"Truly?" returned Shechem. "Tell me."

Hamor continued, "Do you remember the caravan from Haran that stopped here some ten years ago? You were away at the time, but we told you about it."

Shechem responded, "I think I do recall your telling me—a very wealthy caravan, you said."

His father continued, "The head of that caravan, Prince Israel, came again today. His dress and his camel trappings are even more impressive now; they are laden with silver, gold, and jewels. You should see the size of the emerald in his headdress! It is truly a marvel to behold! And now he wants to buy land and live among us!"

"Tell me more about him, Father."

Hamor went on, "His father is the old, blind chieftain who lives way to the south near Hebron. He is called Isaac and he is very wealthy. Isaac's father was Abraham from far-off Ur of the Chaldeans. You have surely heard of him— this Abraham, the Hebrew?"

"Of course, I have heard of him. Everyone has."

Hamor nodded and continued, "This Prince Israel left our land many years ago. At that time he was called Jacob. He lived in Haran, to the north, for many years, where he acquired two wives, eleven sons, and much wealth. When he came back to this land, his God had changed his name and his nature, and he is now called Israel, prince of God. All this he told me when he asked permission to pass through our land ten years ago. Seeing him again today made me remember. I know he has grown even more wealthy in this land. We can surely get much gold if we sell to him."

Shechem reflected on what his father had told him. "But which land would you sell, father? And if he lives here, will he not profit from the land more than we?"

Hamor answered, "He has not indicated which land he wants to buy; I am sure he and his sons are looking over the land even now. Surely if his God continues to prosper him, we will prosper as well."

"Suppose he should grow stronger than we and fight against us?" Shechem's logical mind was considering possibilities, but his father was concerned only with the gain he could get.

"No, he comes from peaceable people," he answered. "He will not fight. If our people intermarry, then his wealth will become ours; doubtless, we will make such agreements."

They rode through the gates, returning the gatekeepers' bows and greeting. They rode on in silent thought until they came to the broad stone steps of Hamor's house. They dismounted, threw the reins to servants who bowed and smiled their pleasure at Shechem's return.

As they went up the steps, Hamor asked, "Are you not pleased that we can acquire much gold for the land now and also take their wealth in years to come?"

"My father is wise," Shechem answered evasively. "I am sure you will trade well and do what is best. I am tired and hungry, my mind dwells more on my belly than on bargaining right now."

"Of course you are weary, my son," returned Hamor, noticing the lines on the darkly handsome face of his son as they reached the lighted hallway. "We will talk more of it tomorrow and you can tell me of the cattle you went to buy."

Hamor went back to the steps, deep in thought as night fell and the stars appeared through the branches of the tamarind trees in front of the house. He was disappointed that Shechem had not exhibited more enthusiasm for the bargain they could surely make with Prince Israel. *Why, when I was his age,* thought Hamor, *I had already taken three wives and had five children—Shechem and the four girls!* Sadness crossed his face as he thought of Shechem's beautiful mother who had died at his birth. With an effort, he turned his thoughts to happier things, the gold he could surely get for his land, the ways he could get wealth through Prince Israel. *Surely the God who blessed his father Isaac and his grandfather Abraham is also blessing him. If he lives among us, we will be blessed by his God as well. I have heard it said these people worship only one God—Jehovah—who they believe made heaven and earth. I have even heard they burn perfect animals on piles of stone as sacrifices to Him, and are quiet in their worship, looking to heaven as they beat their breasts and talk to Him. Perhaps we shall learn much more of all this as they live among us, and we can worship this Jehovah also, so He will make us to prosper, too.*

Just thinking what might come their way if he sold the land to them and they settled among them made Hamor happy. There would assuredly be intermarrying. Well! He would talk to Shechem in the morning, not only about the land but also about taking the man's daughter as wife. If he would not listen to reason, then Hamor himself was not averse to having another wife. Likely the little girl who had visited his daughters long ago would have grown into a beautiful young woman. How he hoped she would come with her father when he returned! Hamor smiled, moistened his thick lips, and as was his habit, rubbed his hands together, hungry with anticipation over all the possibilities he foresaw.

Shechem presented himself, well-rested and refreshed, to the family the next morning. He greeted his father cheerfully, kissed his two stepmothers and his four half-sisters. He talked with them of the places and things he had seen on his journey, and he enjoyed answering all their questions. He assured his father he had bargained well for cattle, and that old Elihud and the other herdsmen would likely be home before nightfall. They would be bringing twenty fine bulls and a hundred cows which were the largest and fattest he had ever seen.

"From these," he told his father, "our herds will improve and multiply greatly. And I did not even need all the silver you gave me." He pulled a bag from his multicolored robe and gave it to Hamor, who accepted it with pleasure, jingling the coins, his eyes gleaming.

"You bargained well, my son. Now let us go into the garden where we can talk of other matters."

They went through a side door and into the large, rectangular garden that was enclosed by a high stone wall. They sat on stone benches under a graceful willow tree, where yellow leaves fell around them as a gentle breeze rustled the high branches. Along the wall were well-pruned trees—fig, pomegranate, apple, apricot, and almond. In the four corners were gnarled, old olive trees, their leaves showing silver as the breezes blew over the wall. In the center was a circular stone pool containing dark green water; bright, sweet-smelling flowers, and herbs bloomed in profusion around the pool. Many stone tables and benches had been placed at intervals around the area. It was calm, secluded, lovely— one of Shechem's favorite places, and he inhaled the mingled scents with delight as his father began to speak.

"Now that you are rested, we must decide about the land to sell and drive a hard bargain. I tell you, the man is wealthy! I can hardly wait to see his flocks and herds! They must be numberless. He rides the biggest white camel with the finest trappings I have ever seen. Magnificent! And those of the sons and servants are hardly less impressive. Even his harness is inlaid with gold and jewels. They all wear many grand jewels."

Hamor paused to see if Shechem was impressed by all he had told him. Surprisingly, his son was silent, thinking. After a little while Hamor continued casually. "The Prince has a daughter who visited us when they passed through before. He says she is a young woman now and may visit your sisters again when he returns."

Shechem turned toward him and asked, "How many sons did you say the man has?"

"He had two with him yesterday; he said there were nine others. He would not stay, he said he just wanted permission to pitch his tents before nightfall. He did not say where he had come from. It must have been from the north, or the caravan would have passed close enough for our lookouts to have spotted it. By now he has probably ridden in all directions to decide which land he wants. Maybe we should sell that parcel farther to the west, where the land is not so good, but where he will be fairly close to us. Our merchants here can do business with him. Is that not best?"

Shechem was quick to answer, "The west is best for us to sell, but this may not be what he chooses. It is where I would have chosen, for the land is not entirely poor, it has few stones, there is water from the two springs and the stream, and there is that rock outcrop for shelter from the wind and for building."

"If he chooses thus, what price should I ask?" Hamor asked.

"Ask a hundred pieces of gold, Father, and then you can haggle over it," Shechem returned quickly.

Hamor smiled, pleased at the thought of all that gold. He sat silently, savoring the thought of the coming sale, then rose and told Shechem he had business with the town elders. "You can find me with them should Prince Israel arrive before I return," he said as he left his son in the garden.

It was mid-afternoon before Hamor, finished with his town business and resting in the dappled shade of his wide front steps, heard hoofbeats. He jumped to his feet and stood looking toward the city gates expectantly. Soon three riders came into view, and in a moment Hamor saw that one was a woman, sitting sideways. His excitement mounted as they came closer and he saw how gracefully she rode. He cursed silently when they were close enough for him to see that a veil covered her face.

He bounded down the steps toward them and as they halted, he smiled, bowing deeply. "Ah, Prince Israel, my friend, you are welcome to the city and to my home," he said.

Jacob dismounted and bowed to him. "You are gracious," he returned. Looking toward the veiled figure, Jacob continued, "My daughter Dinah." Then he turned back to his host, "Hamor, Prince of Shechem."

The girl had drawn back her veil, and Hamor's heart skipped a beat at her delicate beauty— her pink and white oval face with large, deep-set gray eyes was framed with curling, dark red hair. She smiled, showing even, white teeth between red lips. Her eyes met Hamor's . He bowed low, and when he raised his head, the veil had again covered her face.

The third rider dismounted, and Jacob spoke again. "My son Simeon. He was with me yesterday." Both men bowed and Simeon helped his sister dismount. Hamor took Jacob's arm, and they proceeded toward the house, with Simeon and Dinah following, as a servant led the camels away.

When they reached the top of the steps, Hamor bowed again and said, "Welcome to my humble home." Letting Dinah go on ahead of them, he continued, "The women will be delighted with so lovely a guest."

"It will be pleasant to see them again," responded Dinah, "after so long a time."

They moved on down the hall. A servant waited by an open door on the right and showed them into a spacious, dimly-lighted room, with plain but massive furniture. As Hamor seated them, his eyes took in the tall, slim loveliness of Dinah, which the richly flowing, jeweled robe only served to enhance. She drew back her veil and smiled, as Hamor said, "Be comfortable, my very welcome guests." Turning to the servant, he said in low tones, "Bring my wives and daughters." The man bowed and left.

"We shall not tarry long," said Jacob. "There is much to do at our camp. We cannot determine the far borders of the land I wish to buy. I came to see if you will be so kind as to come and mark it with me tomorrow, if you agree to sell it."

"Which lands did you consider, Prince Israel?" Hamor asked.

"To the west—there," answered Jacob, pointing.

"Ah, so you have found the lands by the stream and the great rocks!" Hamor answered. "Very good they are, and they extend far. We will see their boundaries tomorrow."

He had remained standing, and now turned as huge double doors at the far end of the room were opened and two plainly dressed but pretty girls and two older women entered.

Hamor nodded toward the dark, pretty woman. "Adah, my wife."

She looked at them all, smiling and bowing. Then Hamor pointed to the very small, younger, plump woman. "Basha, my second wife," he said. She bowed also.

He beckoned for the girls to come forward. "Bashemath and Tamara, my daughters." They smiled shyly as they, too, bowed.

Hamor introduced the guests. "These are our neighbors, Prince Israel, his son, Simeon, and his daughter, Dinah." Turning back to the women, he went on, "I am sure you remember Dinah from the visit she made to us long ago, when she and the girls were small."

Adah spoke, "How good to see you again, but you have changed. You are so grown-up and so lovely. Welcome, welcome."

Her soft voice was sincere, and Dinah replied, "Thank you. It is good to see all of you again also. Bashemath and Tamara have grown up too. And they are beautiful." The girls flushed with pleasure and bowed, as pride shone in the eyes of Adah and Hamor. Everyone was pleased, for they seldom had visitors, and never had they been hosts to one so lovely who was from such a far-off land.

Dinah spoke, "I seem to remember two other little girls when I was here before."

"Yes," responded Basha. "They were my daughters, Mahlah and Hoglah. Right now they have gone into the city."

Adah said to Dinah, "Shall we go into the garden where we can talk of all that has happened since you visited last? The men can talk of business here without interruption. Come, dear Dinah." She reached for her hand as she rose, and they went through an outside door toward the garden, the girls now talking excitedly. Hamor and Jacob watched with pleasure. Simeon smiled self-consciously as plump, dark-haired Bashemath turned and smiled at him as she left.

The women sat under the trees in the garden as the sun sank lower, casting long shadows. The garden was cool and peaceful; a faint breeze was coaxing the leaves to whisper. Dinah removed her veil and headdress at Basha's urging and relaxed against the cushioned back of the stone bench, listening to the leaves and enjoying the breeze on her rosy cheeks. For a moment she closed her eyes, breathing deeply of the spicy fragrance floating to her from the plants around the pool.

"It is so lovely here," she said softly. "I remember the garden from my other visit. How the trees have grown! It seems so long ago, doesn't it?"

"Indeed it does, and it is lovely here, isn't it?" agreed Adah.

"Tell us about Haran again," begged the girls. "We have often spoken of it since you were here."

"I was so young when we left, only about seven or eight, and it was so long ago, I can't remember much, I'm afraid,"

Dinah explained. But she told them all she could think of: her old home, the garden, the city with its temple and priests, the maidens who served there, the sacrifices. The women gasped at the number of sacrifices Dinah's father had told her were offered at the great feasts, and of the custom of the young people in choosing their mates, which her mother had told her of.

Then she told them what she could remember of the long journey to this land, her father's old homeland. She talked of their years at Succoth, of their trips to worship Jehovah at Bethel, where her father had once had a wonderful dream and had promised to serve Jehovah always if He would bless him. She continued, telling of her father's wife, her own Aunt Rachel, who died at Bethlehem when her younger son, Benjamin, was born, of their living then farther north for many years, of Joseph's death, of their recent journey here. It all seemed a great wonder to the women, who had never been beyond twenty miles from home in their lives.

As Dinah talked, Shechem came through an outside gate, and was near them before Dinah was aware of his presence. When she saw him, she stopped talking abruptly, but realized it was too late to replace her veil, so she merely cast down her eyes, as though to hide her face.

Shechem seemed to be awed by her presence and he stopped in his tracks. Adah turned toward him, stood and bowed. "This is Dinah, daughter of Prince Israel. Your father told you of him?" she asked.

Shechem bowed low to Dinah as Adah continued, "This is Shechem, our oldest son. I believe he was away when you visited the last time."

Shechem managed to find his voice. "Welcome, daughter of Prince Israel. My father did indeed tell me of your father. May you be happy in our land." Dinah bowed her thanks. Shechem's black eyes boldly searched her face, noting her slenderness and the lovely rise of her breasts under the blue robe. He struggled inwardly to suppress a lustful impulse.

Dinah flushed, and to hide her embarrassment,

murmured, "You are kind. May Jehovah bless all of you." Then she bowed gracefully.

It was an awkward silence that followed. Shechem looked at Adah, but he realized he could find nothing more to say. Then he turned and looked at Dinah again. His half-sisters giggled and looked away, as Dinah raised her head. Their eyes met; they both smiled.

Basha finally said, "Prince Israel and his son are with your father inside. Will you go in to meet them?"

Shechem bowed and turned toward the house. Relief spread over Dinah's face. She realized her heart was racing as she and the others watched him go through the door. She found the young prince attractive.

The girls begged Dinah to continue talking, so she told them about her family, their customs, and their God, Jehovah. When they asked, she offered details concerning her clothes and jewels. They were so engrossed that she talked on and on. Then abruptly she realized they had told her nothing of their land or of themselves.

"But I've talked only of myself!" she exclaimed! "You must tell me of your city, your customs, your people."

"There is little to tell," Adah said, rather wearily. "You see the city spread before you" — here she indicated the houses below them, all crowded together, with the city wall visible on every side. "The city is small, the houses are small, and beyond the wall the land is bare except for the trees where the streams run."

"But it is beautiful," protested Dinah. "The brown grass, surrounded by green vegetation and the pretty trees by the streams. Look at the wonderful colors of the setting sun! And the city makes me think of Haran, with the houses so close, the many people, the wall. I miss seeing people, since we have only our family. My brothers go away with the animals sometimes and then it is very lonely."

The eyes of the girls showed interest each time she had mentioned her brothers. Bashemath asked, "You say you have eleven brothers? They are all grown up?"

"All except Benjamin—we call him Benji; he is almost

six," answered Dinah. "Joseph was about sixteen when he—when he left us." Pain crossed her lovely face.

Basha said, "I am sorry."

"Eleven brothers!" exclaimed Tamara. "We have only Shechem and three younger brothers—children, really."

"Your brothers have wives?" pursued Bashemath.

Dinah laughed. "No. They were young when we left Haran, and here there are no women of our own kin. Remember my father had to go to Haran those many years ago to find my mother and Aunt Rachel among his kin."

"Must you marry only kin?" asked Adah.

"Oh, yes. My father would be very displeased otherwise. His twin brother, my Uncle Esau, married daughters of Canaan, and my grandfather, Isaac, and grandmother, Rebekah, were not pleased. He was a few minutes older, but he lost the birthright, partly because of his marriages."

They were all silent for a while, thinking, and Dinah closed her eyes, trying to regain the happy, peaceful mood she had before Shechem disturbed it. The others studied her face, her hair, her clothes. *How beautiful*, each thought.

Finding she could not shut out Shechem's face from her thoughts, Dinah roused herself and smiled, facing the sunset, with its vibrant, glowing red-to-rose-to-blue shades, now casting purple shadows near the distant trees.

"One can see so far," she said, "and there is so much beauty. Oh, that sunset! Only Jehovah could make such a design!"

The others were clearly amazed at her joy in their surroundings, since they rarely noticed them. Adah smiled. "We are glad our guest finds joy in our land. It is plain you like this place. Your father will build a house here?"

"Yes," answered Dinah. "I think so—a big one, to fit our large family! Our old home near Succoth was good, with room for all. And there were many houses for our servants. It will take many months to build enough here."

Tamara was looking at Dinah. Suddenly her face brightened and she became almost beautiful as she smiled, showing even, white teeth. Her black eyes danced. "Why can't we have a big feast soon, Mother?" she asked. "Then Dinah and her brothers could come and meet our people here. They could make many friends and feel at home in our land. Would you not like that, Dinah?" She turned to Dinah, whose face flushed with pleasure, thinking that no doubt Shechem would come.

"Oh, I would, Tamara! How kind of you to think of it!"

"Could we, Mother? Oh, please! Maybe tomorrow night, or the next? The moon will be bright; we can play and talk under the stars."

Adah thought it would be ungracious not to comply. Anyway, why not? They had little pleasure here, and a feast would break the dullness. She smiled as she nodded her dark head. "Basha, let us ask our husband when he comes." Basha smiled approval.

The girls clapped their hands, and Basha said, "I know he will let us. Oh, Dinah, we are so glad you came!" There was sincerity in her voice.

Dinah responded, "How kind you are!"

Just then her father came out the big door, followed by Hamor and Shechem. They walked toward the women, and as they did so, Dinah's heart rose into her throat once more as she noted Shechem's handsome face and graceful movements. Then she remembered her veil and headdress. She put them on but did not cover her face, and she wondered if her father would be displeased and whether he would permit her to come to a feast here. Certainly he would not if he knew how her heart raced at the sight of Shechem! She dropped her eyes and her veil as they came near.

"Come, my daughter," he said fondly. "It is late. We must find our way back to camp before nightfall." He bowed to Adah and Basha as they stood together. "It is good of you to receive my daughter. She sees few of her own age. You will surely come to visit her soon?"

"You are gracious," replied Adah, smiling. "We will come." She turned to her husband.

"The girls would like a feast for Dinah and her family so they may introduce them to their friends here. Do we have your permission?!"

Hamor was thoughtful. He was looking at Dinah, and Adah did not miss the look. She continued, "Soon? Tomorrow night?"

"Why not?" shrugged Hamor. Turning to Jacob, he asked, "My friend, would you come?"

Jacob noticed that Shechem was watching Dinah intently and it disturbed him. He did not like the look of admiration—and what else?—on his face. He did not want to bring his family here, but did not see how he could graciously refuse.

"Of course we can," he answered, looking toward Dinah and then toward Hamor. "It is gracious of you to ask. I'm sure the young people will especially enjoy being together. And now we must take our leave of you. Come, my daughter."

Again, he turned to Hamor. "The time was pleasant, my host. And it was good to meet your family. I know my daughter has found delight in their company. Thank you very much."

Dinah had risen, her veil moving aside a little. Shechem bowed to her, smiling.

"We shall await your company tomorrow night with pleasure," he said to her, then turned to her father and bowed also. Dinah thanked him shyly and then bade farewell to the women.

They went through the garden gate where Simeon and a servant waited with the animals. Shechem helped Dinah to mount, as Hamor said, "We look forward to meeting your wife and, please, feel free to bring your servants as well."

"We will," answered Jacob, mounting. "Thank you." He and Simeon bowed and Dinah waved a slender hand as they rode into the deepening dusk.

"I do not like it, Leah," Jacob complained to his wife in their tent before they went to where the servants were laying out the morning meal. "Yet I could not refuse. We are near these Canaanites now, and we must not offend them. But we must not become a part of them, either. They do not worship Jehovah, but many strange gods—trees, rocks, the sun and also a god they call Baal and a mother-god of fertility they call Ashtoreth. I learned much from talking with Prince Hamor yesterday; some things I do not like. And the looks the prince's son cast upon our Dinah I liked least of all, though he seems to be a good young man. You shall warn our daughter to be wary of his attentions. She must not visit there often."

"Jacob, I fear we should not have come here," Leah responded, her weak eyes almost shut against the sun's rays as they left the tent. "Somehow I feel this is not where Jehovah wants us. Did you inquire of Him, truly?"

It was unlike her to question Jacob and he grew defensive. "I could not stay any longer in that place where both Rachel and Joseph were lost. I remembered this land was good. Why should it not please Jehovah?"

Leah said no more as they approached the table where their sons were already gathering. It was a cheerful scene, with the early morning sun burning the mists away; the birds were chattering and flying under the still tamarinds and oaks; laughter and murmurings floated from the servants' quarters, and the food smelled inviting. The sons joked among themselves and jostled each other. When Dinah and a still-sleepy Benji finally came outside, they all sat and had a happy meal together.

Afterwards, Jacob stood and addressed the group. "Since we must be certain not to offend Prince Hamor, we will attend the feast he will be giving for us tonight. Make ready your best garments and jewels. But I tell you now we must not become too friendly with these heathen Canaanites. It is Jehovah's command that His people keep themselves apart. See that you remember this."

His sons nodded and Simeon grinned and winked knowingly at Dinah. She lowered her eyes as her father looked directly at her. Leah took note of all this and her face showed concern. Later she talked to Jacob. "I do not like this merry-making tonight. We do not know if our sons will fall into bad company. We do not know the customs of these heathen people."

Jacob agreed, but added, "Yet, as I said, we dare not offend them, since we are in their land. We will just be careful. Our sons are of an age to become friendly with these heathen girls. And, as I told you, I did not like the way Prince Hamor's son looked at Dinah last evening. Yet, I felt she was pleased."

Plans were carried out through the afternoon, and as sunset tinged the western sky, an excited, finely dressed group set out in a sizable caravan of well-groomed, richly harnessed camels. As dusk fell, they were riding through the gates toward Hamor's home. They passed well-dressed people, old and young, walking up the slight hill in the same direction. Soon they saw lights on the terrace and people moving about.

Prince Hamor greeted Jacob warmly, and when all had dismounted and the animals were led away, he presented his wives and daughters. They greeted Leah and the handmaids graciously, and happily welcomed Dinah once more. They bowed to Jacob, and the girls eyed the handsome brothers without shyness. Dinah looked for Shechem, but did not see him.

Soon all of Jacob's family had met the other guests. There were so many gathered there for the festivities that they could not possibly have remembered all their names. The large terrace and an open space beyond was well-lighted by hanging lanterns, so the guests could see each other well. Music, strange to Jacob's family, floated on the air from a dozen players near the open space around a great bonfire with crackling flames that licked the night air. Servants passed wine in silver goblets to the guests, who milled around talking, or sat on the many stone benches around the terrace. Soon laughter began to drown out most of the strange music.

Leah and the handmaids, Dinah, Adah, Basha, Bashemath, Tamara, and the two daughters who were not present the afternoon before, Mahlah and Hoglah, sat together with several other women and girls. Adah turned to Leah and asked, "What is that pleasing perfume you wear?"

Leah smiled as she answered, "It is called deaxylon. It is a small, white flower that grows profusely in Haran. In this land it is sometimes found in shady, damp places, such as the spots where springs overflow. No doubt you have seen it. The blossoms must be gathered at just the right time and dried in the sun. Then it can be stored in covered earthenware pots for long periods of time. When dampened and rubbed on the skin, the scent lasts for hours." Dinah promised Adah and her girls that she would bring them some when she returned again to their home.

The women were interested in the robes, sandals, and jewels of Dinah, Leah, and the handmaids. They especially complimented them on the way their hair was piled high on their heads and held with jeweled pins, combs, and golden chains. These women all wore their hair long, hanging to their shoulders or below, pinned away from their faces on both sides. Dinah thought it was very becoming to their faces with their wide foreheads, deep-set, dark eyes, and high cheek bones. When she said as much, they flushed with pleasure and smiled their appreciation.

Dinah and Leah, Bilhah and Zilpah, in turn, took in every aspect of the dress of these Canaanite women, and their menfolk. They noted that the robes were more loosely flowing than their own, with no sashes at the waists. The colors were bright: rose, pink, blue, green, multi-colored, but there were none of the rich purples such as they wore. Almost all of them, both men and women, wore long scarves, tied at the neck and of a different color from that of their robes. Some of these were richly embroidered, as were the sleeves and hems of many robes. A few men wore turbans, with their long, heavy, dark hair flowing from beneath them. None of the women wore veils, so Leah and the other three women soon removed theirs.

Prince Hamor's young sons and a few others played near the fire, occasionally running in and out among the guests and chasing each other round and round the long table, laughing and shouting. Leah and Dinah noted with pleasure that Benjamin seemed at ease, joining in their play and laughter.

Jacob and his sons were gathered with Prince Hamor and the other men on the far side of the table, away from the women. Dinah, searching for Shechem, was disappointed that he hadn't appeared and that none of his sisters had mentioned him. Leah observed that Jacob seemed to be enjoying the company of Hamor and the other men. She could hear enough of the conversation to know he was being questioned about their life in Haran, their journeys around this land, their customs, and their God—Jehovah. She heard Jacob's clear voice above the others and now and then his laughter as well. How good it was to know he was really alive again! She realized that she herself was enjoying the company of these people, after being so long with only her own family.

Soon a tall figure came from the back of the house and approached the men. When Prince Hamor saw him, he said, "Here comes my son, no doubt to tell us the food is ready. He has been overseeing its preparation. Ah, Shechem, come and greet our friend Prince Israel again and meet his sons."

Shechem bowed to Jacob and to Simeon, and to each son as Jacob called their names. He greeted the other men and said, "All of you are welcome." Then his father led him around the table and over to the women. He smiled and bowed to Dinah, "How good to see you again." Leah saw that his eyes said much more than his words, and that her daughter glowed under his perusing glance. To the rest he gave the same welcome he had given the men. He turned to Hamor. "The food is prepared, Father. If you are ready, I shall have the servants bring it to the table."

"Indeed, we are ready. Please start now," returned Hamor. Shechem hurried back toward the house, while Hamor invited the women to come to the table.

Soon many servants were bearing huge platters of steaming meats, breads, vegetables, fruits, cheeses, cakes, and honeycomb to the long table. At Hamor's urging the guests were filling shining brass platters with foods of their choice. The older guests and Hamor's wives filled their platters first and went to sit at a smaller table nearer the fire. Later, Hamor joined them.

The young people and children sat around the long table, after all had served themselves and servants had placed the remaining food at one end. They were a merry lot, and there was so much talk and laughter that Jacob's sons and Dinah felt comfortably at home with them. Shechem had brought the best food to Dinah and then seated himself next to her. Many of the other young men could not keep their eyes away from her lovely face, and when she smiled at them, their faces glowed with pleasure until they noticed Shechem's dark looks.

Bashemath had chosen to sit next to Levi. Reuben and Tamara sat across the table from them, and Dinah soon noticed how taken he was with the much younger girl. Farther down the table, Mahlah was unabashedly popping fat grapes into Dan's mouth, and both were giggling. Hoglah had singled out Gad and they were sitting next to Dinah. She noticed that girls from the city had chosen Naphtali, Zebulun, Asher, and Simeon. When she finally spotted Judah far down the table on the opposite side, she saw that he was completely charmed by the prettiest girl of all, one with large, deep-set eyes and a perfect widow's peak above a wide forehead. All this she was aware of with some remote part of her mind, while her senses were centered on the dark, handsome Shechem beside her, giving her all his attention, while his eyes told her plainly how deeply he desired her.

The musicians began a loud and lively tune, and the people became silent, listening and keeping time with their heads and hands. Then they began to play slower, rather sad music, and all the guests sat quietly, with thoughtful faces, sipping their wine.

Soon Prince Hamor suggested that the older guests should go to the garden where they could talk in peace. On his way outside Jacob noticed how close Shechem sat to Dinah and how she smiled up at him as he spoke quietly to her. Leah had noticed it too, and she had to restrain herself from warning Dinah to be cautious. As they passed farther down the table, they saw their sons were talking and laughing with the girls beside them. The children had finished eating and were having a lively game of tag in the open space at the far end of the table. Jacob was happy to see Benjamin having such a good time and seemingly so at ease with strangers.

As the older ones moved on toward the garden, Leah whispered to Jacob that she hoped the young people didn't pair off here like they had in Haran. Before he could answer, their host caught up with them, and was remarking about what a good time the young people seemed to be having. "How glad I am you came." he said. "My daughters see so few people, except those from the city. It is good to have your sons among them." He laughed and then continued, "And as you saw, Shechem has eyes only for your beautiful daughter."

"Perhaps," responded Jacob rather shortly.

Leah asked, "Shouldn't they, and the children, also come into the garden?"

"Oh, they'll enjoy the music more where they are. The servants will see to the children."

Once in the garden, the women soon gathered around Leah and the handmaids on one side of the pool, while the men clustered on the other side. There was another fire burning in the open end away from the house, and many well-placed lamps illuminated the flowers, casting their reflection in the pool. Mingled fragrances wafted on the slight breeze. As they sat on the stone benches, Leah couldn't help but marvel at the quiet, beautiful scene. Soon the women were plying the three of them with more questions, and they chatted cheerfully.

Leah's fears for Dinah continued to nag her even as she talked and laughed with these women. Otherwise, she would have enjoyed this gathering, for she had been so long away from all but her own family. She was interested in the customs and dress of these people, and she enjoyed sharing her own with them.

She was conscious of Jacob's voice and his laughter coming to her from across the pool. *Oh, how good to hear his laughter again! Perhaps in this land he will come to be as he was*

40

before we lost Joseph.. Perhaps he will even learn to love me a little. She smiled wryly to herself. *There I go again—always hoping he will return my love! Must it go on forever—this longing?* Even as she thought, she knew it would. She drew her bright shawl closer against the cold ache in her heart that rivaled the chill of the night.

With an effort, she turned her thoughts back to the women and soon became so engrossed in the conversation that she forgot her concern for Dinah. Sometime later, Benjamin and two or three other children came into the garden. He was visibly upset as he called out and ran to her. Rising, she went toward him, asking, "What is it, Benji?"

"My brothers are all gone," he said, "and so is Dinah. When I couldn't find them, I was afraid you had all left me and gone home." His voice faltered; he was near tears.

Leah patted his curly head, "Now, Benji, you know we would never leave you." She started to draw him close, but he saw Jacob coming toward him and he pulled away to run to him.

His father took him up in his arms, reassuring him that of course they would never go home without him. Then he turned to Prince Hamor, who had followed him around the pool. "But where would the young people be?" he asked.

Hamor answered, almost too quickly. "Oh, they've just wandered off somewhere around the city. You know how the young like to be away from their elders."

"So they do," returned Jacob, worriedly, thinking of the customs of Haran. "But it is late. We should be starting home. Could we send servants to find them? I'm sure my sons and Dinah have forgotten the time, as I did."

"Very well," agreed Hamor, "but we wish you would not hurry. We are enjoying your company." He called to a servant who had followed them to the garden with more wine. He spoke to the man in low tones, and the servant bowed and hurried away immediately.

Jacob set his son down, tousled his hair and bade him return to play with his new friends until his brothers came back. "I promise we won't leave without you when they arrive." The child smiled and chased the other children out of the garden, as they all shouted and squealed happily.

Jacob went to Leah, and Hamor followed. Then the other men moved toward their women also, and Hamor asked, "Shall we all go back to the fire and sit until the young people return?"

Both Jacob and Leah answered together, "Yes, please. That would be good," and they moved toward the gate.

Back at the fire, the musicians resumed their playing when they saw Prince Hamor returning. At his gracious insistence, his guests seated themselves again at the table while servants poured more wine and brought bowls of fruit from the larger table. Hamor and his wives made a valiant effort at conversation and Jacob and Leah tried to respond, but their interest was now focused with concern for their children's, and most especially, Dinah's, whereabouts and actions. Leah's eyes kept straying in the direction of the city, searching for the return of any of them.

After some time had passed, a few couples came drifting back from the direction of the city, and other areas as well, four of Jacob's sons among them. They sat on cushions around the remains of the fire, as they sang with the music. Leah's fears were allayed somewhat and she began to listen to the songs. She couldn't really understand their meanings, but she thought they must be songs of love because of the slow, plaintive melody and the way some of the couples looked at each other as they sang. *Oh, why doesn't Dinah come?* her heart kept asking. *I told her to beware of Shechem.* Then she remembered the way they were looking at each other when she had passed the table earlier, and her heart was gripped with fear.

Several more young people joined the group around the fire, laughing and teasing. The anxious eyes of both Jacob and Leah searched each returning group. Of his sons, only Reuben and Levi had not yet returned. Still no Dinah. Leah wanted desperately to question them all about their sister, but she knew it would be embarrassing to them and to Prince Hamor as well.

Finally Reuben and Tamara returned, followed by Bashemath and Levi not long after. Each couple was holding hands and talking softly as they joined the larger group around the fire.

Soon afterwards, Jacob said to Hamor, "All of my sons are here now. It is certainly time we were leaving. Forgive me if I go and ask about their sister and send them for our mounts. It is late and we must leave."

"But, of course," agreed Hamor. "I'll go with you." Both he and Jacob rose and walked over to question the young people. None had noticed in which direction Dinah and Shechem had gone, and none had seen them as they walked through the town. They all agreed they had not gone outside the walls.

"Then get our animals and we will search for your sister," commanded Jacob. His sons immediately took leave of the girls they were with, though with obvious regret. Prince Hamor sent two servants with them to get their mounts, and four others to look around his grounds and in the city. Several of the young men volunteered to look also, and set off in the semi-darkness, the moon having sunk so far that at this hour it gave little light.

When the camels were brought, Jacob and his sons rode together through the still-open city gates, then scattered in all directions, two by two.

After perhaps an hour they all returned, Jacob with Simeon and Levi, last of all. Leah's agitation had mounted steadily and Hamor's wives had taken her and the handmaids inside to rest before their long ride back to the camp. Hamor, seemingly not concerned, stayed outside and waited for the searchers' return. When he saw Jacob's great white beast coming at a gallop, with two of his sons close behind, he hurried immediately toward him. Jacob stopped and dismounted.

"Have none of you found your sister?" he asked.

They all shook their heads, some muttering angrily under their breaths.

"Don't be worried, Prince Israel," soothed Hamor. "I'm sure they will come soon."

"But we need to go *now*," returned Jacob. "Where are the women?"

"They went inside to rest," Hamor answered.

"Father," Simeon spoke up, "if it please you, Levi and I will stay and continue to search. We will bring Dinah when we find her. You and our mother and the others can leave now."

Jacob thought for a moment, his brow furrowed with concern. Then he said, "Very well. I will leave her in your charge."

Hamor offered quickly, "Why not let the girl stay with us the remainder of the night? Indeed, we would gladly have all the women stay—and you also, of course."

"Thank you, but no," answered Jacob. "We will go now and leave these two to find their sister and bring her to our camp."

By now the women were coming down the long steps. Leah called out, "Did you find Dinah?"

"No," answered Jacob, "but come, Simeon and Levi will stay in order to find her. We will leave for home now." He turned to Hamor. "Please have our animals brought to us now."

"Of course," returned Hamor, and he sent a servant to fetch them.

The guests from the city had begun to leave, and many were already going down the hill when the animals were brought.

Jacob and his family thanked Hamor and his wives for the feast, expressing regret that their daughter had caused so much trouble.

"Oh, it is no trouble," assured Hamor graciously. "I'm just sorry you are so worried. I assure you my son is taking good care of her and that they will return soon. Do not be concerned. We want you to come again soon."

"Thank you," returned Jacob. He helped Leah to mount, while Asher and Dan helped Zilpah and Bilhah. He turned then to Simeon and Levi, "I leave your sister in your care. Go now, find her and bring her to us."

After Prince Hamor had lifted small Benjamin up behind his father, the two rode quickly ahead, while the others followed. Hamor and his family stood watching and waving until they were out of sight.

4

The Bargain With Hamor and Shechem

And his soul clave unto Dinah the daughter of Jacob, and he loved the damsel, and spake kindly unto the damsel. And Shechem spake unto his father Hamor, saying, Get me this damsel to wife. . . . But in this will we consent unto you: If ye will be as we be, that every male of you be circumcised: Then will we give our daughters unto you, and we will take your daughters to us, and we will dwell with you, and we will become one people.

(Genesis 34:3-4, 15-16)

At daybreak, Jacob was shouting, "You didn't bring your sister? After I trusted her to you! Why? What has become of her?"

The two sons were ill at ease under their father's angry questioning. Simeon looked at Levi, and Levi answered, "My father, we looked for Dinah. Truly we did. Everywhere, inside the city and out, until the moon was gone and we could not see. We went back to the house, but everyone was gone. We even dared to wake Prince Hamor. He insisted that Dinah should stay with his daughters when she and Shechem returned. We came home. We did not know what else to do."

Jacob's voice was shrill with anger and fright. "Not know what to do? Not know what to do? You could have ridden over the whole city crying out for her. You could have told Hamor he must find her at once or we would come and take his city! You could have searched Hamor's house!"

Servants were running about now, trying to discover what their master was so upset about, and Leah was crying softly in the tent door.

Simeon remained silent while Levi continued in a placating tone, "But, my father, you went there because you did not want to offend the prince! How much more would a threat of violence have offended him!"

Suddenly the anger drained from Jacob's face, and only fear remained. He said wearily, "You are right. And he must not be offended now. I shall go myself and fetch your sister—this very morning! See to your animals and have a servant bring my camel while I dress."

Leah continued weeping, attempting to wipe her eyes on her sleeve.

"Do not weep," Jacob said, not unkindly, going past her into the tent. "I will find Dinah."

"But suppose you cannot?"

"Oh, I shall find her," he assured his wife. "It's just that I am afraid of the state I may find her in."

"Jacob!" Leah now pulled at his sleeve as he was dressing, turning him to face her. "What do you mean?" Her voice trembled, her eyes were fearful.

"Never mind. She will be all right." Jacob moved from her grasp, finished dressing, and went toward his waiting camel.

An hour later Jacob sprang from his mount and bowed curtly to Prince Hamor who was coming down the steps of his house.

"Ah, it is good to see you again so soon, my friend. Come in! Come in!"

Jacob did not move, but held Hamor's eyes. "Prince Hamor, I have come for my daughter. I suppose she stayed with your daughters last night. Where is she now?"

Hamor's gaze shifted before the question.

"Ah, but my daughters have not yet risen, for they were

late to bed. It may be that your daughter is with them." He clapped for a servant, excused himself, then spoke in low tones to the servant in the hall. Jacob caught snatches of his speaking: "See if Prince Israel's daughter is with mine...." The voice trailed to a whisper, the servant left. Hamor returned to Jacob, visibly ill at ease.

"Sit down, my friend," he invited, motioning to a skin-covered seat on the wide porch. "How blessed you are," Hamor continued, "to have eleven strong, well-favored sons. You will become a great nation. But they must find wives. Perhaps they favored some among our daughters?"

"I have not spoken with them," answered Jacob. "They are tending my animals this morning."

Loud voices came from the hallway. Prince Hamor ignored them as he spoke of how pleased he was to have had him and his family at the festivities last night. Jacob was civil enough, impatiently thanking Hamor again for his hospitality, assuring him they had enjoyed everything.

"But I cannot understand why my Dinah would have remained here, why the two brothers I left did not find her." His voice was anxious.

Prince Hamor tried to reassure him. "Do not think that anything is amiss, my friend. You know how the young are. They have little sense of time when they are together. It is likely she was with some who strolled into the grove of trees outside the wall, or farther into the town than they realized."

Jacob now heard rapid footsteps and looked up to see Dinah. Her face was almost covered and her robe was disheveled as she rushed through the door. Hamor and Jacob rose. She bowed to Prince Hamor and went on to her father. "I am sorry I have worried you, my father. Will you please take me home now?"

Jacob saw that she was upset. "Yes," he said. Then he spoke to Prince Hamor, "We will go. My thanks to you. Please have a servant bring my daughter's camel."

"I will," returned Hamor, and he clapped for a servant. When the animal was brought, Jacob helped Dinah mount as Hamor said, "May you both return soon."

Jacob thanked him and bowed, mounted his own camel and the two rode away, leaving Hamor to watch them until they were out of sight. Then he went inside and asked the house servant, "Where did you find the girl?"

"With Prince Shechem, master," replied the servant, his face carefully blank.

Hamor cursed. "Shechem should have known better," he muttered. "Bring him to me at once."

As the servant hurried down the hall, Hamor stood scowling, stroking his beard until Shechem arrived.

"You fool! What have you done?" Hamor demanded angrily, his beady eyes flashing. "Could you not wait? Our friend is angry. He may decide to go away."

Shechem sprawled on the low couch by the wall, as he calmly answered, "Father, I love the girl. She was willing. I did not force her."

"But will her father believe that?" demanded Hamor, still angry. "She will tell him you forced her, and he will believe her. Why could not her brothers find her last night? Where were you?"

"Dinah wanted to see the city. We went so far—to the grove at the other side—that we didn't see anyone hunting for us. When we returned, her people were gone, and your household was asleep," Shechem answered defensively, standing up to face his father.

"Then you should have taken her home yourself!" Hamor was shouting at his son now.

"You think her brothers would not have killed me if I had taken her home alone? Besides, neither of us knew the way. Will you not go and bargain with her father? I must have her for my wife!" he begged.

"If they would have killed you, will they not kill me?" Hamor was almost screaming now. "By now she has told her father you forced her, and he will tell her brothers as soon as he can!"

Shechem tried to calm his father, reaching out a bronzed hand which Hamor ignored. "But you told me you wanted us to marry into their tribe and gain their wealth. Now they will have to consent."

Hamor lowered his voice, "This is not the way it should have been done."

"Well, it is done," returned his son. "I cannot change things. We will just have to make the best of it. I must have Dinah for my wife. Let us take some townsmen and bargain with them."

"I must think," answered Hamor. He strode out to pace back and forth in the garden. Shechem smiled and lay on the couch again, dreaming of the beautiful Dinah and remembering the night they had spent together. He thought, *I must have her as my wife.*

An hour before sunset, Jacob watched a group of men ride quietly into his camp. He was sure he knew what they had come for. He had been seething all day, but now his anger of the morning had abated somewhat. Dinah, with many tears, had convinced him that Shechem had not forced her, that she had been willing to lie with him. She had begged her father to give her to Shechem in marriage. "I know he will come to ask for me," she confidently declared.

Jacob's resentment had built all day long. *The girl should have known her behavior would be against Jehovah's will.* Still, he could not remember having warned her about this; indeed, he thought of her as little more than a child. It had never occurred to him she would think of giving herself to any man, much less to a stranger and a heathen. *O, Jehovah, I waited seven years for Rachel, yet here my own daughter gives herself to another within three days! It is too hard for me to bear.* Even as he thought, he remembered how completely he had loved Rachel the minute he saw her. Perhaps it had been the same for the young man Shechem, and for Dinah also.

As the visitors dismounted slowly, Jacob sent a servant to ask them to enter his tent, as he himself moved leisurely toward them, noting the rich dress they wore, especially Hamor and Shechem. He bowed when he reached them. "Welcome to my humble tent," he invited, endeavoring to hide the bitterness he felt.

The men entered hesitantly, and they looked about warily as Jacob and the servant found places for all eight to sit. He observed their admiration for the fine furnishings of his tent.

Prince Hamor wasted no time in stating his business. "It is regrettable what happened to your daughter, Prince Israel. Please pardon my son's somewhat—hasty behavior. He longs for her exceedingly. I beg of you to give her to him as his wife, and overlook his ah,—indiscretion."

Jacob's eyes searched the young man's face, as it flushed faintly under its tan. His eyes, however, did not flinch under Jacob's gaze. "I do indeed love your daughter, Prince Israel," he avowed. "I must have her for my wife."

Jacob could not trust himself to speak calmly. Prince Hamor continued, "I beg of you, Prince Israel, make marriages with us. Give us your daughter and take our daughters to you. The land is enough for us all to dwell together in peace. Behold, it is before you. Trade here and get possessions here."

Before Jacob could answer, voices could be heard outside, and his son, Simeon, came to the tent door. His eyes swept around the room, coldly. He neither spoke nor bowed to the visitors. To Jacob he said, "My father, we wish to speak with you alone." He turned abruptly and walked away. Jacob excused himself, as his guests rose, looking fearfully at each other. Each knew what all were thinking: *We are at the mercy of these people, and that one is angry.*

Outside, Jacob herded his sons farther away from the tent. He noticed their swords and daggers as he spoke placatingly, "These men are peaceable; they are in our midst unarmed." There was muttering among some of the sons as they flashed their weapons. He continued, "Prince Shechem did not force your sister. By her word, she was willing. He wants to marry her. His father insists that our family join with his people, promising that the land will be shared with us. I have not told him we may not join in marriage with heathen."

"*We* will tell him," Simeon said angrily. "And then we will kill this one who dared to treat our sister as a harlot!"

Jacob raised his hand to ask for silence. "No!" he

commanded. "Do you want the whole city against us? We are few in their eyes. Besides, such a deed would displease Jehovah."

"Does not this treatment of our sister by the heathen displease Him also?" asked Levi angrily.

Jacob answered, "What if she were willing? I tell you she says he did not force her and that she loves him."

"She is little more than a child," Judah spoke up. "How could she know what she wants? We must avenge her!"

"We will remain peaceable." Jacob spoke with authority and finality. "There is surely a way to settle this. I must go back to my guests and bring them out here so we can somehow deal rightly and peaceably with them." Jacob started toward his tent.

The faces of the brothers were sullen and they spoke in low, angry tones.

After some time, Jacob stepped outside his tent door and stood beside it. The men filed out, with Hamor and Shechem exiting first. Jacob led them to an open space in front of the camp, where his sons had gathered. Their faces showed no sign of hostility now.

I wonder why the change, Jacob thought as he spoke. "Listen, my sons, to the words of Prince Hamor."

He bowed to Hamor, who began to speak slowly, persuasively. "My son loves your sister and would have her for his wife. I beg you to give her to him and we will pay whatever you ask. I beg you also to make other marriages with us. You need wives, and our daughters are fair. Did you not find them so?" He looked at each of the men for an answer, and he noted their nods and smiles. He continued, "You shall dwell and trade in the land just as we do. See, it is before you. Choose where you will."

Shechem then spoke, "Let me find favor in your eyes. Ask whatever dowry and whatever gifts you will, and I will give them, for I must have your sister for my wife."

Jacob was surprised when his second son, Simeon, answered. It was usually Reuben or Judah who spoke for them all.

Though Simeon's voice was peaceable, Jacob knew something was amiss; this was too much of a change from the anger of a few minutes earlier.

"We cannot give our sister to one who is uncircumcised." He looked from one to the other. "You understand my meaning?" The men nodded, and he continued, "That would be a reproach unto us. But this we will do, if you consent. If you will become as we are, with every male of you submitting to circumcision, then we will give our sister to you and will take your daughters to us. We will then dwell with you and become one people with you." He stopped, noting the hesitancy on their faces.

Jacob said nothing, but he still could not understand this change in his sons. Simeon spoke again. "If you do not heed this requirement , we will take our sister and our possessions and we will be gone."

Jacob and all his sons studied the faces of the men. Shechem and his father nodded to each other. Jacob thought, *He must indeed love our Dinah. He looks like such an honorable young man. Perhaps it is truly with him as it was when I first saw Rachel. And what will become of Dinah? She is defiled and can marry no one else. O, Jehovah, we know we are a separate people, but what about all this? Why should this be? Did You not want us here? Could these people really become as we are? Can we trust them?*

As Jacob thought, he could see the men with Hamor were beginning to consider the proposal, and then Hamor spoke. "My son and I consent to do this thing now, and we will do as you say. We cannot speak for the men of our city, but we will talk to them tomorrow. Give your daughter to my son now and she shall go with us if she wishes."

Shechem's face brightened, as if the sun had shone upon it, as he said, "I am sure she will go." He turned toward Jacob, "Prince Israel, please consent to this and ask her at once."

Jacob looked at his sons. They began to nod their approval, especially Simeon and Levi, and again he wondered at their change of attitude.

"It is well," he answered Shechem. "I will speak with my daughter at once." He bowed slightly and turned away, in his heart seeking Jehovah's will. As he went toward Dinah's tent, he prayed, *If this is not the right decision, may the girl refuse.*

5

The Bargain

Shall not their cattle and their substance and every beast of their's be our's? only let us consent unto them, and they will dwell with us. . . . and every male was circumcised . . . And it came to pass on the third day, when they were sore, that two of the sons of Jacob, Simeon and Levi, Dinah's brethren, took each man his sword, and came upon the city boldly, and slew all the males. . . . and took Dinah out of Shechem's house, and went out. . . . They took their sheep, and their oxen, and their asses, . . . And all their wealth, and all their little ones, and their wives took they captive, and spoiled even all that was in the house.

(Genesis 34:23-26, 28-29)

Early darkness had fallen and the stars were coming out as Hamor, Shechem, and their friends galloped away from Jacob's camp, taking Dinah and her maid Milah with them.

There was consternation and some weeping in the camp, for Leah was very unhappy that her daughter had *wanted* to go away from her and Jacob—and with strangers at that. This was not at all what she had wanted for her only daughter.

Many of the servants wept also. Jacob sought to calm and reassure them all, "Our daughter will be all right. She loves the young man Shechem, as he does her. I am sure he is a good man, and this is really the only thing we can do. You know she is defiled and can marry no one else." He thought, *I'm so glad Benjamin is sleeping through all this.*

Leah interrupted him, her distress making her bold. "Why could she not have stayed here until we prepared her for marriage? She should at least have had a wedding." Her weeping broke into loud sobs.

Jacob sent the servants away and sat beside her in Dinah's tent. He put a comforting arm around her heaving shoulders as he promised, "She shall have a wedding later, if you wish, but I have Shechem's and his father's pledge that they will consider her as his wife just on our agreement. They will give whatever we ask as dowry when we've had time to decide on it. Maybe we should ask for the part of the land we want. All will be well, I know. I even feel Jehovah approves and will bless us all, or Dinah would have refused to go. Dry your tears now and be happy for her. This will be her wedding night. Milah will take care of her, and we will carry more of her possessions to her tomorrow."

Leah still wept but tried to control herself.

Again Jacob encouraged her, "Stop weeping now. This is best and our daughter will be happy. Come, let us go to our own tent."

He helped her to her feet as her tears subsided. They went outside where they could hear the sons in their tents jesting lewdly and laughing. Again Jacob wondered why they had so readily consented to let Shechem have their sister. Were they planning some crude revenge? *They always seem to have some evil in mind, as Joseph told me.* His heart ached as he thought of his beloved son. *O Jehovah, why did he have to be lost? Why are the others so evil? And now this unintended alliance with the heathen. Where have I failed? I have tried to serve You, to teach my family to serve You.* He could find no answers as he and Leah entered their tent and tried to sleep.

Shechem came to his father on the porch of their home late the following morning. He was smiling.

"Ah, I see you had a good wedding night, my son."

"Indeed we did," Shechem answered without embarrassment.

Hamor continued, "It is late. We must get to the task at hand, so you can keep your bride. Come." They walked to the great gates where the men of the city waited. As he saw them, Hamor said to Shechem, "Our friends have kept their word. It looks like they have gathered all the men of the city. Do you think they will consent to this agreement?"

"Oh, they must!" exclaimed Shechem. "I cannot live without Dinah. We must persuade them. How did your friends feel about it last night?"

Hamor answered, "They were afraid. How could they not be? It is such a strange custom and will no doubt be painful. Surely Prince Israel and some of his sons will perform the rite, since it is new to us."

They came near the men, who stopped talking and bowed to them with respect to their prince and his son who would be prince after him.

Hamor and Shechem bowed in return and Hamor said, "My thanks to you for coming. A matter has come up that I hope we can agree on, so our city will not be divided."

He paused, looking around the group as they sat on stone benches in a half circle, then proceeded, "As you no doubt have heard, a mighty and wealthy prince has come to us from Haran to the north. He is the grandson of Abraham of the Chaldeans, whom you older men will remember."

A few nodded and Hamor continued. "Abraham was very rich. He bought the cave of Mach-pelah from Ephran the Hittite, our own ancestor, who dwelt in Hebron to the south." Several men again nodded assent. "There he buried his wife, and there he is buried. His son Isaac dwells there still. It is his son, Prince Israel, who has come to us. He left his father's house when he was young and found wives among Abraham's kindred in Haran. He returned to this land some ten years ago, and built a house in Succoth to the east. Now he would buy land and dwell with us."

Hamor noted that the men were listening carefully, their eyes intent. "Some of you saw him and his family two nights ago at my home. I'm sure you noticed the fine clothes they wore and their gold and silver and precious stones. I have seen the furnishings of his tent, as have some of you, and the trappings of his camels. He has many servants and tents and his animals cannot be numbered. He is indeed a mighty and wealthy prince. If we let him dwell among us and trade, shall not his cattle and substance and every beast be ours? We can take his daughters to wife and we can give to them our daughters, so we shall be one people."

Hamor was aware of the pleased looks, the assenting nods. He felt sure now they would consent to his proposal. After a moment, he spoke again. "My son was—ah, what shall I say? He was indiscreet with the prince's beautiful daughter." Some of the men smiled and snickered and Shechem's face flushed as he glanced downward. "They have given her in marriage to him, but they say they will take her and all their substance and be gone if we do not consent to become as they are by each one of us being circumcised."

Again Hamor paused and looked round at all the men. Now they were nodding or smiling, each looking at his neighbor to see how he felt. One finally asked, a little shyly, "Just what is this circumcision you speak of?"

Hamor answered slowly, trying to find the right words so the men would not be against it. "It means that the foreskin from each of our male organs is removed. It will not be too painful, I presume; the soreness should surely last for only a few days."

He could see they were thinking seriously about this. Then a man asked, "Who would do this circumcising?"

Hamor answered, "I'm sure it would be done by Prince Israel and some of his sons. It is nothing to be afraid of, and just think how we would profit by having them in our midst—all their wealth and their daughters. Surely that alone will make us forget a little pain!"

Some of the men smiled knowingly now, and Hamor

perceived they were coming around to the idea. He spoke more encouraging words and soon the men, even the older ones, were laughing and slapping each other on the back as they contemplated their good fortune.

Hamor looked at Shechem; they both smiled because they knew the men had been won over. They knew they could ride to Prince Israel's camp this very day and tell him they had consented to his family's proposal. They could also decide on the land and the price as well as the dowry Shechem would give.

Shechem now expressed his gratitude, "My thanks to you, my friends. You will not regret it, and you must all have the pleasure of meeting my new wife very soon."

Hamor added his thanks, and then told the assembled men that he would give their answer to the prince this very day. He and Shechem then walked toward their home in order to get their camels ready and ride to Prince Israel's camp.

Hamor and Shechem arrived at Jacob's tent just as he was leaving for the midday meal. He welcomed them and invited them to eat with his family, but bade them to first go into his tent while his servants prepared for them.

Inside the tent, they all sat on thick cushions, and Hamor again took in the rich, luxurious furniture that was imbedded with jewels—the golden candle-holders and lamps, the wall-hangings, the colorful woven mats. He could hardly turn his eyes away from the magnificent trappings used on Jacob's camel. Unconsciously, he rubbed together greedy hands and almost smacked his thick lips, thinking, *Soon we too will have wealth like this.*

Having made them welcome, Jacob asked Shechem, "Is my daughter well?"

"Very well, Prince Israel," the young man replied. "It was well for us both on our wedding night."

Jacob smiled. He understood the assurance Shechem was giving him. He was struck by Shechem's grace and beauty, by his honorable bearing. *Little wonder Dinah loved and trusted this man so quickly,* he mused. As he turned to Hamor, he noted the resemblance—the same heavy hair and bronzed skin, only slightly more wrinkled, and the beard a little lighter, the deep-set, dark eyes, the full lips. He asked, "Did the men of your city consent to our proposal?"

"They did, indeed," Hamor assured him. "We ask only that you and your sons come and perform the rite for us, as we know nothing about it."

"We will come," promised Jacob. "You will see that it is not a hard thing to go through."

Shechem inquired, "What will it please you to have as dowry? We will give whatever you say."

Jacob remembered fourteen years of hard labor he had given his uncle Laban for his beloved Rachel, and Leah. He answered, "You may choose either to labor with my herdsmen for five years or to give me all the land around the big rocks where I would like to build my home."

Shechem looked to his father. "Which pleases you, my father?"

Hamor answered immediately, "We shall give the land. I need you to manage our herds."

Jacob looked at Shechem. "It is well, my son. So it shall be." He reached to clasp his hand to seal the bargain. Shechem was pleased. Then Jacob turned to Hamor. "I should like to purchase all the land that joins that part unto this land here by the stream where I have pitched my tents. I will show you after we have eaten. Come, my friends."

They went outside and around to the large table in the center of the tents, where his sons had already gathered, laughing and jesting. They became quiet and bowed to the guests and their father as they came to the bountiful table.

After Jacob had given thanks to Jehovah and they began to eat, he told his sons that the men of Hamor's city had consented to their agreement. Several of them said, "It is well." Jacob noticed that Simeon and Levi exchanged knowing glances before they smiled and voiced their approval. He wondered again if they were up to some wickedness; he knew they were always together and seemed to agree on everything. *They will bear watching.*

When they finished the meal, Jacob invited his guests to sit or lie under the trees nearby, but Hamor declined. "I know it is very hot for riding," he said, "but we would like to see the land you want to buy and get back to our city as soon as possible. There are many things to put in order before the circumcision disables us for a few days. And I believe Shechem's eager to get back to his bride."

Shechem smiled and blushed, "Indeed, I am," he agreed.

"That is good," returned Jacob, smiling also. "Come, then, we shall get our mounts and go. Judah, please see to them. I wish you to ride with us."

"I will, my father," responded Judah and hurried to find his camel and his father's, after directing a servant to bring those of the guests. The other sons ambled lazily over to the trees and sprawled upon the ground, as Jacob, Shechem, and Hamor approached Jacob's tent.

Jacob had ridden that morning with Reuben, Judah, and Benjamin around the land he wanted, so he knew exactly where to ride now. For some two hours they rode, stopping now and then under clumps of trees to escape the sun for a few minutes and drink from their water-skins. There was much about the land, the distances, and directions that Jacob wanted to ask about, and Hamor was obliging. The two younger men were pleasant to each other, talking of many things as their fathers discussed the land.

By mid-afternoon, they rode back and went inside Jacob's tent, where a servant brought refreshments. There was some further talk and then Jacob asked, "Prince Hamor, what price do you ask for the land we covered?"

He noted the glint in Hamor's eyes at the mention of price, and thought of his uncle Laban. Quickly, Hamor answered, "It is worth a hundred pieces of silver, my friend."

Jacob knew this was too much, that Hamor expected him to haggle and insist the price be lowered. *Well, I shall surprise him,* he thought. He said, "It is well. I will pay you the hundred pieces. I will bring it to you when we arrive for the circumcising, if that pleases you."

"It does please me," responded Hamor quickly, his

countenance jubilant at having gotten more than he had hoped for.

"Name the day for me to come." requested Jacob.

Hamor was thoughtful, then answered, "I think the day after tomorrow would be good. That should give all the men enough time to take care of their work before the circumcision is performed. And now Shechem and I will leave. We thank you for your kindness, Prince Israel, and we will seal the bargain when you come." He and Shechem bowed.

Jacob said, "So we shall. And you are welcome here anytime. May I send two servants with you to carry my daughter's possessions? They do not know the way."

"Of course," answered Shechem. "We can take some ourselves."

"Thank you, but our camels are ready," returned Jacob. He spoke to a servant who brought the camels and two male servants. Again Hamor and Shechem thanked Jacob, bowed, and they all rode away.

Jacob went to Dinah's tent to make sure all her belongings were taken. He found Leah standing inside, weeping, and he put a comforting arm around her. "Do not weep," he begged. "We will see Dinah often. Remember, she is happy. Her husband said all was well on their wedding night. He seems to be a very considerate young man and he loves our daughter very much."

Leah tried to stop crying. "But I miss her so much already. It is not as if I had another daughter left with me. Dinah is so cheerful, so comforting. Benji is missing her too and he has been crying." Her tears started anew.

"But you have your maid, Zilpah, and Rachel's maid, Bilhah. You won't be alone. Come, let us see where our house shall be built on the land Shechem gave as dowry. I also bought all the land on this side of it, reaching from here to the stream." He went to the tent door, called a servant, instructed him to bring Leah's and Benjamin's camels and his own. Leah's tears subsided at the prospect of riding with her husband. He patted her shoulder, then led her outside his tent, and over to her own.

"Get something that will shade you from the sun," he commanded gently, and she went inside. Almost immediately she returned with a light-weight white shawl over her head and shoulders.

"That's a good choice, and it looks very becoming," said Jacob, smiling. Leah beamed with joy at the realization that he noticed her looks. A servant brought her camel and got the trappings from her tent. Another servant did the same for Benjamin. Jacob called loudly, and his beloved son came running from near the stream. Benjamin's eyes were red from weeping. His face brightened with a smile as his father said, "Go and mount, my son, and you may go with us to where we shall build our new home."

He answered, "Oh, thank you, Father," and trotted toward his camel. A servant helped him mount, while Jacob assisted Leah before mounting his own camel. They rode toward the great rock outcropping. It was Jacob's third trip to that site that day.

The next morning, just as the sun streaked bright fingers across the sky, Jacob called for all male servants that could be spared to go with him to gather rocks near the site for the new house. Ten soon set out on foot, carrying tools, following Jacob, Judah, and Benjamin who were riding ahead. The child felt quite grown up and was very pleased at being allowed to go. Jacob thought it would ease his sadness over Dinah's absence; he also knew he would be helpful in moving many of the smaller stones.

When they reached the rock outcropping, it was almost mid-morning. Jacob put two brawny men to work breaking the huge rocks in pieces with the heavy tools he and Judah had brought on their camels. Benjamin and the servants began gathering smaller stones from the ground at Judah's direction.

Jacob wanted the house built around a courtyard, just as the one they had built long ago in Haran had been. He knew exactly what to do and the work progressed quickly. The servants and Benjamin soon had the ground completely clear of stones, and the servants began to shape the broken ones at the outcrop into rectangular, flat, foundation stones. By the time the sun became so hot that they could not work, almost half of the foundations were laid. It was time for a rest. They drank from the cool, sparkling waters of the stream, as it flowed over many stones. The servants rested their tired backs by lying on the ground, while Jacob and Judah propped against trees with Benji sprawled between them, listening as they discussed the next stops they would take in their building program. The child soon slept, weary from his early rising and the work he was unaccustomed to. Jacob smiled as he noticed him, and put his rolled up turban tenderly under the boy's curly head.

Two servants on swift mounts brought their midday meal. After lunch they all slept until mid-afternoon. Then they resumed their work until sunset. While the others went to the stream again, Jacob drank from his water-skin and surveyed the day's work, debating in his mind whether he should make any changes. He was still considering these matters when the others came back. He looked up, said to the servants, "Go on ahead; you know the direction now. We will catch up soon." To Judah and Benjamin he said, "We must bring your mother before we go further. We've talked about what she wants—this is really to be her house—but she may want changes when she sees the actual foundations. I want her to be pleased."

Judah smiled, glad to know his mother's wishes were to be honored, "That will be wise," he said. "It will be easier to change anything now than later."

Benji was hopping around the flat foundation stones. When he reached the end, he followed the stakes and cord all the way around and came back to his father and Judah. "It is so big," he stated, stretching his arms out as far as they would go. "I know Aunt Leah will like it. Dinah would like it too." His face clouded. "But she won't be living in it now."

"Oh, she will visit us. She is not so far away. Come, let's get our camels and go to camp. Aren't you hungry?"

"Indeed I am," answered the child, clapping his hands.

The sun had not risen far in the heavens on the appointed day, when Jacob's party of six dismounted at Prince Hamor's steps. Hamor came toward them. "Welcome, my friends. You are early. Come in, come in!"

"You remember my sons, Reuben and Judah," Jacob said.

Hamor returned, "Oh, yes. Fine sons they are, too."

Jacob continued. "These others are trusted servants, who have helped me with the rite before. Are your people ready?"

"We are," answered Hamor, as they entered the door a servant held open for them.

"First I should like to see my daughter," Jacob requested.

"Of course," responded Hamor who sent a servant for her. "Sit, my friends, while we wait for her."

Jacob said, "We wanted to start early, so you'd not have too long to—well, perhaps dread the rite. If it pleases you, we will take your household first, then get to the other houses as we come to them. Perhaps you can send a servant with us, and we can perform the rite on him last."

"It is well," agreed Hamor. "Shechem and I will be first. You say we will be well in a few days, surely within a week?" For the first time since they had agreed upon the circumcision, Hamor seemed a little apprehensive.

Jacob sought to reassure him. "Not more than a week, that is certain. Do not be afraid. It will not be as bad as you think."

Dinah hurried in, her eyes catching the blue of her robe, her shining hair swinging. She ran into Jacob's arms as he rose. "Ah, my daughter, is it well with you?" he asked fondly, holding her away from him and kissing her on each cheek.

"Indeed, I am well—and happy." Her lovely, smiling face verified her words. Jacob noticed a new radiance about her and remembered the way Rachel looked when she first became his wife. She hugged her brothers in turn and greeted the servants warmly before asking, "How is my mother?"

"She is well," responded Jacob. "She wanted me to tell you she misses you and wants you to visit soon."

"Oh, I will, I will," she assured him. "And is Benji well?"

"He misses you too and cries sometimes. He was still sleeping when we left."

"I miss him too, and all of you. But I am so happy with Shechem. Everyone is so good to me here."

"I am glad, my daughter."

Shechem came into the room. He bowed to his father-in-law and to the brothers and servants, but his face seemed tense as he went to stand beside Dinah.

"Shall we get started with the business at hand?" Jacob asked.

"Yes," answered Hamor, rising. "Come, we will go to my room first."

All but Shechem followed him, as Jacob said, "We will see you before we leave, my daughter."

"Oh, please do," she begged. "I shall write a note for you to take to my mother."

Shechem stayed with her; his eyes were full of love, and he seemed reluctant to leave her for even a short while. They held each other closely, kissed, and spoke in whispers until a servant came and said his father was calling for him. As the servant left, they kissed a last time and clung to each other. Then Shechem followed the servant.

Reuben and one servant went in one direction to Hamor's servants' houses, and Judah and the other servant hurried in another direction to the houses farthest away. They each carried instruments and several ointments. Jacob and his trusted Ziph performed the rite on Hamor first, then on Shechem, each in his own room. They then went to the rooms of the house-servants, each in turn. Jacob whispered to his servant as they left Shechem's large, airy room, "He bore it more bravely than his father. Prince Hamor was plainly upset, and so the pain was greater,"

Ziph nodded as he said, "Yes, master. And he will not heal as fast either."

"You are right, Ziph. You and I have seen many of these, haven't we?"

Again Ziph nodded, as Jacob continued, "I am glad the rooms are fairly cool and that they have plenty of wine. It will help to deaden the pain. The servants will not fare so well."

Bera, the servant Hamor had appointed to accompany them, hovered near, looking pale and frightened after what he had seen, dreading when his own time should come.

Within a few minutes, they had finished with the last house-servant. Judah and Reuben were coming into the back of the house. Bera led them back up the long hall, where they could hear the women's low voices coming from several rooms. They saw no one as they went outside and Bera led them to the first houses in the city. The sun was very hot and they all dreaded the task ahead, but each team went first to one house, and then another until far into the afternoon. They did not even stop to eat, knowing they'd have no appetite anyway. Now and again Bera would ask at the houses for water for them all.

At last, hot and very weary, Judah and his servant finished in the last house and all of them trudged back up the hill to Hamor's house. As they entered, Jacob said kindly to the tired Bera, "Bring my daughter to me here; then go to your own room, eat something, drink some wine and lie down to rest. We will come to you soon."

When Dinah came, she led them into the big front room, where they seated themselves. She called her maid, who with one of Hamor's maids, brought basins of water and cloths for them to wash their hands and wipe their sweaty faces.

Dinah asked, "Now would you like some food? Perhaps some bread and cheese, my father?"

Jacob answered for them all. "No food, my daughter. We have no stomach for it yet. But please bring some fresh water, and a little wine." When it was brought, they sat drinking slowly and telling her about beginning the new house and, again, about how her mother and Benji missed her.

When they were somewhat refreshed and had given Hamor's servant time to rest, Dinah showed her father and

Ziph to the servant's room and bade them good-bye. They went in and got on with the task at hand, then stopped by Prince Hamor's room on their way out. They found Shechem with him. Both had stopped bleeding and did not seem too uncomfortable.

"Shechem will remain with me till we are well," said Hamor. "We will be company for each other and our wives can bring food and visit. Will you not stay for a while?"

"Thank you, but no. It is late and we are tired. My sons have gone for our animals, so we will go. I am glad you are doing well."

"I shall bring your daughter to visit you as soon as I am well," Shechem promised as they left.

At dawn the next morning, Jacob took the same sons and servants who had gathered and broken and shaped rock before, and they set out for the house site. This time, both Reuben and Leah rode with them. Jacob wanted Leah to make any changes she might want before they proceeded further, and Reuben was to then accompany her back to the camp. The other sons had gone with the herdsmen, as usual.

When they reached the site, Jacob helped Leah to dismount and immediately began showing her the beginnings of their future home. She wore no headdress at this early hour and her heavy hair was tied at the nape of her neck. Her eyes shone with anticipation. Jacob thought she looked very young, very pretty. He was happy to see her so excited. He explained where each room would be. The largest room would extend across the length of the longest side of the rectangular courtyard. The cooking room would open onto it and also onto the courtyards so it would be handy. Their own room would be at the opposite end. "Is it large enough?" he asked after Leah and Benjamin had walked around the stakes and cord that marked it off. As Leah hesitated, he added, "We could well make it longer."

Leah considered the suggestion a few moments, then said, "I think so. Perhaps this much," and she took several steps to show how much to add. Jacob changed the stakes and cords, with Benji—to make the child feel useful—while Leah wandered around, still considering the plan carefully. She finally decided on two or three minor changes and the moving and enlarging of the cooking room's chimney.

When Jacob had moved the necessary stakes and cords and showed Benji where to gather stones, he said to Leah, "Come, let us go to the stream for a fresh drink."

He guided her around the stones. "We'll clear a path later," he promised.

She smiled up at him as she said, "I know I will love the house, Jacob. Already the plans please me. I am glad you let me come."

"You notice it will be larger than the ones in Haran or Succoth, though Dinah is gone, and we have the same number of sons, with Benji in place of Joseph. His face clouded as he recalled Joseph, and Leah took his hand.

"It is good, Jacob. If our sons marry, we will need even more rooms."

"So we will," agreed Jacob. "We'll build a long row of rooms for the servants outside the back wall of the courtyard. Later, we can build separate houses as families grow."

They reached the stream and Jacob took a huge leaf from a tree, folded it together to make a cup and dipped water for Leah.

"Oh, it is so good," she breathed, wiping her full, red lips. "How glad I'll be to always have fresh water near the house."

They sat on flat rocks, watching the water as it tumbled over a jagged gray rock into a small sparkling waterfall, listening to its splashing onto rocks below.

Soon Jacob rose, pulling Leah up with him. "The sun is getting hot. You and Reuben should be starting back."

They joined the others and Reuben brought their camels. Jacob helped Leah to mount as he instructed Reuben to return as soon as he could after taking his mother safely home.

When Jacob, Judah, Reuben, Benji, and the servants returned to camp after sunset, the other sons were all knotted under a huge oak near the table. After Jacob and the others had bathed in their tent, and gone to the table in clean robes, the boys were still under the tree, talking in low tones.

As soon as the meal was finished, first Simeon and Levi ambled off into the darkness, then Dan, Naphtali, and Zabulun left together. Soon Gad, Asher, and Issachar followed them. Jacob said nothing, but he wondered what mischief they might be considering.

Reuben asked, "Shall we leave for the house site about sunrise, father?"

Jacob answered, "We must. There is so much yet to be done."

Judah rose. "Then we'd better get to sleep soon. Goodnight," he said, as he started toward his tent.

"Sleep well," responded his mother. She then called for the servant who cared for Benjamin to put him to bed, as he had already fallen asleep with his head on the table. Reuben bade his parents good-night and went to his tent also. Leah and Jacob walked awhile in the faint moonlight, loving the quiet beauty around them and the coolness. They could hear only the night sounds and occasionally, far off, the sounds of their sons' loud laughter.

As they went to their tent, Jacob wondered aloud. "What is going on with them? They acted strangely tonight."

"I don't know," answered Leah as they went through their door, "but they seemed to be planning something when they came for the noon meal and they spoke in low voices when they rested afterwards. It was not the laughter and jesting they usually carry on. Would they be jealous that you chose Judah and Reuben to help with the house?"

Jacob blew out two candles, leaving only a small one burning as he began to undress. "I think not. Tending the animals is so much easier. Have they mentioned Dinah or the bargain we made with Prince Hamor?"

"Not a word to me," answered Leah as she folded her shawl and removed her robe.

Jacob lay down on the heaped-up mats that served as a bed in the tent. "They are up to some mischief. I feel it. But

I am too tired to try and figure out what it is now." He drew in a long breath and was already asleep when Leah blew out the last candle and lay down beside him. For the hundredth time, she thought, *Oh, I wish we had moved our sons away from Haran and my brothers' evil influence long before we did. Only Reuben is not like the others; he is more like Joseph and Benjamin, bent toward good. Perhaps only those born of real love can be good. Though Reuben is my son, still Jacob thought I was his beloved Rachel when he was conceived. And my own Dinah is good, but then she is a girl—no, a woman now—at the mercy of her husband. O Jehovah, I pray that Prince Shechem will be kind to her and will love her the way I have never been loved. And with the new house, which will be ours together, with no reminders of Rachel or Joseph, may Jacob come to love me a little, at least.* Leah's tears fell on her pillow in the silence of the night, and she did not hear her sons return to their tents from the evil they had planned.

Jacob took the same sons as before to the new home site in the early morning, while the others went to tend the animals. Simeon and Levi, however, never reached their animals, but turned their camels toward Hamor's city as soon as they were out of sight of the tents. They rode hard and came early to the city gates. For once the burly keepers were not at their posts. Two maidservants were there instead, and they soon convinced them they had come to help Prince Hamor and Prince Shechem, their sister's husband. They also asked that they permit their other brothers to enter when they arrived.

Once inside the gates, they rode quietly to Hamor's house, secured their mounts, and slipped in at the back. Their drawn swords were in their hands. They knew the men would be sore and weak on this third day after their circumcisions. They would have no trouble surprising and slaying them. They would kill Hamor and Shechem first, then the menservants of the house. If they hurried, and no one cried out, no one in the servant houses would know; they could enter one house at a time and none would hinder them.

They accurately guessed which room was Hamor's.

When they pushed the door open, they found both him and Shechem asleep. With two swift strokes, they killed them both without a sound, and ran quietly back to a door they had passed as they entered. Simeon opened it enough to see several men lying around on mats; some were asleep, but two or three were awake and talking in low tones. "Get those who are awake first," Levi whispered to Simeon and they burst into the room, killed two before they could cry out, and a third as he started to scream. All the others were slain before they were awake enough to know what was happening.

As they slipped out of the house, their swords were dripping with blood. Not one of the maidservants, who talked and laughed as they prepared the morning meal, had any suspicions of wrongdoing. Levi and Simeon ran toward the first servant-house. When they burst into it, the women screamed. Three men in a room toward the back were alerted, but they could do nothing and they were dead in a matter of seconds. The brothers ran out and took the other two servant-houses in the same way. There was wailing and screaming from women and children as Levi and Simeon ran past their camels and on to the first house near the city gates. They found and killed the only two men there, ran to the next house and the next, leaving frightened and screaming women and children in their wake.

And so it went in half the houses of the city. By then the other six brothers and several herdsmen had ridden through the gates. They tied their animals under trees nearby and began herding the terrified women and children together. Some had been running wildly in the streets, some were screaming in the houses, some were cringing silently in closets or under bed mats, and some were crouched over their dead, wailing and moaning. The six brothers were thorough about getting them all out and herded together so they could be guarded by the herdsmen.

On and on Simeon and Levi ran, with the other brothers close behind them, getting the fear-crazed women and children to the herdsmen's group. Before they had finished their bloody work, many of the women had fainted from their horror and fear. Others were hysterical, screaming and tearing their hair. A few of the women were trying in vain to quiet and console children. There were no boys above twelve years of age, for they had been circumcised with the men, and now they were being slain with them also.

Before midday, it was all over, and Simeon and Levi, sweating and cursing, joined the other brothers and the herdsmen in getting the still hysterical women and children into three or four of the houses nearest the gate. Once inside, the grieving people were made to sit on the floor and they were ordered to stop their screaming. They were given water and were promised that they would not be harmed. The men explained that they would be taken to Prince Israel's camp as soon as it was cool enough. A few at a time, under careful guard, were allowed to go to their own homes to get some of their clothes and food for the children. In the first houses, some of them found their dead husbands and sons, but they could do nothing but scream and weep. From then on, one of the men would go into each house first, drag the dead men into one room, and close the door before the women entered.

As the women searched for necessary clothes and food, the men who were guarding them searched for valuables and piled them in heaps in the street near the gate. They also carried food and wine to a huge tamarind tree, where some ate and drank while others guarded the women and children. They planned how to manage the animals, which were still bound in stalls and folds outside the gates and were now lowing and bleating for food and water. They would have to wait until near sunset to move them to their camp, or they would die from the heat. But how could they get them there before dark, since they would move slowly? And how could they take animals, people, and spoils at the same time?

They took their fill of food and wine as they cursed the heat, the women, and even the dead, until it was cool enough to begin moving the people. Six brothers loaded as much of

the valuable spoils as they could onto their camels. With the
herdsmens' help they forced the women and children to
carry all the food and wine they could manage, telling them
to eat what they wanted as they walked. As they were forced
outside the gate, some of them became hysterical. They
looked back at their homes for the last time, realizing their
dead were inside. Many fainted, had to be revived, and then
they were dragged away. Finally the group was moving,
with three brothers riding ahead, three behind, all
brandishing their swords.

The herdsmen began to move the hungry, thirsty,
frightened animals, but they made slow progress. Simeon
and Levi helped them as best they could on foot.

Back at Hamor's house, the day had been one of
complete horror. Adah had gone to Hamor's room with the
morning meal for both him and Shechem. Her screams at
what she found brought Basha and the maidservants. Their
screaming brought the daughters and the smaller children,
but a maid stopped them at the door. Another maid,
moaning, ran to the servants' room, and several followed
her. The carnage there sent all but two back into the hall
screaming. Two had husbands in that room and they fell
upon the bloody, still-warm bodies with shrieks and moans.
Just then, several women from the servant-houses burst in
the back door, screaming also.

At that moment Dinah, wakened by the noise, ran into
the hall. She cried out, "What is wrong?" Nobody answered
her, so she ran down the hall, grabbed a screaming maid,
and shaking her cried, "What is going on? What has
happened?"

The terrified woman shrieked, "The men—dead! They
have all been slain!"

At that, Dinah screamed and pushed through the
howling, terrified daughters and children to Hamor's door.
Her maid, Milah, ran up and gently pulled her back. "No,
no, my mistress. Do not go in! It is too awful!"

Dinah brushed her away, pushed through the door,
screaming, "Shechem! Shechem! What is it?" Then she saw

him. His face was drawn and white in death. He was splattered with his own blood, his clothes were soaked. With an awful cry, she fell upon him, kissing his face, smoothing his hair, keening inconsolably. Milah, sickened by all the blood, stood behind her, weeping at her mistress' grief, conscious of Prince Hamor's wives wailing over his body close by. Their maids also stood helplessly by, their eyes averted from the horrible scene as cascades of tears flowed everywhere.

In the hall, the wailing and screaming grew louder as others came from the servants' houses and looked at the horror in the servants' room.

The older servant in charge of the prince's children came to herself enough to move the children and the daughters to the front of the house. Seeing this, two servant mothers gathered up their own children and the other servant children and followed. Someone closed Hamor's door and the door to the servants' room in order to let the widows grieve in privacy.

The screaming and wailing in the hall eventually quieted, and soon those few who had lost no men or sons went to Hamor's door and stood whispering. Finally they opened the door and slipped inside. After a long time, they and the handmaids prevailed on the three widows to leave the room, almost dragging them, as they wept and screamed, into the hall and then to their own rooms.

The head woman-servant then took charge and after many hours, she and the maids who had lost no one, washed the bodies and covered them with clean covers, master and servants alike.

They reasoned that the same awful thing had happened in the houses in the city, but since they didn't know who had done it, nor if they would come back, they were afraid even to go outside the house.

Hour after hour, they stayed shut inside as the heat mounted steadily and the moaning and wailing went on. Somehow they fed and quieted the smaller children, and later prepared food for the older ones. They got water for the bereaved women and helped them bathe and dress. All the while they wondered, silently and aloud, what had really happened, and why. And then their questions turned to what they were going to do, how to bury the dead, what would happen to them with no men. They all wept even as they worked.

Dinah lay where she had fallen on the bed, and wept till it seemed she could weep no more. Her maid, Milah, sat watching, filled with distress for Dinah, trying to comfort her, even as she herself wept all the while. At last Dinah fainted from grief and the heat. Milah ran to get water, then hurried back and sponged her mistress' pale, swollen face. Dinah slowly came to herself. Dazedly she sat up, the horror rising afresh in her mind, and began to weep again.

"My mistress," pleaded Milah, "you must stop weeping. Let me help you bathe and dress yourself. We know not what may happen next. You should be dressed."

"Yes," Dinah agreed. "You are right. Please bring a pitcher of water for me."

While the maid did her bidding, she rose shakily and began to look through her things, still weeping. Some part of her mind that had been numb seemed to come alive as she chose a garment to wear. Just then a thought hit her so suddenly she dropped to the floor. *It is my brothers who have done this thing! They were angry with Shechem for lying with me. They planned the circumcising and this horrible slaying as vengeance on him. I know they did. They are so evil. Oh, what have I done? Why did Shechem and I yield to our love? Now he is gone forever and I am left alone! What shall I do? What shall these women and children do? Oh, why didn't they kill us all?*

Her thoughts continued as Milah came with the water. *They will come back for me. My father will make them, I know.*

She rose from the floor and found clothes suitable for riding. With Milah's help, she bathed and began to dress, even as her tears continued to fall. She whispered to Milah her suspicion that her brothers had done this terrible thing. The maid was horrified. "No, my mistress, surely they could not have been so cruel!" she cried.

"Sh-h-h," cautioned Dinah. "These people must not know. They will kill us for bringing this upon them. Just please put all my things back into the chests and the bags. Find your things and bring them here also. I know they will come for us."

Her sobs started anew. "But how can I go and leave Shechem? I shall never see him again." Her voice broke and she fell upon the bed, weeping uncontrollably.

After a few moments, Milah gently shook her. "Mistress, your husband is dead. You could only see him buried if we stayed."

"But who will bury him?" Dinah asked brokenly as Milah pulled her up. "The women cannot—you know that—and the men in the city are surely all dead too. Oh, what shall we do?"

"Mistress, you must stop crying and finish your dressing. We must be ready if your brothers come. Please, I will help you," reasoned the frightened girl.

"No, get my things packed. I—I will try to dress, said Dinah as she stood.

"That is good," Milah encouraged her as she began to gather her mistress' clothes and other possessions.

Dinah continued to weep as she hurriedly completed dressing and combed her hair. She saw that Milah had her things in the chests and bags and had gone for her own things.

She wondered how Adah, Basha, and the girls were bearing their double loss. And what of the children, and the servants? *O Jehovah, It is too awful to bear! What have my brothers done? What have I caused?*

She couldn't bear to be alone in her agony and ran to the door to look for Milah. As she opened it, she heard muffled moans and wailing, and the screams and crying of the children. She herself began to weep again. Then Milah came up the hall with two large bags holding her possessions, biting her lips to keep from crying out, while tears streamed down her contorted face.

"Mistress, don't listen! Don't listen! Go back into your

room and close the door!" she begged as she came near.

Dinah obeyed, and Milah went in after her and laid down her bags. Dinah fell into her arms, and they wept together.

When Milah recovered somewhat, she led her mistress to one of the two leather-covered chairs and gently pushed her down. "I shall find some food and some fresh water for us," she said.

"No, no, I cannot eat. I can never eat again!" protested Dinah.

"Mistress, we must. If your brothers come, we will faint from weakness before we reach the camp. Just sit here now and I will be back soon." She quickly left the room, even as Dinah was saying, "Don't leave me. I cannot bear to be alone!"

Dinah fell back into the chair, covering her swollen face and eyes with trembling hands. She began to take deep breaths and gradually grew calmer. Then she thought, *Milah is right. We must eat. I am already so weak I could not even mount, much less ride the long distance to the camp.*

Thinking of the camp made her remember her mother, and she wept again. *Oh, my mother, if only you were here, you would comfort me, you would know what to do with all this horror! Will I ever get back to you and my father again? O Jehovah, help us, help us!*

Milah came in with bread, cheese, and honeycomb on a tray, and a pitcher of water in one hand. She set the pitcher on one table, then dragged another low table to her mistress' chair in order to put the tray upon it. She poured water into two pottery containers she had found and brought them to the table also. Then she sat on a mat across from Dinah, saying, "Mistress, you must eat now and drink also, whether you want to or not."

Slowly Dinah took some of the water. It felt good to her dry lips and tongue, and she drank it all.

Milah, watching her, was pleased. "Now try the bread and cheese."

Obediently Dinah tried, but could get down only a few bites. She laid the remainder back on the tray.

"Mistress, drink the rest of the water and try again, please," begged Milah.

Seeing the girl's concerns Dinah tried again; only a few more bites would go down. She drank again.

"Now try the honeycomb. It will give you strength," insisted Milah.

She put a small bite into her mouth. It was soothing. She chewed the comb until the honey was gone, then laid it upon the tray and took more.

"That is good," said Milah, actually smiling a little. Dinah drank more water, ate some more, to please Milah. Then she pushed the table toward Milah and got to her feet.

"You eat the remainder," she said. "I will pour more water." And she did, spilling a little because her hands were shaking. Then she lay on the bed again, willing herself to not weep while Milah ate.

Soon she dozed into a fitful, exhausted sleep, only to be awakened by loud banging at the front of the house and screams from the back. She jumped up, frightened, looking for Milah, who was replacing the small table near the window. "What is it?" she asked, then answered her own question, "Oh, yes, that will be my brothers. Come, let us go and let them in."

"Mistress," said Milah, hanging back as Dinah started for the door, "what if it isn't?

What if—"

"Of course it is my brothers." There was hardness, bitterness in her voice, hoarse from weeping. "Come with me." She opened the door and Milah followed her.

The banging and screaming was louder from the hall, and they hurried to the front door. "Is it my brothers?" Dinah tried to make her voice heard over the noise, but had to repeat the question twice before the banging stopped and Simeon said, "Yes, it is Levi and me. Let us in. We have come for you."

Dinah opened the door and they came in, swords sheathed by their sides. Anger overcame Dinah's horror and grief. Her eyes blazed as she hurled her bitterness at them.

"Oh, you wicked, wicked deceivers! You vile murderers! How could you do this to me? I loved my husband, and now you have killed him! Now I will always be alone. Oh, I hate you, I hate you!" She was screaming hysterically and beating on Simeon's chest with clenched fists, and scratching at his blood-splattered, cruel face.

He grabbed her hands, taken aback by her anger and her hysteria. Levi stood behind him, too surprised by the viciousness of his normally gentle sister to speak. Holding her hands, Simeon shook her roughly. "Hush!" he commanded. "You don't know what you are saying! Can't you see we did this all for you, to avenge your honor? Could we let him treat our only sister as a harlot?"

Dinah was trying to get free of his grasp, kicking him with all her strength, screaming over his rough voice. "You don't care for me! You wanted an excuse to kill! All of you are murderers! You think I don't know you destroyed Joseph because he told father of your wicked deeds? Of course you did! May Jehovah curse you all!"

Levi had recovered from his surprise enough to be angered by her words. Coming up behind her, he grabbed her by the shoulders, tore her from Simeon's grasp, and flung her roughly to the floor, where she lay weeping.

"Foolish woman!" cried Levi, towering over her. "Don't you dare accuse us! I don't want to hear another word from you, or we'll use these swords on you as well!" His eyes blazed as his hand grabbed his sword.

Simeon caught his arm. "Enough!" he said. "Calm down. She is distraught, and rightly so." He turned to Milah, who was cowering against the wall, "Tend to your mistress and get her things together. We shall take you home—along with all the women and children who are left. Where are they?"

When the terrified girl could speak, she answered, "In the rooms, behind closed doors." She stretched a hand toward the hall. "They are frightened. Hear the children crying?"

He listened. He could hear not only the children, but the moans of the women as well.

Turning from Milah and Dinah, they both drew their bloody swords. Simeon said over his shoulder, as they started down the hall, "See that you calm our sister; get her ready to ride."

When they came to the first door, they beat upon it and cried out, "Open the door. You will not be hurt." Behind it, the crying and screaming grew louder.

Levi shouted, "Stop it! Stop the noise so we can talk to you!" He could hear the women attempting to quiet the children. He went on, "You will not be hurt if you do as we tell you. Open the door." They waited; it was quiet but the door did not open. Levi cried, "If you will not open it, we will break it down." He began to kick the door and beat on it with his sword.

They could hear the women talking with each other in hushed and fretful tones. Presently the door opened slightly. Levi pushed it wide open, then stepped in with his sword held high, as Simeon went to the next door.

"Listen to me. We won't hurt you if you will do as we say. We will take you all to our camp where you will be cared for, all of you. We will give you a few minutes to get food and water for the journey and whatever clothes and possessions you can carry. Do you all have mounts?" Basha nodded. He continued, "Then you may carry your children on them and whatever possessions you can. Now hurry!"

He stepped outside, stood at the door with his sword, as the terrified women scattered to their rooms for clothes and also to get food and water. The children stayed in the room with their maid, crying again. Levi noticed that Simeon had gotten the next door open, and was speaking with the house-servants there. He went on to the next door, persuading those servants to open it. They soon understood what they must do, and scurried like frightened rats to gather their possessions.

Simeon had now gone to the next doors so Levi went past him and opened the door that was barred from the outside. He knew it held the dead Hamor and Shechem, but he made sure no one was hiding there. Then he went to the other barred door where the bodies of the male servants were. No one was hiding there. He ran outside to the servant house, but no living people were there either, so he hurried back just as the women were rushing out of the last room, while Simeon stood at the door with his sword drawn. He was warning them to make haste.

Levi called out, loudly enough for everyone in the house to hear, "Hurry! Hurry! Only a little longer! Take your things to the front of the house."

Just then, Dinah ran down the hall; her face was streaming with tears. Milah was following her. "Simeon," she called, "let me see my husband. Please, I must see him just once more before I leave him forever!"

Simeon hesitated; pity vying with the hardness of his face. But Levi called from farther back. "No, no, you may not see him. It would only upset you. Go back to your room! Now!"

The distraught girl shrieked, "You killed my husband! Now you refuse to let me see him! I hate you! I hate you!" Anger blazed in her face.

Simeon went to her. "Go, Dinah. It is better if you do not see," he said kindly.

She looked at him a moment, as resignation slowly replaced the anger in her pale, swollen face. She turned and walked dejectedly back to her room with Milah's supporting arm around her.

Basha and Adah, along with the other women, had heard Levi's denial of his own sister's request. None of them asked to see their dead a last time, but silent tears coursed down all of their faces as Levi herded them toward the front, loaded with all they could carry.

The brothers emptied each room of maids and children as they came to them, and each child ran to its mother. The little ones were crying, and the older ones were silent, as they helped to carry some of the possessions. Terror covered each face.

Levi pushed them all into the large, front room as Simeon brought out Dinah's chests, while she and Milah dragged their bags.

Levi said, "Simeon, stand here while I get the animals." He brandished his sword toward three stalwart maids. "Come," he said, and they went out ahead of him. Milah and Dinah, weeping quietly, stood by Simeon in the hall. The other women sat weeping in the big room. Some of the children cried, while mothers and maids tried to comfort them.

Dinah swayed as if she would fall. Simeon said, "Here, sit on the chests." She sank down on one and motioned for Milah to sit on the other.

It seemed that a long time had passed before Levi called for them to come outside. When he did, Simeon said to those in the room, "Go out now and stand there until we tell you to move."

When the last one was out, he told Dinah and Milah to go, and they dragged their bags behind them down the long steps, while he carried one chest behind them. When he put it down, he went back for the other one.

Somehow, amid the heat and weeping, Adah, Basha, the four girls, and the smaller children were mounted on their own camels, while some of the maids and smaller children were put on the camels that had belonged to Hamor, Shechem, and the two head menservants. As many belongings as they could carry were put beside the women. Each woman held food and water.

Older women were put on donkeys and held smaller servant-children in their arms. Bundles of belongings were put on the remaining beasts. Several older children and some maids were told to walk. They helped Simeon load Dinah's chests and Milah's bags on Milah's camel, as Levi guarded everything from his own mount, his sword still in hand.

Simeon helped Dinah and Milah to mount Dinah's camel, then he threw Dinah's bags up behind Milah. He mounted his own beast and rode ahead of the frightened, weary, weeping group while Levi rode behind.

Afterwards, Dinah could not remember clearly the awful ride to her father's camp. The anguished moans and screams as the women passed through the gates of their city for the last time, leaving their unburied men behind them, came to her as in a dream. Her own weeping joined with theirs without her being really aware. She recalled with confusion that Levi, cursing, was trying to rush those on foot, while Simeon, ahead, was holding back the riders, especially the ones on camels. She knew they stopped many times when someone fainted and had to be revived, and once when a child fell from one of the donkeys. At times she lost consciousness and it was only Milah behind her who kept her from falling. Somehow, her maid was able to wipe her face with some of her clothing she had moistened from a water-skin she had remembered to fill. As if it was coming from some far-off part of her mind, she heard Simeon cry to Levi that they were in sight of the people from the city, and to hurry so they could catch up, at which the wailing grew louder. Once she caught a glimpse of a multitude of animals to their right, and heard their mingled cries as the herdsmen urged them on with whips, yells, and curses.

She was vaguely aware of stopping, of being pulled from her mount, of Milah beside her leading her to some unknown destination. Then she heard her name being called and knew it was her mother's voice. She collapsed at Leah's feet and when she came to, she was in her own tent, with her mother bathing her face and weeping softly as Milah told her what had taken place. As Dinah began to weep anew, Leah gathered her in her arms and they embraced each other tightly, sharing a grief too deep for words.

Dinah's mother began to comfort her. She told her to stop weeping, that she must rest now. Then, as exhaustion and sleep began to overtake her, she heard her mother's voice as if from a great distance. "Milah, lie here and rest with your mistress. I must go to the other grieving women and children. I must give them fresh water, and find places for them to rest." Leah agonized to herself, *O Jehovah, how could my sons have brought so much horror to so many in one day! What will this do to Jacob?* Blessed sleep finally claimed Dinah's exhausted body and soul.

6

Jacob Moves to Hebron

And Jacob said to Simeon and Levi, Ye have troubled me to make me stink among the inhabitants of the land, among the Canaanites and the Perizzites: and I being few in number, they shall gather themselves together against me, and slay me; And I shall be destroyed, I and my house.

(Genesis 34:30)

And Jacob came unto Isaac his father unto Mamre, unto the city of Arbah, which is Hebron, where Abraham and Isaac sojourned.

(Genesis 35:27)

If Dinah could <u>not</u> remember clearly her awful ride home, Leah <u>could</u> remember vividly every detail of the terrible night that followed. It would stay in her mind forever.

She and her servants had gone to the weeping, terrified people the sons had left under the trees while they cared for the animals. Leah spoke to Basha and Adah, loudly enough for all to hear once they quieted themselves. "Do not be afraid. We will care for you. It is a horrible thing my sons have done to you, and I know their father will punish them. I would do anything to change this, but it is done. I know

87

your grief is great and I can't erase that. But I can tell you not to be afraid. You will be hurt no more and you will be well cared for. You, wives of Prince Hamor, and your children, will be treated as such. The women of the city will be respected and cared for as they have been accustomed to, and so will the maidservants and the children. Try to stop weeping now, sit or lie on whatever you have with you. Eat what food you have and we will bring more, and fresh water, and milk for the children. We will find tents and mats for sleeping. Rest now and do not fear."

Basha and Adah could not speak because of their weeping, but they bowed in thanks to Leah, and their daughters and the younger children bowed also. Then they all began to lie down upon the bundled clothes they held or upon the bare ground. Leah and her servants hurried away to take care of their needs, for night would soon come.

At Leah's order, every servant—man and maid—set about to the tasks at hand. The noise mounted as tents were raised and the sons and herdsmen tried to get the disturbed animals settled for the night. A very large tent was put up near where Leah, Bilhah, and Zilpah were feeding and caring for the people, and when the tent with sleeping mats was ready, Leah invited Prince Hamor's family to it. She went inside with them and helped straighten out their tangled belongings and find things to sleep in. She helped the children to undress and put them to bed. When this was done, she turned to Adah and Basha. "Can I do anything more to help you tonight?" she asked.

"No," answered Basha. "We will be all right. You have been more than kind." Her voice broke and she began weeping again. Leah pulled the broken woman to her. As she held her she said, "I tell you again how sorry I am that this happened. We will care for you."

Adah and the girls were weeping also. Leah spoke to them all, "Try not to think. Try to rest. I will leave you now, but call if you need me."

Outside, she found that Zilpah and Bilhah and the servants had placed the last family, townspeople and servants alike, into the long row of tents under the now-dark trees. She went toward her own tent near the camp's entrance, peering into the near darkness, wondering why Jacob and the others had not come, yet relieved that they hadn't.

She almost choked when she thought of how Jacob would surely react to this horror, and she knew it would be easier for her to bear now that the pitiful captives were cared for. She went quietly to the door of Dinah's tent. There was no sound. *Thanks be to Jehovah,* she thought, *that the weary, heartbroken girl is sleeping.*

She got a lamp from her own tent, lighted it, passed through the camp entrance and walked some distance in the direction from which Jacob would come. Holding the light, she stood waiting, trying to calm her thoughts, wondering how to tell Jacob. Just then she heard hoofbeats and voices. She was relieved to know her men were all right.

Seeing Leah with a light, Jacob called with alarm before she could see him, "What is wrong?" He urged his camel on and the sons followed. Momentarily his great white beast stopped before her and he dismounted. "Leah, is something wrong?"

Leah answered, trying to keep her voice calm. "Jacob, please try to hold your anger. Something is very wrong—so wrong I hate to tell you!"

"Speak up! Tell me," commanded Jacob with fear in his voice.

"Jacob," Leah began hesitantly, "Our sons have killed Prince Hamor, Shechem, and all the men of the city! They —"

Jacob interrupted loudly as Judah and Reuben rode up and dismounted, "Woman, what are you saying? It cannot be true!" The alarm in his voice showed that he feared that he had heard correctly.

"It is true, Jacob. They are all dead and our sons have brought the women and children captives, along with all the city's animals!" Her voice was clear now, very calm.

"What of Dinah?" Jacob cried out. "Have they harmed her?"

"They have not harmed her, Jacob, but she is heartbroken and in utter collapse from the horror and the long ride home. I have taken care of her, she and Milah are asleep in her tent." She stopped as Benjamin rode up, dismounted and came toward them.

Jacob began to cry out, to pull his hair, and tear his clothes.

"My father!" cried the child, "What is wrong with you?" and ran to him. "Can I help you? Father!"

"No, no, my son. Nobody can help!" He brushed the boy away and fell face-down upon the ground, beating his breast and crying out to Jehovah.

Leah said to Reuben, "Take Benji to his tent and call his nurse. Perhaps she can help him understand while she feeds him and puts him to bed."

Reuben obediently took the child by the hand and reached for Judah's reins. He led both camels and Benji away, still holding his own camel's reins in his other small hand.

Judah and Leah moved closer to Jacob.

Leah pleaded, "Calm yourself, Jacob. You cannot change what has happened. You can only harm yourself."

But Jacob only cried out the more and beat his head upon the ground. Leah thought, *This is the way he was when Joseph was being born and again when he lost him. He is older now. His heart will give out with so much emotion. Still it is better this way than the way he was when Rachel died. I could not bear that again!*

Judah was on his father's other side, trying to get through to him. "Father, Father, you must stop this!" he called loudly and reached out to hold him still.

Jacob, not even aware of what he did, pushed Judah away and kept crying out, "O Jehovah, what have my evil sons done? Now I will be hated of all the people of this land, and since I am few, they will kill us all! What have I done that this, after the loss of Rachel and Joseph, should come upon me? Why? Why? Did You not let me come safely to this place? Did You not let me enter into an agreement with these people? What else could I do when I was here among them? I could not know my sons would use the agreement to bring death! What shall I do now? O Jehovah, hear me! Help me to know what to do!"

He continued to cry out, to roll upon the ground in his distress. Reuben came back and he and Judah stood helplessly by, while Leah continued to talk to their father, to no avail. She knew, however, that his agony and frustration would calm when his energy was spent.

She waited and at last he lay still, weeping. She rose and told her sons to help him to his tent. Jacob did not resist and soon he was lying in his tent and the sons had gone to get food. Leah sat by Jacob, bathing his face, speaking soothingly until he stopped weeping. Then she gave him water, called a servant to bring food to the tent for them. They were both silent until the food was brought. She helped Jacob to the small table, coaxed him to eat and to drink some wine.

Gradually, as they ate and drank, he stopped trembling, becoming a bit more rational. "Tell me more of this terrible deed, Leah," he commanded.

"There is little I know, Jacob" she said, "but I will tell you what I could get from our weeping daughter and her weary, frightened maid. But promise me you will hold your anger in check. Anger will not help."

"I promise," Jacob said, thinking he was too weary for anger.

"It was Simeon and Levi who did the killing—with their swords. You remember they all left early this morning, even before you did. All of them must have gone to tend the animals, except those two. They must have gone directly to Prince Hamor's house, for Milah said they found all the men dead while it was still early—Prince Hamor, Shechem, and all the menservants. They saw no one, heard nothing, so the sore, ill men must have still been sleeping."

"O Jehovah!" sighed Jacob, as shock and shame registered in his face. "How could they have killed defenseless men?"

"All day the women and children stayed shut up in the

house with the dead, not knowing who had done this thing, afraid they would come back and kill them also. Only in the afternoon did Dinah, in her grief and horror, think that it had been her brothers, that they would come back for her. They did. It was Simeon and Levi."

"But the women and children—how did they bring them here?"

"Hamor's wives and children rode their own camels. Some old servants and some small children were on donkeys when they got here; those who could, walked. Oh, what a weary, thirsty, pitiful sight they were!"

Far into the night, Leah and Jacob talked and wept in sorrow for the bereaved and homeless women and children. They wept in shame when they thought of the evil their sons had done. Jacob said they must surely leave tomorrow, before the other cities learned what had happened, or the inhabitants of the land would kill them all.

"But can we get ready to leave by the time it is cool enough tomorrow?" asked Leah. "Think how many more there are now, how many of their animals have to be moved also."

"We have no choice," Jacob said with finality. "We must leave, whether we are ready or not. Even then may be too late."

When Judah and Reuben left their father's tent, they went to the table where lamps were burning and weary-looking servants were preparing food. It was later than their usual time for getting food ready, because they had helped their mistress with the captives. Some of the other brothers and a few herdsmen were already eating, and others were coming. They were speaking in low tones.

Judah and Reuben sat down and began to eat. Everyone stopped talking and looked at them with seeming contempt. Judah looked round at them. The faces were weary and grim; their clothes were dirty, some were even still splattered with blood. Gad and Asher straggled in, sat down, and began to grab food, eating greedily. Two more herdsmen came and did the same. No one said anything. Then came Simeon and

Levi, grimier, dirtier, more blood-splattered than the others. They all ate in silence, gulping their food, drinking much wine. Judah thought, *We would not eat this way if our father were here. But I am glad he is not here, in his weary, distraught state. Perhaps he is calmer by now.*

When all of the food and wine were gone, they left the table and sprawled upon the ground, Reuben and Judah with the others, some distance away, not far from the captives' tents. For some time no one spoke and Judah was aware of low moans and wailings coming from the tents. *How wretched, how frightened these people must be,* he thought. *Why, why would Simeon and Levi do this awful thing? How did they keep it from Reuben and me?*

Finally Reuben could bear the silence no longer. "Will someone tell us what happened today?" The men looked at each other. Everyone remained silent.

"Tell me!" Reuben roared.

Levi said grimly, in low tones, "I'll tell you what happened. Simeon and I took our swords, rode to Prince Hamor's house, killed him and Shechem and all the men and boys who had been circumcised. Then we did the same to all in the city." His voice grew louder, more belligerent. "Should that cursed heathen treat our sister as a harlot and not pay for it? We have only avenged our sister! We did what was right!"

Judah protested, "But it was only Shechem, not the others. And he married her! We made the agreement; our father consented to it! Don't you know what you have done to him? Don't you see that the people of the land will find out about this and band together and kill us?"

"We shall leave this place tomorrow, before any other people know what happened," said Simeon.

"It would be good if you left now, before you have to face our father's anger!" declared Reuben. "He was so shocked and angry when our mother told him. You have shamed him by your evil deed. It was worse than when we brought Joseph's coat to him. And Dinah is in a pitiful state as well. How could you bring this on her? How could you do this to these poor women and children who had not harmed you? Listen to them wailing in the tents!" Reuben's outrage grew as he talked, and he was hissing at his brothers now, trying to keep his voice down.

"Don't you judge us!" Levi spat back at him. "You should have been helping us avenge our sister. But we knew you were not man enough to help, so we didn't tell you. We remembered it was you who wanted to save Joseph. You even wanted to tell our father what we did to him, but you were afraid of us!"

Gad broke in fiercely, "We knew you would have told our father about our plans for this, so we didn't tell you! You are cowardly, yet you tell us what we shouldn't have done!"

Several others agreed, cursing at Reuben, calling him effeminate..

At this, Reuben jumped up, charged into them, swinging at them with his big fists. They fell upon Reuben, kicking and punching and hurling profanities at him.

Judah spoke loudly, but with calm authority. "It is enough. Stop! Have you not done enough evil for one day? Did you not tell me you were planning this horror for the same reason? No, don't answer. It matters not; I would not have agreed to such a foolish deed, so we'd have to move on again. And with these captives and the extra animals! How can we do it?" There was muttering and grumbling among the brothers, but they never went against Judah in anything. And in this, they knew, too late, that he was right.

He went on, "Can you not see what you are doing to our father? Do you not yet know how losing Joseph has aged him, taken his strength from him, in these few months? I know now we were wrong in what we did. I fear Jehovah will punish us, and rightly so. And think of our mother. She is no longer young. She was so happy in the realization that she was to have a house at last that would be hers alone, with no reminder of Aunt Rachel or Joseph, that our father would come to love her finally. Can't you open your eyes and see anything, even yet? And now you have ruined things for us all!" His contempt and anger were so strong that no one said a word. Soon, one by one, the brothers moved off to their tents, leaving Reuben and Judah alone.

"I should not like to face our father's wrath in the morning, if I were Simeon or Levi," said Judah.

"Nor I," agreed Reuben. "But at his age, it is not good for him to be so angry. We must stand by him."

Yes," returned Judah, "so we'd better sleep now." As they went to their tents, he said, "Take your sword tomorrow."

Jacob and Leah rose early, despite the fact they had slept little. Jacob, splashing water on his face from the pottery basin on his table, said, "I wish I did not have to confront my sons this day. The more I say, the angrier I shall become, for this evil is the worst they have ever done. But they must know they shall not go unpunished for so great a sin against us, against these people, against Jehovah. They must ask forgiveness and I must sacrifice and pray to Jehovah to forgive them."

"I know," agreed Leah. "But not today. We must prepare to leave today. Jacob, I have told Prince Hamor's family they shall be treated well. We met many of the townspeople that night and were friendly to them. It will not be right now to treat them as servants." She still sat on the bed in her nightdress.

"You are right," agreed Jacob, drying his face carefully. "They shall be treated the way they are accustomed to being treated. Only the servants will become our servants, and they shall be treated as our own."

Leah was silent as Jacob dressed. Then she asked, "Is there no way we can remain here? I hate to leave the beginnings of our home. Besides, where can we go?"

"We cannot stay, Leah," Jacob answered with finality in his voice as he tied on his sandals. "We shall go to my father in Hebron, unless Jehovah prevents us from doing so. Prepare to move out as soon as it is cool enough." He turned to go outside. Then he went back to Leah and put his hands gently on her shoulders, as she looked up at him, squinting in the morning light. "Leah, I am sorry about your house. I promise I shall build you one like it when we reach Hebron. We must hurry before it is too late."

"Thank you, Jacob. We will be ready," she said, smiling sadly.

As he turned and went out, she snatched up her robe and ran to her own tent to dress. *Yes, Jacob, we will be ready,* she thought, *and I will be happy in my house in Hebron.*

Only Reuben, Judah, and Benji, sleepy-eyed, were at the table when Jacob sat down. He greeted them, then turned his eyes heavenward. "Jehovah be praised. We give You thanks for our food. Help me to know what is right to do. Help these people whom my sons have so wronged. Forgive their sin, if it is not too great." He stopped speaking and his eyes filled with tears. He began eating, and soon asked, "Where are your brothers this morning?"

"No doubt they have gone back to the city," Judah answered. "I know they could not bring all the spoil with them yesterday."

Jacob was thoughtful. "Whatever they have brought, whatever else they bring, it shall be given to these pitiful captives, for it is rightfully theirs. It will be little enough to pay for the horror they have been through, for the grief they will always know."

"Yes," agreed Reuben. "Listen, some of them are wailing again." They were quiet, hearing the desolate, pitiful sounds.

Benji began to weep as well. The child cried, "Father, Reuben told me what my other brothers did to the men. But why? Why would they hurt them, why would they kill the fathers and leave the children to weep?"

"My son," answered Jacob, "it is a sad story and you would not understand now. Later, when you are older, I will try to explain it all to you. It is a terrible thing my sons have done, and I am glad I do not have to deal with them this day, when so much must be done."

Just then Leah came up, greeted the sons, began to eat some bread and cheese without sitting. She called for Zilpah and Bilhah and gave them instructions for the day's work. Jacob, Reuben, and Judah left to find the herdsmen. They had to make hurried plans for moving the animals and carry them out in such a little time. Judah let Reuben and his father plan as they hurried along. His thoughts were on the captives. He kept hearing their wailing in his mind. It reminded him of Joseph's pitiful cries when they had sold him to the Midianite traders. The boy's terrified face came back to haunt him once again, as it had many times in the past three months. His father's sorrow was always with him, too. *How could we have done such a thing, and to our own brother? Why didn't I listen to Reuben when he begged us not to harm Joseph? How can I judge Simeon and Levi for this awful deed, when I am guilty as well? I would tell my father now what really happened, but he would grieve even more to think of his beloved son being a slave.*

Somehow the long, busy, frustrating day passed, and two hours before sunset the huge caravan lined up, ready for Jacob's call to move forward. Somehow during the day, Jacob found time for him and Benjamin to visit Dinah in her tent. He was stunned at her pale, swollen face, at her heartbroken weeping as he tried to comfort her. Her pitiful question as to why it had to happen tore at his heart and he wept with her, holding her trembling body close to him. It took a long time before his words of comfort helped her to stop weeping. When she saw small Benji, she wept again. She hugged him, then rumpled his curly, coppery hair in the way she used to.

"Don't cry, Dinah," he pleaded. "You still have us to love you. We are glad you are back with us. Do you know we are moving again this very day?"

She managed a wan smile. "Thank you, Benji, and I still love you. Yes, my mother told me we are leaving. I know it is best."

Jacob and Leah also found time to visit the captives together, to reassure them that they would be treated respectfully as they had been before, and would be cared for. To Adah and Basha, Jacob gave the promise that their family would be as his own, that they would travel with his own wife and Dinah. And even as Leah had, he told all the captives that it had not been his will for this thing to happen, that their goods would be restored, and his sons would be punished.

Leah and the servants had somehow managed to pack food they hoped would last for the whole journey, with what the captives had brought with them. The menservants had taken on the extra duty of seeing to the captives' tents, of packing their belongings and the spoil on the extra animals. The herdsmen who hadn't gone with the brothers to the city, fed, watered, and did their best with the restless beasts of burden.

And now the caravan was lined up, with the captives, except for Hamor's family, just ahead of the servants at the rear. The members of Jacob's family were at the front, on their fine beasts with their best trappings and all the personal belongings each could carry. Behind them were Hamor's family, the wives and daughters also on fine camels, some holding children. The younger women and older children were on foot. The servants, with many heavily laden beasts, were last.

Jacob had started the herdsmen with the animals an hour before, promising to overtake them by dawn, when they would make camp if they found water and shade. Now Jacob, Judah, and Reuben were riding up and down the hot, noisy, restless line, checking to see that all was in readiness. As Jacob rode finally to the front, he noted the tired lines on Leah's face and the tears on Dinah's. *How hard this has been for them both,* he thought. He smiled at Leah, and her face lifted. He spoke kindly to Dinah, waiting between her mother and her maid Milah. "Try not to weep, my daughter. It will be better soon." She gave him a faint smile.

To the child Benjamin, just ahead of Leah, he said, "Well, my son, I think we are ready."

The boy asked, "Father, will we not wait for the others?" Dinah wept anew for someone had told her where they had gone.

"No," he answered. "It's likely they will catch up to us farther on." Just then, Judah rode up on one side, with Reuben on the other.

"All is in order, Father," Judah assured him.

"Then we ride," said Jacob. "If your brothers find us, well. If they don't—"he shrugged, his face was hard. Judah and Reuben fell in just ahead of Benjamin, and Jacob, on his great white beast, looked down the long line of expectant faces. He raised his hand high, shouted the familiar command—"Forward"—and the caravan moved out as one man, toward the south.

The caravan snaked along, winding around low hills, down into shallow valleys, where, even there, the grass was sparse and dried. Suddenly they faced a wide, flat plain and once the caravan had approached it, they saw high, dark hills in the far distance to their left, and level ground to the horizon on their right. Jacob was the first to sight smoke low on the horizon, far to the southwest. *That is Prince Hamor's city burning,* he thought with a jolt, but he was silent. *I hope Dinah and the captives will not see it. It will hurt them too much. At least my evil sons were sensible enough to wait till late in the day, so we can be far away before the other cities notice the smoke.* Just then Judah saw the smoke and rode up beside his father, started to speak of it and point. Jacob stopped him. "It will be too painful for the captives," he whispered. "Don't draw attention to it."

But great billows of black smoke rose high, and they did see it. A pitiful moaning and wailing began with Hamor's family and spread to all the others. Dinah cried out, covered her face, then sobbed aloud, rocking back and forth in her grief. Leah and Milah reached to steady her, and Benji began to cry at her distress. The caravan slowed, leaving Jacob and Judah far ahead. Reuben urged his mount on and caught up with them. "Shall we stop for a while?" he asked.

"No, no," answered Jacob. "We must hurry them on, so they won't have time to grieve for their city, and their dead, burning."

Judah and Reuben wheeled their mounts and rode down the line on either side, urging the people on. Jacob motioned and called to his family to hurry forward. Soon, the whole caravan was moving faster than before, a long straight line on the flat land.

Just before sundown, Jacob's other sons and the herdsmen were spotted on the horizon, smoke still billowing behind them. They were riding hard toward the caravan, but it was almost twilight, with a few stars showing above the red haze when they reached it. The herdsman split from the sons as they came near and rode toward the end of the caravan. The sons rode up beside Jacob and the others, but Jacob made no space for them to fall into their accustomed place, and no one spoke a word to them. Their camels were piled high with more spoils, and the odor of cooked meat and fresh fruits drifted around them on the still air. *I suppose they roasted stray lambs and calves when they returned to the city—feasted on them and brought the rest to eat on the journey*, thought Jacob as his mind literally seethed with anger at the sight of them.

The night became so dark that Jacob could not tell whether the caravan was veering off-course. He could hear children crying in the rear and some donkeys braying. He asked Judah, "Son, should we stop to rest until the moon gives us more light?" Judah agreed, and turned to tell Leah, Dinah, Benji, and Reuben. Then he rode forward a little, turned and shouted, "Halt!"

The line stopped abruptly and an audible sigh ran through it. Jacob, Judah, and Reuben dismounted and began to help the women. They continued to ignore the other sons, as they rode to the back of the caravan to dismount. Reuben volunteered to hold all the reins near the front. The grieving women, stiff from the long ride, stretched themselves listlessly. Servants from the back were lighting lamps, putting bread, cheese, dried figs, and wine on trays, which they soon brought to the front. The loaded beasts ceased their braying, glad to stand still awhile.

The crying children were fed, and soon everyone was sitting or lying on the ground in little groups, talking among themselves and laughing. Most were unaware that they were escaping from sure retaliation for the awful deed the sons had done. The sons stayed together at the end of the caravan, eating some of the food they'd brought from the city—

talking, jesting, and laughing coarsely. Jacob and Leah could hear them where they were resting and eating at the front. They tried to keep Dinah and Hamor's family occupied so they wouldn't hear the laughter. Most of them were bravely trying not to weep, still thinking of the burning city. Benji sat close to Dinah and talked to her about the new house they had started to build. Soon he turned to his father to ask if they would build a house when they got to his grandfather's. Jacob assured him that they would, that he should have a big room for himself, and that Dinah should have a fine one, too. The girl tried to smile as she thanked her father, but her voice broke and tears filled her eyes. Prince Hamor's wives began to weep softly, and their daughters tried to comfort them. The night was chilly now and their shawls were drawn close around them.

Just then they heard voices in the distance, and slowly approaching hoof beats. Jacob, Judah, Reuben, and most of the menservants farther down the line jumped up, checking their swords and daggers, listening intently. Seeing their alarm, the sons sent a herdsman from the back to tell Jacob that it was only the three herdsmen they had left behind bringing a drove of stray animals, including several camels, that had wandered back to the city during the day.

"They have seen our lights and are coming to join us," explained the herdsman. Nevertheless Jacob remained tense until he could see the animals being herded to the back of the line.

Several herdsmen who had managed to get some rest, rose and took charge of the animals, while those who brought them dismounted, stretched their sore and stiff muscles, and were given food and wine. With the arrival of strange animals, there was a lot of noise and restless moving around. Since the moon was bright by now and the way was fairly light, Jacob soon gave the order to mount and in a matter of minutes he gave the call to move forward. The caravan was moving again.

An hour before dawn, the caravan overtook the animals and the herdsmen under a large grove of varied trees, visible from a distance in the moonlight. As they came near, several herdsmen came to meet them and Jacob urged his camel on ahead. One of the men hailed him with relief and they stood talking for a few moments. "Master," he said. "The stream flows from your left, a little farther down, and bends around a small valley, where the trees are. Then it flows directly south, it is shallow and wide beyond the valley. We can follow it for a night or two, and the animals can graze along its banks."

"It is good," said Jacob.

Another herdsman spoke. "We've watered the animals and taken them part of the way down the stream. If you just circle the caravan around the upper trees, you'll come right into the little valley. It will be a good place to camp."

"That we will do," responded Jacob, and turned his great white camel back toward the caravan, now very near. He spoke with Judah and Reuben and they rode down each side of the line to give directions and help. Then he went forward, circling the caravan in a wide arc around the grove. The herdsman waited where he had left them, so they could help with the animals.

At the break of dawn, the donkeys were unloaded, and they and the camels were watered and moved down the stream with the other animals. People bedded down in the valley under the trees, and most of them were already sleeping. They were very weary and it would be mid-afternoon before most of them would rise and begin the task of preparing food and getting ready to move on again before sundown.

Thus it went for many days, as they traveled mostly by night, sleeping by day. Jacob had begun to breathe easier, for he felt sure if anyone had suspected them of the killing, looting, and burning of Shechem, they would have overtaken them by now. He continued to ignore his own sons, who stayed to themselves, for he was not ready to confront them with their evil as yet. Indeed, he had not yet decided on their punishment, but he thought perhaps ignoring them would, in itself, be an effective part of it. He did know that, once they were settled near his father, he would give back to the captives all the spoils they had taken. He assured Adah and Basha of that, and asked them to spread the word to the other captives. That alone should be some comfort to them, to assure them they would be treated well. Most of them were bearing up well under the strain of the traveling, though they were not as accustomed to it as Jacob's household was.

On the night before they reached Hebron, Jacob sent two servants to let his father know they were coming later in the morning. It was an hour before noon when the walls of the small city of Hebron came into view. The people were hot and weary, but there was loud cheering when they saw the city. Most of them did not know Jacob's father's house was some distance beyond the city, farther to the southwest.

It was noon when they went around a grove of terebinth, oak, willow, and pine, with dense undergrowth of myrtle and branches and vines, and a broad, clear, shallow stream flowing through it. Just on the other side, was the sprawling stone house. Jacob had visited his father three or four times since coming back to this land, and he had been struck by its similarity to the old home in Beersheba that Jacob had left so many years before on his journey to Haran. His heart pounded rapidly, and his excitement mounted when he saw the house again and knew he would soon be embracing his father whom he respected so deeply. His heart's grief over the fact that his mother wouldn't be there resurfaced, however. And this time, Joseph and Rachel wouldn't be with him, as they had been each time before. Leah saw tears in his eyes as he turned to tell Benjamin he would see his grandfather soon. The child, in spite of all his weariness, was so excited he could hardly contain his emotions. He shouted and clapped his hands. Even Dinah smiled at his joy, and Leah's relief at nearing the end of the grueling journey showed on her face and in her eyes.

Jacob led the caravan carefully through the shallow, narrow part of the stream. The animals did not shy at the crossing, and the people welcomed the cool waters on their hot, tired feet. The herdsman, with their enormous herds, were behind the caravan now and would arrive perhaps an hour later.

As soon as the last person and animal had crossed, Jacob gave the command to halt. Jacob, Judah, and Reuben dismounted and helped the women to dismount. The others dismounted also, talking and laughing with relief as they stretched their cramped limbs. The sons who had plundered Shechem lingered in the rear. They had eaten with the family on the journey, but had stayed apart at other times. Jacob had not given them the privilege of riding at the front in their accustomed places.

Just then, Jacob looked toward the spacious and serene house under the row of great tamarinds that rose behind it and at each side. He saw his old, blind father, led by a young servant, coming out to meet him. With a glad cry, Jacob threw his reins to Judah and ran to his father.

"It is Jacob, Father," he said, as he gathered the old man in his arms, rocking him back and forth. Both men wept, and Isaac said, "I know your voice, my son. Let me feel your face, I want to know that it is really you." He ran his shaking, gnarled fingers carefully, lovingly over his son's face. "Jehovah be praised!" he exclaimed. "I have you again before I die."

"Father, I have brought all my family, all my servants and goods, all my animals. I want to build a home near you where we can stay."

"Oh, it is well, my son; it is well. Jehovah be praised!" Isaac wept with joy.

Benjamin approached, followed by Leah, Dinah, and all the sons.

"Father," said Jacob, "here is my youngest son, whom you have never met. This is Benjamin."

"Benjamin," quavered the old man, "come to me." He took the boy in his arms as tears of joy coursed down his wrinkled face and into his long, white beard. With trembling hands, he felt the young face and Benjamin was pleased, for

Jacob had told him this was the way his blind grandfather would "see" him. "I am glad we will be with you, Grandfather," the boy responded, with all sincerity.

Jacob pulled Dinah forward. "And this is my daughter, Dinah, whom you met when she was very small. She is grown up now, and very lovely." The weeping girl hugged her grandfather, then waited while he felt her face. Then Jacob brought Leah forward for the old man to "see."

Suddenly Isaac asked, "And where is Rachel? The one who is so like my Rebekah?" Jacob hesitated; his face sorrowful, and Isaac went on, "And Joseph, her beautiful little son? I know he is grown up now, but I remember him well."

Jacob began weeping and answered in a breaking voice, "My father, Rachel died when Benjamin was born, and now these three months, Joseph—is not."

"Oh, my son, my son!" cried the old man. "I did not know. Why did you not send me word? Why have you not come these many years? How sad for you! How sorry I am!" He wept loudly.

"We will talk about it later, my father. Please come greet my eldest, Reuben. You met him a long time ago."

"It is good to be with you again, Grandfather," Reuben said warmly.

When Isaac had felt his face also, Jacob presented Judah. "You saw him once also, Father, as you did the other eight."

He went on to present all the other sons in turn.

"We have other people with us, also, Father, but we are very hot and tired, and you can meet them later. Our herdsmen will no doubt be here soon with the animals."

At that moment Isaac's chief servant came up and said, "Master, food and drink are ready for your son and his family. We have spread it under the trees. And servants will unload his goods and see to the animals."

"Good, good," said Isaac. Then to Jacob he said, "This is Jonah, steward of all my house, and a good one he is." Jonah bowed to Jacob, and Jacob, to him.

"I am glad my father has a trustworthy steward to look after his house," he said.

Isaac spoke, "Come, my son, with all your people. How hungry you all must be! My servants have been preparing a meal since your messengers arrived early this morning. I am sure there is plenty."

"How good of you, my father," responded Jacob, and he and all his household followed the old man and his servant around the house to the tables under the trees.

And so began the new life of Jacob and his family with his old father, Isaac. For three days the family rested and ate and talked. Even the servants and herdsmen were allowed as much time away from their work as possible.

Jacob and his father talked about and wept over the tragedies that had befallen Jacob's family. They talked, also, of their times when Jehovah had talked with each of them, and mused over His ways to the children of men, of how they were the chosen line to bless the world, which had started with Abraham and of which they themselves were the second and third persons. They wondered which of Jacob's sons would be the fourth. Would it be the firstborn, Reuben, or as in Jacob's case, would the younger be Jehovah's choice?

Jacob asked his father's advice as to what punishment his sons should receive because of the evil they had done to Prince Hamor's people. What would best chasten them, bringing them to repentance before Jehovah for their wickedness?

Jacob spoke of his mother and her untimely death, of how hard it was for Isaac to go on without her. This time Jacob could comprehend his father's grief, as he never could before. They talked of the loss of Joseph, of how Jacob had been so sure he was the one to carry on the line, because he was the older son of Rachel, whom Jacob considered to have been his true wife. She had been sensitive enough to appreciate the blessing and the birthright. They talked of Dinah's sadness, of what should become of her; of whom the sons, now of age, could marry besides the heathen people around them.

At times they talked of the land near them, some of

which was Isaac's, some of which belonged to people in the city of Hebron nearby; some, farther off, to the ruined cities of Sodom and Gomorrah. These were not far from the Sea of Salt, and it was in Sodom, Isaac reminded his son, that their kinsman, Lot, had once lived. They talked of Abraham's days, of the time when he had rescued Lot and his family from four kings who had captured them and taken them away. They talked of how Jehovah had spared Lot when the city of Sodom was destroyed. Isaac was sure Jacob could buy lands with well-watered plains from that direction, and from the Philistines to the west of them.

Benjamin loved his old grandfather from the first moment he saw him, although he was distressed by his blindness. The boy often sat near him and held his hand as the two men talked. He never grew tired of the stories they told, tales of the tribe's earlier years, most of which were new to him. Some of the time Reuben and Judah sat with them and listened also, but the other sons stayed apart, except at mealtime.

Leah, Dinah, and Prince Hamor's family got along well together and Leah was able to bring much comfort to them. They and their servants worked with Isaac's servants to prepare food for the large crowd. Jacob and Leah saw little of each other except when they went to their room at night, the room Isaac said was the one he and Rebekah had shared. Jacob assured her he was looking over the nearby land every day, trying to decide on the best site for their house. When he had found a place, he would show her. If it did not seem suitable to her, they would find another. He also talked with her about the punishment of their sons.

She said, "I have thought much about it, Jacob. Seeing the grief of these captives, seeing Dinah's deep sadness, her young life ruined, I have come to feel even more the barbarity of what they did. Surely they too will come to see the deed for what it is, and will note the grief of the captives, the sadness of their sister, for whose vindication they said they did this evil thing. I shall surely remind them at every opportunity. Perhaps Jehovah will somehow help them see the awfulness of what they did so that they will repent. Seeing what they have done to others should be some part of their punishment."

This was a long speech for Leah, and Jacob listened attentively. He knew how deep her own concern was over the evil done by the sons, how her compassionate heart ached for the grieving families. He had been amazed at how she had managed with them in the hours before he came back to the camp on that fateful day. And he remembered how she had been so calm, had comforted him and given him strength when he was so distraught that he was almost out of his mind. Had she not done the same when the sons had brought him Joseph's bloody coat? In many respects, she had even taken charge of the tribe during the months when Jacob's grief at Rachel's death had so engulfed him that he could do nothing. He had given no thought before to who had managed everything, but now he realized it was Leah.

What a strong and wise person she is, he reflected. He would certainly think about what she had said concerning the punishment of their sons. His new-found admiration for his wife sent a thrill of desire through him.

Someday, he thought, *when we have our home and there is peace and quiet, perhaps I shall come to love this woman who has shared so much of my life. I have come to admire and appreciate her so much.* Later that evening, Jacob was so passionate and tender with Leah that she dared to hope once more, as she had so many, many times through the long years. Her greatest hope was that she would be able to rest in the love that, she hoped, her husband would show to her.

7

Life in Hebron

Early on the fourth day after arriving in Hebron, Jacob sent Reuben and two herdsmen to look after his own animals, as well as Jacob's and Judah's. He and Judah, with Benjamin alternately tagging behind and playfully running ahead, began to search for a house site. They went first to the south of Isaac's house, on the same side of the stream. They searched in vain for a high hill or an outcrop of rock that would be like the other site they had had to leave. The area was covered with rocks of all sizes; there was flat land and a few low hills, but no high rock ledges, no hills high enough to protect a house from floods and other weather-related problems. There was one bend in the stream, not too far from Isaac's home that would have been ideal, except for the fact that the land was flat for miles on every side, offering no protection from the wintry blasts Jacob knew would come.

After half a morning's walk, they crossed the stream and turned back toward Isaac's house, covering land between it and the city of Hebron, so far away that they were never in sight of it. They were about to give up, and Benji's short legs were getting very tired, when it occurred to Judah that they had not looked on the far side of the stream from his grandfather's home, almost parallel to it.

"Father," he called, pointing, "let's explore that grove. There must be a well or a spring there. See how large the pines and terebinths grow? And there are some palms on the other side."

"So there are," agreed Jacob. "And look how dense and green the underbrush is."

They quickened their steps and were soon going up to it on the far side. As they got closer, they found moist ground, and a little farther on, small puddles of clear water. Benji splashed into them, sandals and all, shouting in glee, forgetting his tired legs. They followed the pools, noting the great height of the palms and the dense myrtles, brambles, small oaks, and shrubs, even wild grapevines, and suddenly came to a high, rocky cliff that the trees had hidden. From its base, a small, clear spring bubbled from under the rocks. The ground on the side opposite the big palms was flat and bare except for rocks. Behind, the cliff extended for some 200 feet, then tapered off into level land as far as they could see.

Jacob was elated. "What a perfect site! Strange, I don't remember it from my other visits. But then I never explored much, just visited with my father."

Judah readily agreed that this was the right spot. "This dense grove on the west," he said, "and the rocky cliff on the north will give protection and privacy—and by the time spring comes, water will be close and plentiful." They examined the soil, finding it dark and rich under the covering of various sizes of stones.

"Looks right for fine gardens, and if the spring is steady, there will always be plenty of water. Let us go to ask my father about that. He will surely know."

A few minutes later, old Isaac was assuring them that he had not known the spring to dry up in all the years he'd been there. "Indeed," he said, "we would surely have planted a garden there long ago if we weren't closer to the stream. I would have put the house there, but your mother chose this site."

Jacob could hardly wait to tell Leah, and so he took her there to look at the place as soon as the afternoon was cool enough. She liked it immediately, and the more they considered its possibilities, the more enthusiastic they both became.

Jacob said, "If you are sure this site pleases you, then we will begin working on the foundations tomorrow. I can use the same plan here that we used before, and if we get everyone who can work involved, it should not take long."

"This is the right place, Jacob," Leah assured him. "I feel it, somehow. And it is close to your father's home, yet hidden from it by the grove. Do begin work tomorrow. Maybe some of your father's servants can help with sheepfolds and stalls and servant-houses. You know how close the cold and rainy season is."

"Yes, I know," Jacob said. "There is need for haste, and there is no reason everything should not be ready before another moon has passed. We will even build for Hamor's family and people."

They returned to his father's house in time for the evening meal, and afterwards Jacob sat with his father and all of his sons under the old tamarinds and discussed all the plans. They determined who should work at each task. Isaac promised many servants and some herdsmen since most of his late harvest was gathered and only a few herdsmen could care for the animals at this season. Jacob even decided that some of his maidservants and some of Hamor's people could be spared from the cooking in order to help gather stones. It would be a major task, since many would have to be brought from farther off.

Judah questioned his grandfather as to how far away the caravan route to Egypt was, and how often a caravan passed. "We shall need roof tiles, windows, and doors, and other things, won't we, Father?" he asked when Isaac had told him the route ran beyond Hebron and that a caravan passed every week or two.

With the help of Isaac's steward, Jonah, and the suggestions of all the sons, a list was made that a servant would take tomorrow, along with silver to a city merchant, who in turn would give it to the earliest caravan master.

To Jacob's amazement and Leah's delight, within a month the house was completed. There had not been an idle hand in either Jacob's or Isaac's households, and only a minimum of rest. Judah and Reuben had seen that their father's instructions were known and carried out each day, not only on the big house, but on the servant's quarters and animal shelters, as well. Stones of all sizes were gathered from far and near. Rocks for the foundations were quarried from a site that Isaac knew about. They were shaped and hauled, roof timbers were cut, some from around the spring, and some from the stream banks. A few herdsman had cared for and fed the animals so that many could work on sheepfolds, booths, and stalls. Servants had realized the need for haste against the coming rains, and they worked steadily. Even the children were enthusiastic and worked beside their elders, gathering stones or doing whatever they could. The women and maidservants prepared all the needed food in the huge cooking room at Isaac's home and even carried the midday meal to the men so they would lose little time due to eating. Along with cooking, washing of clothes, and doing household chores, they managed somehow to find the time to gather late grains from Isaac's fields and store them in brass containers, clay pots, or skins; to dry the late apples and apricots from clumps of wild trees, as well as figs from Isaac's old trees; to glean the last of the grapes for raisins and wines.

Leah, in her gracious way, took charge of the work, even over Isaac's capable Dilsey, who seemed to be glad to relinquish some of the responsibility from off her old shoulders. Whichever children, large or small, could be spared from the building from time to time, she coaxed into gathering the late fruits and grain, and even had them gathering wild nuts. She was concerned that, with the extra people, supplies would grow short before spring and summer could bring new ones.

She was especially glad they had gathered extra dates earlier on their way to Shechem, drying many and making the delicious date honey Jacob loved so much. She smiled at her many tasks when she thought of how pleased he would be to have it to enjoy through the long winter months. And she dreamed of her very own house—a place where she felt she could make him happy, with nothing about it to remind him of Rachel or of Joseph. She even dreamed, with a wildly beating heart, that now at long last Jacob would really love her. All these thoughts kept her going through the endless tasks, through the almost-constant weeping of the widows, even as they worked; through Dinah's sorrowing, through her own grief at what her sons had done, and her anxiety concerning the type of punishment Jehovah, and even Jacob, might bring upon them.

Sometimes at night Jacob talked to her about them, and sometimes she heard him crying out to Jehovah for them, or weeping, even in his weariness. She sensed that the frenzied work was good for them all—herself, Jacob, Hamor's people, Dinah, even her wicked sons, who must surely have realized by now how horrible was the deed they had done. Both she and Jacob were still afraid that the people from Hamor's land would somehow connect the tragedy with their leaving and come seeking revenge. She knew that the men, both Jacob's and Isaac's, kept their weapons close to their sides even while they worked. She knew that, without Jehovah's help and protection, they could never have escaped revenge thus far, that without His comfort and presence, neither she nor Jacob could go on under their load of responsibility, work, and fear. She thanked Him in her heart continually, even as Jacob often thanked Him aloud.

On the day the house was finished, she determined to put her worries away and rejoice. She insisted that all of them, even Dinah and the other widows, try not to weep, but to rejoice at least for the day. Jacob left off work on the few unfinished servant quarters and the animal shelters. The servants, who would have to live in tents awhile longer, were nevertheless happy that their master's house was complete and they cheerfully helped move the family's belongings into their new home.

Leah's dark eyes sparkled and she clapped her hands

with child-like joy when Jacob and Judah brought in two fine wooden chairs, carved with intricate designs. Jacob had them brought from Egypt, and had kept them hidden in his father's house until now. He smiled at how excited she was. "You see, I can keep some things hidden from you," he teased.

"Oh, Jacob," she returned, "don't try to hide anything from me. But thank you for this surprise. They are so beautiful." She sat in one and was delighted to find it was very comfortable. "How we shall enjoy these through the years!" she exclaimed.

Once the moving was completed, everyone ate a light midday meal, rested for a short while and began getting ready for the feast that was planned for that night. The men went to help the herdsman bring in the animals early and get them settled. A few menservants set up a long table in the center of the courtyard. Old Isaac sat nearby, "watching" through the eyes of the ecstatic child, Benjamin, who could usually be found with his grandfather if his father hadn't given him a task to do.

Leah took charge of the food preparation. In her quiet, authoritative way, she directed the women, maidservants, and children efficiently. Earlier in the day, amidst all the moving, she had assigned two menservants to dress and roast fat calves, sheep, and goats in a far corner of the courtyard. Now, when she could leave the others, she hurried to inspect the roasting meat, her large skirts swinging gracefully as she walked. Finding the meat cooking properly, she went back to the house in order to get two maids to shape dough into many loaves and place them in the sun to rise.

Other servants were cooking late vegetables, and two old women were stirring savory stews in large pots hanging over the burning coals in the huge fireplace. Leah sampled some from one pot, and smacked her lips. "It is good," she decided, "just right. Be sure to keep it stirred."

She found two of Hamor's daughters, Hoglah and Bashemath, near their own quarters sometime later and sent them to Isaac's house, with two of his servants, to bring dried fruits and nuts and arrange them on the table. While they were gone, she went to Isaac's garden and found some late vegetables with a few late blooms—stray red poppies, purple wild flowers, and small, white, star flowers. These she carried to the table, arranged in a flat, brown pottery bowl in the center of the table, and piled the vegetables near it. She took some of the pomegranates, late apricots, three long bunches of purple wild grapes the children were gathering and arranged them on top of the vegetables.

A stooped, old maidservant of Isaac's hobbled up just then, followed by two young lads, one bringing cheeses, another bringing wine from Isaac's plentiful store. Under the woman's direction, they placed the cheeses on platters Leah quickly provided and set them at intervals on the table. Then they emptied the wine into two large pottery crocks on a small table near one end of the large table. Leah covered the crocks carefully, and stood back for a good look at the table. She was pleased with what she saw, thanked the servants, sent them away to get dressed for the feast. Then she went inside to do the same and to bid her own maids to finish their tasks before they bathed and dressed in their finest clothing.

Back in the courtyard sometime later, Leah saw to the placing of the food the servants brought out and admired the well-dressed servants and children as they gathered in small groups in the falling twilight. Lamps were lighted and hung around the courtyard, and a huge fire was started in the far corner. She watched her sons amble out, handsome and finely dressed. They were talking to their grandfather whom a servant had led near the fire.

Soon children began running and playing together beyond the table, servant children and those of Hamor's people, and even Benji, who was now ready to leave his grandfather and join in their merriment. Leah smiled as she watched. How good to see her and Jacob's household in a happy mood, and to have his father's people with them to celebrate! The fragrance of flowers mingled with the savory odor of the roasted meat, the freshly baked loaves, the honey and raisin cakes, the perfume the women wore, the anointing oil from the hair and beards of the men.

Reveling in the whole festive occasion, herself lovely in a pale-blue, flowing robe, her black hair and eyes shining, Leah turned from placing the last rosy-red pomegranate on top of the pile of fruit. Jacob was coming toward her from the house, resplendent and very imposing in his finest garments and jewels, his heavy hair falling to his shoulders. *How handsome he still is,* Leah thought, her heart skipping a beat, *every inch the head of our tribe!*

She was aware that he was gazing intently at her as he greeted her and murmured, "You look very pretty in my favorite color," and his eyes held a promise. Leah could hardly refrain from reaching out to him, even with many eyes upon them. She smiled into his eyes and turned with him toward the table. Jacob looked up and down the bountiful table with pride and thankfulness on his face. "How very good it all looks. Jehovah has been gracious to us, and you have prepared it well. Is all in readiness?"

"When the servants come with the last hot loaves," Leah answered. Happiness beamed from her face.

"Then I will bring my father to bless the feast," said Jacob as he went toward the fire and Leah hurried to rush the servants and Zilpah and Bilhah with the loaves.

As they came from the house with the baskets of hot, brown, aromatic bread, Leah struck a bronze gong near the door, and the children stopped their play and gathered excitedly around the table, as their elders came leisurely from all directions. Jacob slowly led his father to the head of the table, and Benji went to stand beside him, while the other sons gathered behind them, and Leah went to Jacob's side. Jacob raised his hand and the noisy group gradually quieted.

"Father, will you thank Jehovah for the food?" he asked.

Raising his sightless eyes heavenward, the old man praised the God of his father, Abraham. He gave thanks for a bountiful harvest, and for his son's returning to him. Then he invoked His continued blessings upon his tribe, and ended with the familiar, "Let it be so." Everyone echoed these words and Jacob invited all to partake. Leah saw tears in his eyes. *Still he grieves for Joseph,* she thought.

Soon happy chatter and laughter could be heard up and down both sides of the table as people filled platters with foods of their choice. The younger ones finished first and moved back from the table, then sat cross-legged on cushions with their platters on the ground in front of them. Several servants moved wooden benches from near the house to the table and the older people sat on them and began to eat, chatting amiably, some feeding small children beside them. A servant brought Isaac's special chair and he sat at the head of the table, with Jacob and Leah on either side, helping him with his food, glad to have him with them, and thrilled to see him being so merry and eating heartily.

Dinah, beautiful in a dark robe, but sad-eyed and pale, sat beside her mother, while small Benji sat across from her, beside his father. Near Dinah, Hamor's wives and daughters sat, very quiet and sad-looking also. Leah knew they were all remembering their last feast before the tragedy. She hoped her sons would note their sadness and repent of their evil.

Farther down the table were the townspeople and, at the far one, their servants joined with Isaac's and Jacob's. Most of them had put aside any lingering sadness at least for this feast time. Happy talk and laughter prevailed among them, as well as among the young people who were farther off. Jacob surveyed the large gathering, then rejoiced that his family was with his father now, and that the house was finished. He tried to put his grief aside along with his worry over his wicked sons. He talked to his father, smiled at Leah and Dinah, even while his heart ached at the sadness on her face. He felt a bond with his daughter that he had not known before. *She has known sadness at a much younger age than I did,* he thought.

Jacob was determined that there would be at least some joy, some merriment at this celebration over the new house.

He began to talk with his father about some of the good times they had enjoyed when he and his brother Esau were boys. Old Isaac soon caught Jacob's cheerful spirit and came up with some humorous stories about the mischief the boys often got into. Benji laughed loudly at what his grandfather shared, and even sad Dinah laughed some and smiled. Judah and Reuben, seated closely enough to hear, joined in the merriment, and reminded Jacob from where they had gotten some of their own earlier mischief. Jacob laughingly agreed, and Leah's eyes lighted with love as she looked at him.

Benji asked, "Grandfather, did you punish my father and Uncle Esau for their mischief?" Jacob laughed at his small son's seriousness, as Isaac answered that he surely did. Then the child begged, "Grandfather, tell us some of the things you did when you were a boy." Old Isaac laughed and recalled a few happy times, some things Jacob had not heard before. Jacob looked at everyone in his family, smiling and laughing. *Even Dinah had forgotten her sorrow momentarily* he thought, and his own heart lifted.

Benji asked, "Didn't you ever get into mischief, Grandfather?" Judah and Reuben and even some of the other sons laughed at this.

"Oh, maybe once or twice, my son." Isaac's voice was serious, but the corners of his mouth twitched. "You see, I didn't have a brother to get me into trouble. Oh, there was Ishmael, until my father sent him away, but he was older and I wasn't with him much."

"Like me," observed Benjamin gravely. "All my brothers are older, too. So I don't get into mischief either. Do I, Father?" he questioned Jacob, who laughingly answered,

"Well, not much, my son."

With that, Jacob noted that everyone had finished eating, and the younger ones were bringing their trays to the table. He stood and raised his hand. When there was quietness, he said, "It is time now for us to worship and sacrifice to Jehovah. Let us gather quietly around the altar."

He and Benji helped his father toward the large stone altar set up not far from the fire, as a servant hurried to move the old man's seat to a place in front of it. Jacob seated him while two servants lifted great shovelfuls of glowing coals from the fire onto the altar and piled on dry wood from the stack they had placed nearby earlier. As it began to blaze up, brightening the whole side of the courtyard and casting moving shadows, two servants came through the gate. Each carried an unblemished lamb. Jacob took his place near the altar and motioned for Judah to join him. As he did so, Leah, Benji, Dinah, Reuben, and the other sons came to stand in a circle behind Isaac's seat. Beyond them the handmaids, Bilhah and Zilpah, and Prince Hamor's family and the townspeople gathered. The servants stood in the rear, their quiet faces reflecting awe and even the children were silent.

The servants piled more wood on the now-blazing altar fire. Jacob raised his hands and one servant brought his lamb close. Judah, beside his father, helped the servant hold the lamb's head back to expose the neck. Taking up a long knife that had been stuck in the ground, Jacob slit the throat with one swift stroke. The crowd drew its breath sharply. Blood spurted out; the animal made no sound. Swiftly, in one deft movement, Judah and the servant threw it into the flames. The sparks flew high and the crowd let out its breath in a sigh, as one man. The servant stepped back, and the other one brought his lamb forward. The process was repeated and the odor of burning wool and flesh filled the space around the altar and drifted out over the people.

After a few moments Jacob addressed Isaac. "My father, will you invoke Jehovah's blessing on our sacrifice and upon us, His people?"

Slowly the old patriarch rose, again raised his head heavenward and spoke with a reverent, yet quavering voice. "O great Jehovah, God of heaven and earth, will You not look with favor upon us, Your people, accept and bless us and our sacrifice? We praise Your name, for You are a great God, the only God. We thank You for this good land You promised to my father, Abraham, and to me and to this my son, and to his sons after him forever. Bless us, as You blessed my father, with the good of the land, and may we, his seed, also be a blessing, as You promised him. Let these sacrifices cover our trespasses against You, we pray. O Jehovah, our one true God, let it be so forever."

As his voice trailed away, he bowed his gray head. Jacob and the people bowed also and repeated, "Let it be so forever." For some time the people stood silent, with their heads still bowed, some at least worshiping Jehovah in their hearts.

Jacob's clear, strong voice streamed out over the people. "Do you know what we have done?" He waited while the people thought awhile, then answered his own question. "We have praised and thanked our God and we have secured His pardon for our sins and His blessings on our tribe for another year. Now we must praise and thank Him in our hearts every day and try to do good and not evil so His blessings on us will continue, and so our tribe will be a blessing someday to all people. Now let us go back to get wine, and return to sit around the fire, for it is getting cold. My father will tell us stories of our people until he is tired."

The people quickly gathered around the wine crocks, and Bilhah and Zilpah dipped wine for all but the younger children. Leah, and Hamor's daughter, Bashemath, brought warm milk sweetened with honey for the little ones. Servants brought out more mats and the young people found the ones they had before. In a short while, young and old were seated in a semi-circle around Isaac who was sitting with his back to the fire, with Jacob and Benji on either side.

When all was quiet but for the crackling of the new wood on the fire, Isaac began. "It was many, many years ago that Jehovah, our God, spoke to my father, Abraham, where he lived in far-off Ur of the Chaldees." He paused and pointed to the northeast. "Ur was a great city, with tall buildings and many people. One building held many books, written on stone tablets. That is how my father learned to write. He had a learned teacher, who also taught him to read. His father, Terah, had many goods so he could afford a teacher for my father and his two other sons, my uncles, Nahor and Haran, and for Uncle Haran's son, Lot. The people of Ur worshiped the moon-god. My father worshiped the same god until the true God, Jehovah, spoke to him in his heart. Then he knew the moon-god was powerless and was really no god, only an idol. Jehovah told my father to take all his people and his substance and leave Ur. My grandfather, Terah, was yet living so my father took him and Uncle Nahor and Lot, whose father had died, and my mother, Sarai, and all his servants and possessions and left Ur. Jehovah did not tell him where to go. He headed in a southwestern direction that took him to the city of Haran and lived there until my grandfather, Terah, died." The old man paused for breath.

"After that, Jehovah spoke again to my father, who was then called Abram, and He told him to come to this land of Canaan. He promised to bless him, and give the land to his descendants after him. Of course, we are those descendants. He also promised that in us would all people be blessed. We do not yet know just how. Perhaps one day one of our descendants will be a great king or a great deliverer. However Jehovah wants it, so will it be." The old man had straightened his shoulders and pride registered in his voice. Benji, seeing him, sat a little taller. So did Reuben and Judah, watching them.

Isaac continued, "Jehovah spoke many times to my father who always obeyed Him. Each time Jehovah spoke, He promised that my father's descendants would be as numberless as the stars of heaven or the sands of the sea. My father believed Jehovah's words, but he and my mother, Sarai, had no child. So my mother finally insisted that he take her handmaid, Hagar, for his wife in order to have a child by her. Thus was Ishmael, my half-brother, born. But Jehovah told my father that Ishmael was not to be the child of promise, but one born of Sarai. Father believed His word.

"So when he was almost 100 years old, and my mother was almost ninety, Jehovah told my father definitely that a son would be born to him and my mother the next year. My father laughed, for they were both 'too old' to have children. But it came to pass. I am that son. My name means "laughter," and I did bring laughter and joy to them. I am the one who was chosen to continue the promised line, and so was my younger son, Jacob." He reached out a shaky hand to touch his son as he affirmed, "He is next in the line. And one of you will carry on the line after him."

Leah saw tears flooding into Jacob's eyes. *He so wanted Joseph to be the one,* she remembered.

Isaac paused, and each son wondered if he might be the one who would carry on the family line. Isaac went on, "I was a happy child; indeed, my parents cherished me, cared for me, and taught me the ways of Jehovah even though they were old. But when I was seventeen, Jehovah commanded my father, now called by the new name Jehovah had given him—Abraham, "father of many nations"—to take me and two servants up to Mt. Moriah to sacrifice to Him. We rode on donkeys for three days. When we came to the foot of the mountain, my father commanded the servants to remain there. He had me take the wood for the burnt offering, and then he took fire and a knife. We toiled up the mountain. I could not understand why we had no animal for sacrifice, but when I asked why, my father said, 'Jehovah will provide a sacrifice.' When we reached the top, my father built an altar with stones I gathered. He wept while he built it, wept as I had never seen him weep before. I was afraid to ask why. When the altar was finished and the wood had been placed upon it, my father, still weeping, took me by the shoulders, looked into my eyes, and said, 'My son, oh, my dearly loved son, Jehovah has said that you must be the sacrifice. You know I must obey.' I was so afraid, and I began to tremble and to weep. My father held me in his arms and we wept together. Then he said, 'My son, you know I must tie you up. Don't be afraid. Jehovah can raise you up, even from death, if He chooses, and remember, He has said you are the one to carry on the line.' While both of us still wept, I held out my hands; and he bound them. Then he stooped and bound my feet, picked me up and laid me on the altar. A great fear gripped me when he drew back the knife." The listeners gasped. "But I did not cry out. Just as he was plunging it toward me, a loud voice from heaven cried, *'Abraham! Abraham!'* I was watching the knife. It stopped as my father answered, 'Here am I!' " Isaac's audience breathed again!

"The voice continued, *'Lay not your hand upon the lad, neither do anything to him; for now I know that you fear God, seeing you have not withheld your son, your only son, from Me.'* I knew then it was Jehovah who was speaking. How welcome were His words to me and to my father! He quickly cut the cords and took me from the altar. I was still trembling; both of us were still weeping. I sat on the ground, but my father looked around. He saw a ram some distance away that was caught by his horns in the briars of a thicket. He went quickly and brought the ram, killed and offered him as a burnt offering instead of me."

Here Isaac's relieved listeners smiled, and small Benji cried out, "How brave you were, Grandfather! How brave was Grandfather Abraham also!" Here the child thought a moment; the people were quiet. He continued, "But I would not have let him bind me; I would have run away!" The crowd laughed, breaking the tension.

Jacob smiled at his small son, through tears. "If you had been Grandfather Abraham's son of promise, my son, you would not have run," he stated solemnly.

"I am glad I am your son," the child responded.

For sometime, everyone was quiet, pondering the importance of the story Isaac had told. Jacob was remembering the first time he had met Jehovah for himself at Bethel, when he had the vision in the night. He had seen the angels ascending and descending the ladder that had reached from earth to heaven. He remembered also the times Jehovah had spoken to him in Haran, giving him guidance. He especially remembered wrestling with the angel at the brook, Jabbok, when he returned to this land and how he had finally prevailed and received a new heart and a new name— Israel, prince of God.

Benji spoke again, "Tell us more, Grandfather." He laid his hand on Isaac's knee and the old man rumpled his grandson's curly hair, smiling, and resumed his story. "After all these things, my father went to dwell in Beersheba, to the southwest, for there was much grass there for our cattle. Oh, how happy we were in Beersheba! I remember how much joy and laughter there was in our tents, now that my parents had me to leave their substance to. We worked hard as I grew to manhood. I could do so much to lighten my father's responsibility as he grew older. Our household became larger and larger, and our animals increased until they were without number. My father sold many in Egypt for gold and precious stones and beautiful apparel, and for trappings for our camels. He was so great and so wise. Jehovah blessed all that my father touched, and we both learned to know Him better as the years passed by.

"Then the grasslands around Beersheba failed, so we came here where the stream provided more water and the grasslands were green. After some years my mother, Sarah, died. She had lived for 127 years, but to my father and to me she was still beautiful and gentle and loving. We were heartbroken at losing her and our whole tribe mourned for many days. We had no place to bury her, for though Jehovah had promised the land to us, the natives still owned it. My father bargained with Ephron of the children of Heth for the field in which the cave of Machpelah is located. It is that field where you recently gathered stones. My father paid 400 shekels of silver for it. There we buried my mother, and there many years later I was to bury my father."

Isaac was silent for a while, as if he were thinking. All eyes were still on his face. With an effort, he continued, "My father and I were very lonely for many years, though Jehovah still blessed us greatly and often talked to my father. Then my father made his oldest, most-trusted servant, Eliezer, swear that he would go to Haran and bring back a wife for me from his brother Nahor's people. It is a long story, how this servant brought Rebekah back for me and I will tell it some other time. But now it is enough to say that I watched day and night for the old man to return, wondering if he could indeed succeed in getting some girl to come to this land, to people she had never seen.

"But Jehovah blessed in this also, and one evening as I was meditating on Him in the field, I looked up and saw two camels coming. Oh, how excited I was! I ran to meet them, and there was my bride and her maidservants with Eliezer. She had covered her face, but I knew she would be beautiful, as my mother was. I took her into my mother's tent, and she became my wife." He paused and turned toward Jacob. "She was very beautiful, was she not, my son?"

Jacob assured him, "Indeed she was, Father."

The old man went on, "I loved her very much, and she brought me the first comfort, the first joy, I had experienced since my mother's death." His face brightened and he smiled, remembering. "We were happy, and my father was very pleased that he had found a wife for me from his own people. He himself took another wife, Keturah, and she bore him six sons—my half-brothers, just as Ishmael is. But Rebekah and I had no children for many, many years. Yet the time seemed short to me, because of the great love I had for her.

"But Rebekah was very unhappy that she could bear me no sons. So I reminded Jehovah of His promise that my father's descendants would be numerous and a blessing to all the world, and that I was the child of promise. Jehovah told me to remember my father's faith when he was much older than I was. I did not worry any more, and by-and-by Jehovah sent us, not one, but two sons. Before their birth we were told that they would become two nations and that the older should serve the younger."

Isaac paused again, then turned to Jacob. "My son, you are the younger, as you know, though by only a few minutes. How your brother Esau came to lose his birthright and blessing you know well. I will let you tell that story to your sons when you will. But your brother will yet be your servant, and the line to bless all peoples will come through one of your sons. It is customary that it should pass through your eldest, Reuben, but Jehovah may have other plans. Listen to Him before you bestow the blessing and birthright."

"Yes, I will, my father," Jacob promised.

The old man rose with difficulty, even with Jacob's help, stood some time with bowed head, as if speaking to Jehovah. The people waited in expectation. He finally raised his head and said, slowly, wearily, "Now the hour is late and I am very tired. No more of the story tonight." The people sighed their disappointment, especially small Benjamin.

After a moment, he said, "We are sorry you are tired, Grandfather. But thank you for the wonderful story. I shall remember it always. Do you think that I might be the one to carry on the line? I am the youngest, like my father." Isaac smiled and groped until he touched the lad's head.

"I do not know that, my son, but you shall indeed be blessed of Jehovah."

His servant-boy came now and began to lead him to his own home. The whole company rose, moved around, then gradually gathered in groups about the courtyard, talking about what Isaac had related to them. Zilpah and Bilhah and a few women servants, guided by Leah, cleared the table. Jacob's sons gathered around him, near the fire and the altar, where the coals were still burning. They asked their father about parts of the story they had never heard before. They were overwhelmed by the faith their great-grandfather Abraham had exhibited.

They were obviously interested in knowing which of them would be chosen to carry on the line. Would it be the oldest, Reuben, or the youngest, Benjamin? Judah, sitting nearest his father, thought, *I have always been the one who took charge, to whom the others have looked to accept responsibility. That is, until the slaughter of Hamor's people, when Simeon and Levi—not Reuben, the oldest—took over. Reuben may be the oldest, but it is certain he's no leader. Already my father has said that Simeon and Levi, because of their wicked deed, shall be given no blessing. If he holds to that, and Reuben is somehow not chosen, then I am logically the next in line. Oh, how I should like to be the one to receive the birthright and the blessing! I have heard from my father how he and his mother tricked Grandfather Isaac and got his brother Esau's rightful inheritance as the first-born. Even so, Jehovah has blessed my father. I must think of a way to discredit Reuben in my father's eyes. Then the blessing and birthright will surely be mine, for I cannot think he would give them to a child like Benji.*

After a while, a few at a time, the people went to their own places. The shepherds and herdsmen departed first, then Prince Hamor's family went to their new rooms, followed by Dinah and Benji, who left together. Then the other sons and servants retired, until only Jacob and Leah were left. They sat awhile near the still-glowing embers, looking at the numberless stars in the heavens. Jacob said, "Jehovah has promised that our descendants will be as many as those stars. Is that not wonderful, something to look forward to?"

Leah answered, "Yes," but to her it was really much more wonderful right now that she and Jacob were alone together, that at last she had a home of her own, a house that held no memories of Rachel or Joseph. *Surely now Jacob will love me and we shall be happy in this new home where Jehovah will bless us.* Her eyes were shining and her heart was singing when Jacob rose, lifted her to her feet, led her to their own new room, and fastened the door.

8

Dinah, Judah, Reuben

Before another month had passed, all the houses were completed, and everyone was settled comfortably. The shelters for the animals had been finished also, and as much grain and provender bought from people around Hebron as they would sell. This was stored in Isaac's partly filled barns, for Jacob had not yet found time to build his own. The family was beginning to feel at home in this land, and in their new dwellings. Even the animals seemed to sense that they had found a permanent place, and had ceased to be restless and unmanageable, becoming sleek and fat on the abundant, though dry, late grass. The herdsmen had also found two more springs whose overflow produced many acres of green grass on the side of the stream which Isaac had given to Jacob. The animals could find much green as they foraged along their side of the stream banks as well.

Jacob was so pleased with the way his affairs were going here in his father's land that he rejoiced, and at times he forgot his sorrow that Joseph and Rachel were not able to enjoy Jehovah's blessings with them. At each meal his family had together, he thanked Jehovah aloud that things were going so well for his tribe. One night after the meal, a herdsman called for him. A straying sheep had been badly hurt by a wolf before the shepherd could reach it. He had managed to fell the wolf with his club and then finished killing it. Would Jacob come to tell him whether the sheep should be put out of its misery? Immediately Jacob and Judah followed the man to the sheepfold where he had brought the stricken animal. It was the first time a wolf had attacked since Jacob had come to this land, and he was disturbed by the threat to his flocks.

It was late when he and Judah returned, for they had decided to "patch" the torn sheep and pour oil on its wounds. It had taken the three of them a long time in the dim light of the lantern. Leah was sitting in one of the beautiful new chairs, brushing her curly black hair, that reached now below her waist. She was wearing a blue night robe that Jacob had not seen before. He looked at her appreciatively as he came in, throwing his cloak across the bed and dropping wearily into the nearby chair. Leah did not miss his look and her heart rose into her throat as she stopped her brush in midair. Then she noted his weariness as he sat, and she laid the brush on the ivory-topped table beside her. "You are tired," she said, as quick concern registered in her voice. "How is the animal?"

"It will live, I think, but it was badly torn. Perhaps we should have put it out of its misery, but it is one of our best ewes. Judah is getting very good with animals; he seems to have real compassion for them. Perhaps the tragedies of Joseph and of Hamor have softened him." A shadow crossed his face.

"Let me get you some wine, Jacob, or some warm milk, to relax you and help you rest," Leah offered, half rising as she pushed back her heavy hair.

"Some wine would be good," he responded, and she hurried out, the robe swishing round her slender, sandaled feet.

In a short time she was back and she handed Jacob a silver cup, half-filled, smiling at him as he thanked her and sat sipping the red liquid. Then she sat and resumed her brushing, conscious of his eyes upon her.

"The air outside feels damp," he remarked, "and dark

clouds are boiling up. I think the rains will start before morning. How relieved I am that our people and our animals are well taken care of. How thankful I am that Jehovah has blessed us in the land at last!"

"Yes," agreed Leah. "It is time that good came and we have found some place to rest and be happy in."

"You've been weary of so much moving, haven't you?" asked Jacob.

"Yes," she smiled. "It is good to stop moving, and how proud I am of our own house at last."

"So am I," said Jacob, draining the cup. Leah reached a slender brown hand for it, set it gracefully on the table and laid her brush beside it.

True to Jacob's prediction, the rains came in torrents before daybreak, and the winds whipped the tamarinds and shrubs in all directions.

Jacob's household rose later than usual, and all the family had a leisurely morning meal together. Dinah and small Benji joined them even later. Dinah seemed to have a subdued joy about her, and her eyes were not red from weeping. Benji's excitement at the rain bubbled up and spilled over. He could not sit still, but kept excusing himself and running over to look out the window.

"Now everything will have plenty of water!" he announced gleefully, clapping his small hands. "Thanks be to Jehovah! How good He has been to us!"

He sat beside Reuben, who agreed with him heartily, and tousled his reddish curls with affection. The whole family smiled, even Dinah, and Judah commented, "It is good to see you smile, my sister. It seems to be a happy morning for us all."

When the rain slackened later, the brothers and herdsmen splashed through rippling puddles to tend the animals. Jacob and Judah went to see about the injured sheep. All of them were clutching their garments about them against the chilly winds.

Leah saw to the food that needed to be prepared for the midday meal, then went to her room to lay out dry clothes for Jacob. Dinah followed her and closed her door. "My mother," she began, and when Leah faced her, she saw that her eyes were shining, the way they had before the tragedy.

"Yes?" Leah prompted her beautiful daughter.

The girl continued with joy and excitement in her voice, "Oh, mother, I am going to have a baby. Shechem's baby! Now I shall always have something of him with me! Is it not wonderful?"

Leak was taken aback, and stood silent, not knowing how to answer. *Why did I not think of this possibility? How can it be wonderful without a husband to rejoice with her? And she is so young, only a child really.*

Then she recovered from her surprise enough to know she must rejoice with her daughter. She must be happy for her, because her child was so happy. "It is good, Dinah, if it makes you live again. A baby is always wonderful! Are you sure?"

"Oh, yes, mother," the girl assured her. "It is now three months that I have missed the time of women. And it will be a boy. I know it will! I will bear Shechem a son to be with me forever, since I had him such a little time." Tears filled her eyes. "How sad that he won't be here to share him with me."

Leah took the girl in her arms to comfort her. "We will be here, your father and I, and your brothers. We will rejoice with you. Why, it will be our first grandchild!"

"Will you tell my father for me? Will he be happy too, do you think?" Dinah asked.

"Of course, I will tell him. And of course he will be happy for you, and proud of a grandchild!"

And so he was. Leah told him as soon as he came in to change his wet clothes by the fire she had lighted against the dampness and the chill. He was as surprised as she had been, and so excited he could not wait to go to Dinah's room and rejoice with her. Later he called the whole family together to tell them, but without Dinah's presence. He was sure of Levi and Simeon's reaction, if not of the others, and he did not want Dinah to be hurt further.

He was right about Levi and Simeon. He was appalled at the bitter oaths that slipped involuntarily from their lips. "Enough!" Jacob snapped. "You will not use such oaths in my presence!"

They said no more, but their sullen looks spoke volumes about their bitterness. The faces of the others were sullen too. Only Benji, whom Dinah had already told, and Reuben showed excitement. Benji clapped his small hands and jumped up and down. "Now I will be an uncle!" he exclaimed triumphantly.

Reuben said, "Now Dinah will be happy and smile again. A baby will take away her sorrow." The others scowled at him, muttering under their breath. Judah showed no emotion at all, and he said nothing. Jacob could not understand. He had been sure Judah would be happy for his sister. He could not know that Judah had secretly hoped to father Jacob's first grandchild.

Jacob looked at each of his bitter sons. His voice was stern, "I have said nothing to you until now. I had hoped to give you time to repent of your evil. I see you have not. I see you have no compassion for your grieving sister nor the other women you have made widows, the children you have made fatherless. Your deed was wicked!" Jacob's voice rose angrily, "It was wicked in the eyes of man and of Jehovah! You shall not go guiltless and unpunished. Sons though you are, your mother and I will never feel the same about you. You shall not have our blessing as long as you are unrepentant, and you shall never have as much of our substance as you would have received. Furthermore, every piece of spoil you took shall be restored to Hamor's people. It is enough that you took their men, who can never be restored. Our work of building is finished for now, and I will have time. As soon as the rain ceases—this very day if it does—they shall go with me to my father's barn where you have stored it. Then each family can claim what it knows is its own. The rest will be divided among them all. It is the least I can do to make amends for your evil, and perhaps it will turn some of Jehovah's wrath away from you." Jacob's voice was commanding, his look was one of authority. The sullen faces quailed before his anger, their eyes fell, their wills submitted to Jacob's decision. He turned to Judah. "My son, see that the people are gathered when the rain ceases."

"Yes, father," Judah responded willingly. Jacob strode out, leaving the group feeling guilty. One by one, the sons went to their own rooms.

By late afternoon, the rain ceased, though the winds continued, and the sun came out. Judah, with the help of Benjamin and Reuben, got all of Prince Hamor's people to the barn. The other sons did not go. It was best that way, Jacob knew. He explained to the people what he wished and, without greediness, they claimed their own possessions, and the rest was divided.

"Each of you may claim his own camel or donkey," Jacob promised, "though it is best they be kept with ours until you need them. The cattle we shall keep with ours and care for, with the help of your herdsmen. For those, we provide you with shelter and clothes and food. That seems only fair to us. Is it agreeable to you?"

The people considered this for a few moments. Prince Hamor's wife, Adah, looked around at them all, saw them nodding their approval, then she turned to Jacob.

"It is well, Prince Israel. We thank you."

Jacob said, "From time to time you will be given some of the price when animals are sold, and you will be paid for any extra work you do. We want to be fair. We want to make amends. Your young sons will be circumcised, and any future sons will be also. Thus you can intermarry and become a part of our tribe. It shall be so for Prince Hamor's family, for the townspeople, and for the servants. Will you agree to this?"

He saw trust in the faces of the women, though the children were too young to understand. Soon the women nodded their agreement.

"Then it is settled," declared Jacob. "You are welcome in our tribe. Now take your possessions to your own quarters and do with them as you will."

Both Adah and Basha, along with the daughters, murmured their thanks, the others smiled and bowed. Jacob returned a smile and left them with their possessions. The sun was going down in a maze of clouds, the sky above them was a vibrant rose, and bright rays burst through cloud openings, flashing in Jacob's eyes as he went to find Leah. His heart was lighter than it had been since Joseph left him.

The rains came in abundance for several weeks. Jacob's household stayed busy inside except when the men tended the animals. Spinning, weaving, and the making of garments and mats, along with the daily cooking and household chores were the responsibilities of the women. The men mended and stored their tents, patched their harnesses, burnished, and mended the trappings for their camels, and built needed furniture. Those who were skilled in pottery made jars, pots, and dishes, even a few beautiful urns, pitchers, and vases. Jacob, Judah, and some of the other sons, saw to the plows and yokes for their oxen and sorted seeds for the fall planting. Fascinated with this, Benji watched and helped them instead of playing with Prince Hamor's children or the others. Leah and Dinah worked much together in Leah's room where a fire always burned. They spun fine yarn for baby garments and blankets, and coarser yarn for Jacob and the sons. Zilpah and Bilhah helped them when the cooking tasks were done. All of them worked at Leah's looms and took yarn to their own looms at night when it wasn't too cold to work without a fire. More looms were made for Hamor's women and they worked steadily at weaving and sewing garments for all their people. Leah encouraged them, knowing that keeping busy would help to heal their sorrow.

No matter how hard Leah worked during the day when Jacob was outside with the animals or with the men at their tasks in the barns and pottery sheds, when he came to their room after the evening meal, her full attention was given to him unless he brought some tasks with him. Then she would help him with them or do light sewing while he worked. More often than not, they sat in their comfortable, new chairs before a blazing fire, and talked over the day's happenings, their sons, Dinah's new glow of life with the anticipated child. Sometimes Jacob reached out and took Leah's slender hand in his, and they sat, quiet and content with Jehovah's blessings. Jacob spoke of Joseph and wept less and less often, as Leah tried to become more and more to him, as he was all in all to her.

After the rains had soaked the dry ground thoroughly and then had slackened, the fall planting was done, on Jacob's land and on his father's, as well. Both Jacob and Judah saw to Isaac's interests and the child Benjamin stayed with the old man much of the time. The tales he told of his own life and the family's earlier history would become a part of Benji for life. The child slept on a small bed in Dinah's room, and often shared their grandfather's stories with her. He kept Dinah from being lonely at night, and also helped her with the spinning. She often told him the little she really knew of Shechem and his people, and talked to him often about the birth of her coming child. Benji could hardly wait to be an uncle and also to have a little playmate.

When the planting was finished, the other work went on during the day, as well as at night, for the rains set in again, and the cold was more extreme as the winter wore on. To break the monotony, the whole family sometimes stayed in the warm cooking and eating space that ran across the entire back of the house, except for Dinah's room on the far end. Since it opened on the courtyard, it was easy for those on the other side or the ends of the courtyard to run across from their own rooms. Merriment and laughter, along with music and singing, were heard everywhere. Jacob and Leah agreed that, except for Dinah's sorrow and the loss of Joseph, their first winter in Hebron was a happy one.

Once, when there was a break in the snow that came when the rains stopped, Judah and Reuben rode in search of the small city of Timnath that Isaac had told them of. They left in mid-morning and found the city atop a high hill shortly after mid-day, just as their grandfather had said. Isaac had not been there for many years, but they found a small shop on the main part of the city just as he had described it. They went inside to buy food and wine. As they waited, a tall, swarthy man in a purple, embroidered, flowing robe came from across the room to greet them, bowing deeply.

"I am Hirah, from the region to the south, called Adullam. I come here from time to time, but I have not seen you before," he said, smiling expectantly.

Judah responded warmly, "I am Judah and this is my brother Reuben. This is the first time we've been here. We only recently came to Hebron. Isaac, the Hebrew, who lives near that place, is our grandfather."

"Oh, yes, I have met his servants here when we all bring our sheep to be sheared. I have heard he has a son in the country of Edom. Your father?"

"No," Judah answered. "Our father is his twin who left this land many years ago and lived in Haran to the north. Now we live near our grandfather. Oh, I'm sorry. Please sit and dine with us."

And so began a friendship that Judah was to cherish always. The three ate together before Hirah showed the other two around the city and the surrounding area. He told them much about the people and their customs, about his own people, his own young family. Reuben was interested enough, but Judah had never met anyone he liked so well. He and Hirah seemed to think the same about so many things. They parted at sunset, after warm invitations to visit each other soon. Hirah rode south, Judah and Reuben west. They had much to tell their father and the others about the city and about their new friend, when they reached home.

After that, now and again when the weather permitted, the other brothers visited Timnath in twos and threes— Simeon and Levi, Dan and Naphtali, Gad, Asher, and Zebulun. Once Reuben and Judah returned, taking Issachar with them. Jacob hoped they would not get into trouble. He knew there would be prostitutes and drinking, probably fighting as well, in the city, and he knew his sons had few scruples and hot tempers. He did not, however, forbid them to go, knowing they occasionally needed a change from the monotony of home and work. Because of what his father had told him of Hebron, he did forbid them to go there at night. They were permitted to go there only in the daytime when something had to be bought for the family.

The inside work still went on when the weather was too cold or wet to go outside. Jacob longed for spring. He took satisfaction in the inside work, and in being with Leah, but it reminded him of the winters he and Rachel had passed together in Haran long ago. Remembering still brought the pain that she and Joseph were no longer with him. *O Jehovah, will I never stop grieving?* he often silently asked. He spent much time with Benjamin, but that reminded him of Joseph when he had been that age, also. He couldn't help noting that the child, though apt and ready to learn about all the work Jacob taught him to do, was not as quick-witted as Joseph had been, nor as sensitive to the teachings about Jehovah. Of course he doted on the child and enjoyed being with him, but something was lacking. He really did not mind that the child stayed much with his grandfather and with Dinah.

As for Dinah, she seemed happy in anticipation of the coming child. Her body was heavy now, so she moved awkwardly, but her face had rounded out and was more beautiful than ever. She and Leah and their maids had everything in readiness, and the whole household was happily awaiting the call to the tribe's midwives, old Shillah, and her daughter Pelah.

Judah had overcome his disappointment that he would not be the one to produce the first grandchild. *After all,* he told himself, *my father will surely pass the chosen line through a son's son, and not through a daughter's. And besides, Dinah's child may be a girl, though she is so sure it will be a son. I must find a wife quickly, before my brothers do.* He began to consider the daughters of Hamor, and even those of the townspeople. After a few weeks of observing, he was sure not one of them could ever please him. Not one of them set his pulse racing. Not even the black-haired beauty he had chosen on the night of Prince Hamor's party appealed to him now. Besides, all Hamor's people seemed to recoil in fear from any of Jacob's sons, except Benjamin, though Jacob had been kind and generous to them. In time, no doubt that fear would leave them, but Judah did not have time to wait, even if he desired any of them.

He remembered how his new friend, Hirah, had spoken of the beautiful women of his land of Adullam and his urgent invitation to visit him. He decided to go, so when the weather cleared and began to warm somewhat in early spring, he spoke to his father. Jacob had no objections; he thought Judah could be spared from work for a few days before the spring planting began. And, yes, Reuben could go also, if he wished. But when Judah asked him, he answered that he really did not care to go. Judah could not but wonder, for usually his brother was ready for a trip. There must be some interest here for Reuben. Had he found a girl among Hamor's people, or perhaps one of the servants' daughters? He was the oldest son, the rightful one to inherit both the blessing and birthright. Was he also going to be the first son to present Jacob with a grandson? Well, Judah would find out about it when he returned. Surely Reuben wouldn't marry while he was gone, not within the next few days.

Judah chose Ziba, a brawny, bowlegged servant with a twinkle in his eye, to make the trip with him. Ziba would enjoy the trip and be a pleasant traveling companion. He was also handy with sword and dagger, in case they met with robbers or with a lion or bear or wolf. They set out early the next day, just as the sun rose on a fair, cold world. They traveled all day, passing through forest and ever-flat grassland, through shallow valleys, around high, wooded hills. Only twice did they see animals and shepherds at a distance, and they passed no houses. Judah noticed all the land carefully. Perhaps they could bring their animals this way later.

They spent the night in a densely wooded area, and were on their way by daybreak. As they zigzagged southward, and the sun rose higher, they soon were wiping their brows as if it were summer. Before midday, they stopped in a coppice of juniper and myrtle, bordered by bare sycamores and thorn bushes. They ate and rested in the cool shade, then pushed on.

An hour before sunset they reached the outskirts of a village Judah was sure was that of the Adullamites. Curious children and two weathered, old men watched them approach the first house. Judah inquired as to the location of Hirah's house. One of the men pointed toward the third one down the cobbled street, and they rode slowly on, observing the few scattered houses. As they approached the third one—a large, sprawling, one-story house—Judah glimpsed his friend hurrying around the far side. Glancing up as he heard hoofbeats, Hirah recognized Judah immediately. His brown face broke into a broad grin, white teeth flashing.

"Ah, my friend Judah! How good to see you!" he cried. "I had hoped you would come. Welcome!"

When Judah dismounted, Hirah hugged him, then held him at arm's length briefly before kissing him on both cheeks. "It is good to see you again, my friend," said Judah. "This is my servant, Ziba."

"Ziba, you are welcome," Hirah assured him. "Dismount, dismount. Here is my servant, Vadok. He will show you where to take the animals."

Ziba bowed low, thanked Hirah, and followed Vadok, who was leading Judah's weary mount toward the back.

"Come, my friend," invited Hirah, "let us go inside. You must be tired." He was leading Judah over the broad, tiled terrace and through wide double doors, opened by a servant. Hirah spoke quietly and the grinning, toothless old man hobbled away. Hirah seated his guest on a low couch and sat beside him.

They talked of what had befallen each since they had parted at Timnath and of Judah's journey here, while a servant set wine, bread, cheese, and fruit before them. Almost before Judah knew it, he was telling his friend of his disappointment at not having the first grandson, and of wanting to make sure he would at least be the first of his father's <u>sons</u> to have one.

Hirah's black eyes twinkled and a teasing smile played on his lips. He asked, "And have you already decided who the mother will be?"

Judah grinned sheepishly and a slight flush crept over his handsome, tanned face. "My friend," he declared seriously, "That is where I hope you can help me. Did you not tell me the women of this place were beautiful?"

"Ah," Hirah laughed, dimples appearing in his fleshy cheeks, "now I know why you have come to me—you are hunting a wife!"

Judah squirmed under the teasing tone, but did not contradict Hirah, who continued, slapping him on the back, "Well, my friend, you have come to the right place. We shall fix you up with one of our beautiful damsels on the morrow. Now tell me what kind of woman you fancy."

And so they sat talking until Hirah's wife came to tell them the evening meal was ready. Both men rose and Hirah made the introductions. Orpah was a beautiful woman, tall and buxom, with heart-shaped face, olive skin, black hair, and full, red lips.

As he bowed to her, Judah thought, *I hope there are some unmarried ones here as beautiful as she.*

After a hearty and pleasant meal in a large, brightly lighted room with a high ceiling, Hirah led Judah back onto the terrace. They sat on stone benches and watched the stars brighten as the sky darkened.

Hirah's three young sons played hide-and-seek with neighboring children among the trees and shrubbery beyond the terrace. His two daughters, almost grown up, sat on the far end of the terrace with their mother.

"Your daughters will grow into beautiful women, my friend. Like their mother," Judah assured Hirah. "And these sons will soon grow into handsome men also. Your oldest already looks much like you."

Hirah smiled and Judah continued, "How fortunate you are. I wish I had one his age."

"Ah, never fear, yours will come soon enough. Tomorrow you shall meet some of the women here," responded Hirah. "I shall have a feast in your honor tomorrow night, and you can have some time with whichever one pleases you."

"You sound so sure, my friend. What if none of them want me?" asked Judah.

Hirah snorted, "Not want you? A handsome man like you, the son of a wealthy prince? Any one of them will want you. Of that I can assure you. You can have your choice, my friend."

Hirah told Judah more about his people as the moon climbed high and cast eerie shadows under clumps of olives, terebinths, and tamarinds. The children ran everywhere, laughing and shrieking as they played. Judah and Hirah watched and listened, and Judah was pleased with all of it— his friend's hospitality, the beauty of the surroundings, the happy children. He thought, *These Canaanites may be heathen, but their home life seems much like our own.*

As the night grew chilly, Hirah called to his sons, assured Judah his servant would be taken care of, and laughingly promised he would find a wife here. They went inside and Judah slept well in the pleasant room his host provided, dreaming of the dark-haired girls he would meet tomorrow.

True to his promise, Hirah took Judah to several homes to meet his neighbors. In most of them, there was at least one beautiful girl who smiled shyly and bowed when her father or brother presented her to Judah. Each time, Judah was aware of Hirah's eyes upon him, watching to see if he was "taken" with any of the girls. He wasn't, though he agreed with Hirah after they left each place that the girls were indeed beautiful.

"There are two others," Hirah told him as they explored the surrounding land in the afternoon, "who will come to the feast tonight. They live in the cave with their father, Shuah. He is away today, and it is not fitting we should visit when they are alone. So, my friend, you have the best to look forward to tonight." His laughter rang out again and Judah smiled.

He thought, *Surely one of these will please me. I need a wife.*

Some time later, Judah helped Hirah and the servants to set up tables in the clearing at the back of Hirah's home. Soon Hirah's wife, daughters, and maidservants piled the tables with many of the foods Judah's family served, along with some dishes he did not recognize. Tantalizing odors of roasting lamb, kid, and calf drifted through the still air.

Just before sunset, Judah and Hirah went inside, bathed, and changed into their finest raiment. Then as dusk began to fall they came outside again, each praising the other's looks. Hirah's robe was light brown with gold braid, and his heavy hair, unturbaned, fell to his shoulders. Judah's thick curls hung halfway to his waist, black against the rich wine of his robe. They strolled between the tables, Hirah making sure all was in readiness. The admiring glances of the servants followed them, while the children chattered and played around them, happy to be admitted to the festivities.

Soon Hirah's Orpah and the two daughters came out, dressed in fine clothes, beautiful and smiling. The taller one, whom her father said was twelve, looked at least fifteen. Her mother could have passed for an older sister in the soft light. Judah did not miss Hirah's pride as he looked at them, nor their admiration for him and Judah.

As the first stars appeared, the neighbors began to arrive, all in their best. Judah guessed from their dress and festive mood that it was not often they all gathered for feasting. He recognized the ones he had met, especially the girls, now more beautiful in their fine clothes, their thin veils thrown back. They and the women, some with babies in their arms, gathered around a huge fire, and sat on stone benches, laughing, talking, giggling. There were many children, and they kept running among the tables and around the fire, shouting as they chased each other. *How like our children at home,* thought Judah.

When Hirah saw three dark figures coming from the cave area, he touched Judah's shoulder and whispered that now the ones he was waiting for were coming. Judah's pulse quickened in anticipation and he smiled.

"Come," Hirah ordered, as he bowed slightly to the other men and led Judah toward the approaching guests.

The shadows from the fire could not hide the tall, slender grace of one of the figures as she seemed to float toward them. Judah's excitement grew. *That one has to be beautiful of face,* he thought, *to match her flowing walk.* And as they came closer, he saw in the half light that she was indeed beautiful, with black hair and blue eyes, fair skin, and the reddest lips he had ever seen. Judah's heart leaped into his throat and he knew immediately she was the one for him. He could hardly greet the three as Hirah presented them.

"My good friend, Shuah, and his lovely daughter Lala." Judah looked toward the tall one who smiled and bowed. *Even a lovely name!* he inwardly exulted, bowing to both her and her father, too excited to speak. Hirah went on, "And Admah."

The shorter girl bowed, smiling, and Judah saw she was beautiful too, with the same dark hair and fair skin, but with dark eyes. He bowed and, finally finding his voice, managed to say that it was good to meet them all. He felt Hirah's gaze on him, and when he met his eyes, Hirah winked, laughed loudly and knowingly, and began to talk as he led them back to the others.

Orpah came forward and welcomed the three, then drew the girls back to the women. Judah followed Lala with his eyes and felt Hirah watching him again. He flushed, glad the firelight covered for him, as Hirah's laugh rang out once more.

The feast began and progressed leisurely, with the wine making people merry. To Judah, it all seemed like a dream as he became more enamored of Lala with each look. Her own shy smiles told him she was attracted to him also, and he hoped young people eventually "paired off" here as they had done at Prince Hamor's feast. *Why hadn't he asked Hirah earlier what the customs were? Or why hadn't Hirah told him?* He was aware that his friend was enjoying his agony at having to wait to be alone with the girl, for he kept winking at him and laughing. *I could choke him!* Judah thought cheerfully. *Why doesn't he help me?*

After what seemed ages to Judah, the women and servants cleared the tables of the remaining food, gathered together with their younger children around one side of the fire. Hirah and the older men ambled off in search of fallen limbs to throw on the dying fire. Blessedly, the young people were left, chattering and laughing, on the other side of the fire. They began to make Judah talk about his people, where he came from, why he was here—all the things young people want to know about a stranger. They seemed fascinated when he spoke of distant Haran, about his family's journey from there to this land. Reality seemed to creep back over Judah as he talked of himself and his family, and he was at ease with these young people. His eyes kept meeting Lala's and his heart would not behave.

At last two young men asked two girls to walk with them, and they went off arm in arm into the now moonlit night, while the others giggled knowingly. This was what Judah had been waiting for. He rose and asked Lala to walk with him, holding out his hand to her where she sat with her skirts spread around her. She smiled her willingness as she took Judah's hand. He helped her to her feet and they too went off into the night.

The next day Hirah brought his friend Shuah back to his home alone, and he and Judah agreed upon a dowry for Lala. Judah insisted on taking her back with him, and Shuah asked for a week to enable Lala to get her clothes and arrangements ready for a wedding.

Judah asked his friend to send a servant with Ziba back to his father's house. He did not want Jacob and Leah to worry about him being gone so long, and he also wanted Jacob to send pack animals for Lala's things and a camel for her. He wanted more of his own clothes and money, along with some of his finest jewels, especially a fine ring, for Lala. Ziba listened over and over to Judah's instructions so he would not forget. He promised faithfully to return as fast as possible, and could not repress a smile at Judah's unbounded excitement. He and Hirah's servant left that very afternoon, the servant riding Judah's own mount.

Judah worked for Hirah by day, when Lala was busy with her preparations, and was with her during a portion of every night. He fell more in love with her every day, could hardly think or talk of anything else, though his friend teased him and laughed at his enthusiasm constantly. Of course, Hirah and the whole village were excited too. Hirah even insisted on having the wedding at his home, since it was larger than Shuah's cave home and all the villagers could attend.

Ziba returned on the fourth day, bringing all Judah had sent for, along with two servants to help with the wedding and one to care for the pack animals. Soon everyone was in a frenzy of wedding preparations, Judah himself buying all the food for a two-day celebration. He would not adhere to the customary week of celebration, for he wanted to get his bride home to his father's house as soon as possible. They would have a week of celebration there. He knew his mother was even now preparing for it, as well as getting an extra room ready.

And so Judah was the first of Jacob's sons to find a wife and take her to his father's house. Jacob and Leah had wished for him to have found one of their own people, but since there were none closer than Haran, or Esau's people in Edom, they were content. They had made arrangements for a week of celebration while Judah was gone, as he had anticipated. Judah and Lala, with her maid and her possessions, arrived one bright, warm mid-afternoon, and the festivities began that very night. First there was a second ceremony, in which Jacob joined Judah and his bride and prayed Jehovah's blessings upon their marriage. Then food and music and merriment were provided for all, servants as well as family.

After the week of celebration, when the family became acquainted with the new bride, and when she and Judah got to really know each other, the spring planting began and the men worked from daylight till dark for two weeks. It was during this busy time that Dinah's baby was born, a fine son as she had known it would be. She called the child Shechem, after his father whom she still loved and mourned. The women rejoiced with her and kept busy with the baby. Dinah was happy with the baby, even though she was sad because he would never know a father.

After the planting was finished and there was leisure time for a while, Jacob and Leah made a feast in honor of their first grandchild, Shechem. It was a time of great merriment and all the brothers except Levi and Simeon seemed happy for Dinah. Benjamin loved the baby and felt very proud and important over being an uncle. Reuben loved all children, and assured Dinah that her son was the most handsome boy he had ever seen. Judah was glad to see his sister being so happy after all her sorrow, and rejoiced to see Lala so interested in the baby. Surely she would want their own son as much as he did. Seeing her holding the baby, he was overcome with love for her and fervently hoped they'd have their own by this time next year.

Toward the end of the feast, when the family was gathered around the fire that the servants had started in the courtyard, Judah noted something that both interested and puzzled him. It was odd that he noticed, since he was so wrapped up in his love for Lala and so aware of sitting near her. Or perhaps it was because of those things. Chancing to look at Reuben, he was aware that his brother's eyes were meeting those of his father's handmaid, Bilhah, sitting on the other side of the fire. Was it lust or love he saw? *What was it? Why did they look at each other in that way? Didn't they know that someone would see them?* Judah looked at the others. Apparently only he was aware of the long meeting of the two pairs of eyes. When Judah looked again at Reuben, he had turned toward his father, seemingly intent on what Jacob was saying. *This will bear watching,* Judah thought.

The very next day, at the evening meal, when Bilhah was serving the savory stew the family liked so much, Judah noticed that exchange of glances again. Again, Judah looked to see if others noticed, but there was no sign that anyone had. Still, Judah knew <u>something</u> was taking place between these two that should not be. When he thought about it later, he became angry. *How dare his brother look at his father's concubine that way?* He would just have to talk to Reuben, and threaten to tell their father if whatever was going on between them didn't stop.

But as he thought about it, he saw in this situation a way to deprive Reuben of his birthright and blessing as the first son. He would simply ignore it and let it go on until his father found out—surely others would notice.

When several weeks passed, Judah felt determined to find out just what was taking place. One night after the family had retired, he told Lala he was going for a walk, and he hid in the shadows at the back of the house. It was not long before Reuben slipped across the courtyard toward the rooms of Zilpah and Bilhah. Staying in the shadows, he crept close enough to see his brother entering Bilhah's door. *I was right,* Judah thought, *there is something between them! How could Reuben go in to our father's concubine? She is old enough to be his mother! How did that get started? Surely he could have had his choice of the younger women, even of Hamor's daughters or the townspeople. Of course, Bilhah is still beautiful. Could Dan and Naphtali not know this about their own mother? Wouldn't they kill Reuben if they did? I must tell my father so this can be stopped! O Jehovah, this evil right in our own family!*

Judah was almost back to his room when again the thought came: *Let it alone. Our father will find out soon enough and then Reuben will never be given the blessing or birthright, even if he is the eldest. And Levi and Simeon will never be. So you, Judah, are next in age, and you are going to have the first son of a son. You must take care of that if you haven't already! No, I will not tell my father. I will even encourage Reuben in his evil.*

The next day he told Reuben he knew about the liaison. His brother responded in a surly manner, "Mind your own business. <u>You</u> have a wife to go to."

"Well, so could you," Judah reminded him. Then he

added, "But I suppose there is no reason for you not to use Bilhah. Our father no longer goes either to her or Zilpah, and Bilhah, though not young, is still beautiful. And why should she not know pleasure if she pleases you?"

Surprise showed on Reuben's ruddy face. "Then you will not tell our father?"

"No, I will not, but sooner or later I suppose he will find out. If she is your choice for now, however, do as you wish. I will not tell."

No more was said, but it was almost a year before Jacob learned of the affair, and even then had to have proof before he would believe it. His anger flared in a way it had not done since he had learned of Simeon and Levi's evil. When he confronted Reuben, he did not deny it, and for once stood up to his father. An ugly scene followed and Jacob demanded that this evil be put away, or Reuben would lose his inheritance.

Reuben spoke bitterly, "Why should I care? You have never loved me as your firstborn. You've never loved my mother either. No, it was always Aunt Rachel and Joseph you loved, though I grew up closer to them and to you than to my own mother and my brothers. Now with Joseph gone, it is Judah you have turned to, not me!"

Jacob, still angry, could nevertheless not deny the accusation, and Reuben continued, "Judah even told me to go on with Bilhah because you no longer wanted her. What kind of life do you think she has had? Oh, I know she's only your handmaid, only used to give you sons when Aunt Rachel couldn't, but it is not right for her, or Zilpah either. I hate the custom! Look what it caused my great-grandfather Abraham to do with Hagar and Ishmael!" Reuben's voice grew louder and he was angrier than he had ever been, his face flushed a fiery red.

"Enough!" his father shouted. "Who are you to judge a custom that started before you were born? Stay away from Bilhah or she will be beaten! She should be anyway!"

Reuben looked at his father for a very long moment. He had never incurred his anger before. He was shaken by his own boldness. "If anyone is to be beaten, it is I, not Bilhah. I started it, not she!" he said angrily, but with earnestness, meeting his father's eyes squarely. "Why don't you just beat me and disinherit me? Then Judah can have the birthright and the blessing—that is what you want and that is what he wants!"

Jacob was stunned at the vehemence and bitterness of his firstborn's words, but again could not deny the truth of what he said. The anger drained away from him as he and Reuben faced each other.

Reuben finally turned and stalked away. Jacob stood awhile looking after him, then went in the opposite direction, head down, shoulders sagging.

As Jacob walked, he considered his son's words and went back over the situation from years ago. It was true; he had neglected both Bilhah and Zilpah. He had never cared for either of them, had never really thought of them as women, just as his wives' handmaidens. But, after all, he had gained four sons by them; he should not have ignored them and still not given them as wives to others. He thought of his grandfather, Abraham. It was as Reuben said—he had started the custom in their tribe. But then when he had sent Hagar and her son, Ishmael away, she had been free to go to some other man if she chose. Not so with Bilhah and Zilpah; they had to stay with him and yet never be used by him. Not that they weren't well provided for; they were treated almost as Leah was, except he never slept with them. After all, he reasoned, he hadn't wanted them in the first place. It was Rachel, and then Leah, who had pressed them upon him by their nagging.

The more he thought, the more confused he became. He had perhaps not done right by them, though he was following the custom of his tribe. *Should he even now consider freeing them to other men, servants of his? What older male servants were in his household that they could be given to?* He could think of none. *Certainly Bilhah could not be given to his own son , even if he had defiled her; he simply could not have his own father's concubine! But what then should Jacob do about it?*

He was head of the tribe; it was up to him. What would Jehovah have him do? Perhaps if he thought about it for a while, God would tell him.

At last Jacob turned and walked back to his house to talk with Leah. She had not heard the rumor of her son's behavior with Bilhah, and was very disturbed about it when Jacob told her. Still, she gave him no advice on what to do; after all, Bilhah was not her maid. She certainly would not have Zilpah given to anyone else, even if the handmaid should desire it, which she was sure she did not.

Reuben came back to the family table that night; his anger seemed to be passed, but he said nothing to his father or the others. He just sat there moody and silent.

And it continued for many days, as Jacob sought an answer from Jehovah. Finally he talked with Leah again. This time she said that Reuben should be given a young bride of his own; then he would no longer desire Bilhah. And Bilhah would be given a choice of remaining in Jacob's house or be given to a servant if any were willing. Jacob thought about this plan, and eventually decided Leah was right. *But where would they find a bride for Reuben?* Leah asked if Jacob had noticed how grown up one of the little girls of Hamor's people had become; not one of the servants, but the daughter of one of Hamor's chief men. She described the girl and Jacob recalled her. *Perhaps she would do,* he thought. *If she were willing and if she pleased Reuben.*

"Leah," said Jacob, "you know that Reuben can no longer be considered to receive the blessing and birthright, don't you?"

"But to which son will they go?" she asked, fearing lest they go to Benjamin, the youngest, as in Jacob's case, and not to one of hers.

O Jehovah, she silently prayed, *If I never have his love, surely one of my sons should carry on the line at least.*

"To Judah," Jacob answered her slowly. "He seems the one who would value it most. Reuben says he encouraged him in the affair with Bilhah, hoping it would discredit Reuben, and Judah would be next in line. Perhaps he is right."

Leah said nothing; she was thinking. *Judah would be the better choice. He's quick-witted, steady, can be depended on. Reuben is much like a child, trusts and loves so easily—that's probably why this thing with Bilhah occurred. He's happy-go-lucky, not responsible.* Though she'd never admitted it even to herself, Reuben had never been her favorite, though he was her firstborn. He had been conceived with Jacob thinking she was his beloved Rachel, and Reuben was a continual reminder of this deception.

Jacob broke in on her thoughts. "I'll not tell Reuben yet. We'll see how he feels about the girl. But whether she suits him or not, I will demand that he stop the affair with Bilhah. It will be easier if she chooses to marry a servant, but I don't care. Will you find her and send her to me at once?"

It was not hard to convince Bilhah that her affair with Reuben must stop, but she did not quail before Jacob. She said she would like to become wife to Jedediah, whose wife had died some months before. That is, if he wanted her.

Jacob later talked to his servant, Jedediah, and discovered he was agreeable to the plan. Jacob felt relieved. *Now,* he thought, *if dealing with Reuben will only go as well.*

It didn't. Jacob found him alone with a flock of goats, far off from the others. He was morose and defensive when Jacob asked why he hadn't wanted a young wife of his own rather than his father's concubine. Jacob's anger over the first confrontation was gone; he tried to be understanding, for he did not want to alienate this son who had been closest to him and Rachel as he grew up, and later to Joseph as well. Reuben finally admitted that he had always admired Bilhah even when he was a boy, because she was always laughing and teasing him. She had been kind and cheerful when his mother was too busy with the younger sons to even notice him.

"I leaned toward her even as I grew up, and I found joy in her company. Then, when Judah encouraged me, I just followed my desires," Reuben reluctantly explained.

"But, my son," remonstrated Jacob, "surely you knew it was wrong. You know it was against our custom, that it would shame me."

"I did not think of it that way," returned Reuben, relenting a little.

"Perhaps you didn't, my son, but you know it must stop. You are never to go to her again," Jacob stated with finality. "She has just said she would become the wife of Jedediah, at my suggestion."

Anger flared in Reuben again; he lashed out at his father. "You just couldn't let me have anything good, could you?"

Jacob was calm, but firm. "You know it cannot be allowed to continue. Your mother and I have decided you shall have a wife, the young and beautiful daughter of Prince Hamor's chief man. She is just growing to womanhood. Tall, slender, dark. You know her? Does she please you?"

"I know the maid you mean, but I never thought of her as more than a child. How do I know whether she pleases me or not?" Reuben questioned.

"Well, think of her as a woman when you see her again. If you wish then, I will speak to her mother for you. If you do not choose her, find another. It is time you had a wife." Jacob's voice was kind, trying to melt his son's bitterness. "I will leave you now, so you can consider my words." Reuben said nothing.

Jacob walked away from his son, feeling tired and old. On his way to the house, he considered what Reuben had said about Judah's encouraging him with Bilhah. *Had Judah really done this to get Reuben disinherited? Did he do this deliberately, as Jacob himself had long ago tricked his own brother Esau?* Jacob's memory traveled back over the years. He once more felt shame at what he had done, at what his beloved mother had helped him to do. His face burned. *Why could they not have let Jehovah work it out in His own way, since it was He who had said the older Esau should serve the younger Jacob?*

And he also recalled how his uncle Laban had deceived him in return, how he came to have his two wives and their handmaids. This trouble with his sons was at least partly caused by all that had taken place with him in his earlier years. He must not judge Judah too severely; perhaps the birthright and blessing meant as much to his fourth son as they had to him. *Judah will surely do much more with them than Reuben, just as I have done more with them and treasured them more than Esau ever would have. Oh, it was all such a tangle, how could I have really known what was right when I was so young? How can I know what is right and best now? O, Jehovah, please help us! Let Reuben choose what is best for us all, even if You won't show me.*

9

Changes and Growth and Trouble

Jacob and his family celebrated the passage of ten years at Hebron with a great feast. Afterwards, when the tables were cleared and family members and servants had gone inside, Jacob and Leah sat on a stone bench by the dying fire. As Jacob stirred the glowing embers, a shower of sparks flew upward. Leah's eyes followed them until they faded, and then she fixed her gaze on the starry heavens. Jacob put an arm around her shoulders and took her hand. After a few moments, he said, "Jehovah promised Grandfather Abraham that his descendants would become as numerous as the stars of heaven. When I looked at our tribe tonight, I realized that we are beginning to fulfill that promise."

"Yes," Leah returned, putting a hand over his, "we are growing. Just think what has taken place in the five years since we came here. First, Dinah gave us our first grandchild, little Shechem, right after Judah brought Lala here as a bride. Now they have two sons also."

On and on they reminisced, thanking Jehovah for His blessings upon their tribe. And they did have much to thank Him for, both at that time and in the years that followed. Throughout this time they continued to prosper and they saw many changes. Bilhah was given to Jedediah. Reuben married the dark and lovely Shirah, and they had three sons.

Each of the other sons, except Benjamin, married and had children.

Dinah's son, Shechem, grew into a fine lad; he was handsome like his father. One of Esau's sons, Joel, came from Edom to visit his uncle Jacob; he fell in love with the still-beautiful Dinah, stayed there, and married her. Judah's sons, Er and Onan, turned eight and nine years of age; they fought with each other almost constantly, rebelling against all discipline from Judah and not always responding to Jacob's gentle admonitions. Jacob grayed at the temples. Leah became a little heavier, but she remained graceful. Her face became actually more beautiful, her eyes seemed less apt to squint than they used to be. She was so industrious and efficient, ran the house so well, that Jacob came to admire her even more. The memory of his beloved Rachel dimmed with the years, and he gradually came to love Leah. He never knew quite when it happened, but Leah knew. Her cup of joy overflowed and she daily thanked Jehovah and forgot the long years of being unloved. She lavished her unbounded love and care on Jacob and they were both happy with each other—happy in their family.

Sometimes Jacob still mourned his lost Joseph, but the years helped to ease his grief and he turned more and more to Benjamin as he grew up. When Benji was almost fifteen, old Isaac died. His son Esau and some of his family came, and he and Jacob buried their father in the cave where Abraham and Sarah were buried. All his father's possessions were then Jacob's. He let Judah move into Isaac's house and gradually take charge of all that had been Isaac's, while Benjamin stayed with his father more and helped with his affairs.

The other sons became less wicked, accepted the fact that, as punishment for their evil to Hamor's family, their father had taken away their right to much inheritance, and never seemed very close to any of them.

Most of them built houses of their own nearby, and those who stayed in Jacob's home had more room. Though Jacob largely ignored his sons' business matters, both he and Leah adored all the grandchildren. Jacob taught the boys probably more than their fathers did. Though his own sons came to know Jehovah as a presence in their lives, it was Jacob who pointed his grandsons to Jehovah. It was he who gave each child ten sheep when, at the age of twelve, each was considered a man of the tribe, and taught them to set aside one out of each ten of their increase as a tithe to Jehovah. He let each one help in selecting the animals for the sacrifices twice yearly, so each learned early which animals were considered perfect.

All the flocks and herds increased, and more and more animals were set apart as tithes. Many of these were sold, and the price was put into the "tithe urns." Twice each year, soon after the tribe's sacrifice ceremony and feast, Jacob, Benjamin, Judah, and whichever grandsons had just turned twelve, took part of the tithe money into the city of Hebron and gave it to the poor, the blind, and the crippled they found there. The remainder of the tithe was stored away against a time when some great thing would need to be done for Jehovah. Jacob was sure that time would come.

One thing that grieved both Jacob and Judah was the behavior of Judah's sons, Er and Onan. They had always rebelled at discipline from Judah, and when each reached the age of twelve, such discipline was flaunted altogether. No amount of punishment availed, and neither did any reasoning or tears. Jacob talked with them often, but even he had little effect. They still bickered and fought with each other, and even fought their cousins or the servant children They did more and more evil, and cursed and swore when something or someone displeased them. Of all the grandchildren, they alone scoffed at the idea of a God they could not see, and they refused to put aside any tithe from the animals Jacob gave them.

Jacob and Judah talked of them much, prayed to Jehovah often on their behalf. Judah was sure it was a punishment designed for him because of his part in selling his brother into slavery long ago, but of course he never told his father this. He simply talked with Jehovah when he was alone. He confessed the jealousy and hatred he had harbored in his heart for Joseph, and could now see that they were unjustified. He was sorry for what he now knew was an awful deed against Joseph, against his father, against Jehovah Himself. As he grieved over the waywardness of his own sons, he came to understand more and more of the agony he and his brothers had brought upon their father. Again and again he confronted them with their evil, begged them to repent before Jehovah, even if they could not tell Jacob. He knew, and they knew, that he would grieve more at knowing the truth than by thinking his son was dead.

Little by little, over the years, the sacrifices and prayers of their father and Judah had their effect. The sons could now all agree sometimes when they were together, away from Jacob and Benjamin, that their deed had been wicked, that it had been against Jehovah. Secretly Judah wondered why his sons alone were wicked, when his brothers had been as guilty as he. Yet he felt sure he was being punished, and rightly so. He was glad that his brothers had realized the wrong they had done, glad that Jehovah was becoming more of a reality to them, as He had been to Judah for many years. He was sure Levi and Simeon had repented of their evil to Prince Hamor.

And even as he grieved and worried over Er and Onan, and prayed they would turn from their waywardness, he thanked Jehovah for his youngest son, Shelah, who was still a child. He somehow felt that this son was a sign from Jehovah that his sin against Joseph was forgiven. He kept Shelah away from his older brothers (they mostly ignored him or were unkind to him anyway) as much as possible. The child stayed much with his mother, Lala, who adored him and taught him how to help with the household tasks. Leah took up much time with the little boy also, and as he grew older, both Jacob and Judah taught him to help with the animals and other tasks.

Jacob's family continued to grow. Prince Hamor's people had merged with Jacob's tribe through marriages with his sons and grandsons, and his servants. All in all, his was a happy, peaceful tribe, with only Er and Onan being openly rebellious. The flocks and herds increased yearly, so that Jacob and Judah marveled at Jehovah's blessings upon them. The crops were bountiful, and more and more barns had to be built, as well as folds and stalls for the animals and more houses for family and servants. The number of animals for sacrifice increased and the money in the tithe urns did as well, though they gave away more and more to the needy in Hebron. Jacob—Prince Israel to the city—was indeed a mighty and wealthy prince, greatly respected, whose family grew to perhaps half the size of the city.

As the wealth of the tribe grew, Jacob lavished gifts upon his adored Benji, and upon Leah, as a token of his growing esteem and love for her. Jacob's sons, especially Judah, gave many gifts to their wives as well. Each time a caravan to Egypt passed by on the not-too-distant route, a long list was carried to the caravan master and the items were dutifully brought back by him. Sometimes it took many donkeys to bring the goods: jeweled camel trappings, household furnishings, building materials (especially windows and roofing material), farming tools, clothes, perfumes, cosmetics, jewelry, beautiful dyed silks, wools and linens, even seeds. Now and again more camels and donkeys would be bought, and sometimes more servants, especially some who could teach the tribe's children to read, write, do numbers, as well as a few gifted in higher learning and the arts.

Jacob's people were an industrious and, for the most part, a happy tribe. Being well-fed and clothed and with Jehovah's special blessing, there was little illness and few died young. In thankfulness to Jehovah, there was often much merriment, many feasts and always, twice a year, the great sacrificial ceremony, led by Jacob and Judah, sometimes assisted by different sons.

When Benjamin was twenty, and the tribe had been in the land some fifteen years, he was given the youngest daughter of Prince Hamor, a tall, dark, lovely girl with gentle brown eyes and a ready, beautiful smile. Benji had been captivated with her since he was seven or eight, and Jacob was glad to have persuaded him to wait until he was twenty to marry. It was a costly and well-prepared celebration, with the whole tribe feasting and not working for a week, even though it was the beginning of harvest.

Zebulun had just finished a new house and moved out with his brood of children, so there was much room in Jacob's house for the young couple. Indeed, only Dinah, with her husband, Joel, and young Shechem, and Dan and Naphtali, with their small families, were left with Jacob and Leah. Since Jacob depended on Benji to help him with everything, as he had once depended on Judah, and so doted on him, he certainly would not have had him live anywhere else. He often watched his son, now grown into a tall, handsome young man, with the dark red hair and green eyes of Jacob's beloved Rachel. He looked very much like Joseph had looked when he went away, so that at times Jacob's eyes filled with tears as he beheld his youngest.

As Er and Onan grew to young manhood, they became increasingly wild and disobedient. They never wanted to work nor tend the animals. Sometimes when Judah made them go out to help the herdsmen, they would slip away and go into the city, taking a sheep or goat when they thought the herdsmen wouldn't know. Then, later, they might go back to the animals, full of wine and talking of the whores they had slept with in the city. Or they would be gone until late at night, leaving their parents worried and sleepless. They still oftentimes fought with each other, or someone else in the tribe. There seemed to be no way to tame them, and both Judah and Jacob despaired of them. Jacob often thought to himself that they were even more unruly and wicked than his own sons had been at their age.

The small city to the northwest of Hebron—Timnath—where Judah had first met his great friend Hirah, was on a caravan route to Egypt. It was known for sheep-shearing and trading. People for miles in every direction came to have their steep sheared and the wool disposed of. Jacob's tribe was no exception, and all the sons went there with their sheep at the beginning of summer. Judah and Benjamin went often for they had to take their father's animals as well as their own.

One day when Benji was ill, Judah persuaded Er to go with him and Gad to take their father's sheep. While the sheep were being sheared, they went into the heart of the city and entered one of the shops. Judah had been there often before, and the shopkeeper greeted him warmly, inquiring as to what refreshments they would like. He seated them at a low table and disappeared through a door at the rear. When he returned, a young girl helped him bring in their food. He said, "This is my daughter, Tamar," and the men bowed to her, while she smiled shyly at them as she placed the bread and cheese, raisins, figs, and wine before them.

She was very beautiful, with dark hair and eyes, fair skin and full lips the color of ripe pomegranates. Young Er could not take his eyes off her. Once she looked up and met his gaze, then returned his smile, blushing faintly and showing two deep dimples. Then she went away as Er followed her with his eyes, taking in her graceful carriage, her slenderness. He ate almost nothing, barely sipping the wine. His eyes went again and again toward the back of the shop, while Judah and Gad exchanged amused glances. Later Gad went out first, while Er lingered behind as his father paid the shopkeeper. The girl never did appear and reluctantly Er followed his father outside and they left.

Judah noticed Er's silence as they later led the sheared sheep back to their own fields. *He really was taken with that girl; what was it her father had called her? Tamar?—yes, that was it! Lovely name, beautiful girl. Er is young to think of marriage but perhaps that would settle him, take away some of the restlessness.* The thought pleased Judah, for despite the trouble and worry Er and Onan had caused him, he loved them and still hoped that one of them would carry on the family line.

Judah was not surprised when Er remained quiet for the next few days. When Onan tried to pick an argument or a fight, he ignored him. He did not go into the city of Hebron.

A week passed, and one day when Judah went to see

about the sheep, Er was alone with them. "My father," he said, "there is something I want you to do for me." He met his father's quizzical gaze levelly.

"Yes, my son?" inquired Judah.

The boy continued, "The girl we saw at Timnath—Tamar, the shopkeeper's daughter. You remember?" Judah nodded. "The girl pleases me much. I can't stop thinking of her. Will you bargain with her father for me? I must have her as my wife."

"But you are young, my son," Judah ventured, knowing it was useless to argue or refuse him.

The boy was firm. He went on, "Nevertheless, I know what I want. I cannot live without her."

Judah remembered Hamor's son Shechem and how he had felt the same way about Dinah. When he thought of what happened as a result, he was afraid. What if something should befall Er? He hesitated and the boy pleaded, "Please, father, will you get her for me? Go to her father tomorrow and pay whatever dowry he asks. I have some silver and I will give half of my flock."

Judah looked at his wayward son closely, at the pleading in his dark eyes. He thought of how he had felt about the boy's mother when he had first seen her. "My son," he said, "I wish you could have chosen one of our own people, for Jehovah is not pleased when we join with others, although your mother has been a good wife to me. Perhaps this girl will be likewise to you. But what if she or her father refuses?"

"She will not refuse, I know it," Er responded confidently. "If her father refuses, just offer him more dowry."

Judah tried to reason, but his son knew what he wanted: he wanted this girl to be his wife, and he wanted her now! Judah promised to go to her father in the morning.

There was a look of gratitude on Er's face as he said, "Thank you, my father. I will give you the money tonight and you may tell her father he may have the sheep or I will sell them and give him the money.

Judah, beholding his handsome, wayward son, felt great love for him. He responded, "Keep your sheep, my son. I will pay the remainder as a wedding gift."

The boy bowed and answered, "Again I thank you, my father. You will not regret it."

So it came about that Judah's firstborn married the beautiful Tamar from Timnath and she came to live under Judah's roof. Er became less wild and headstrong, and he and Judah remained on good terms. The whole tribe loved Tamar and made her feel welcome. All except Onan, that is. He was rude to her from the start and from then on ignored her. He picked fights with his brother even more often, though Er tried to be peaceable, and he went more often to Hebron, alone.

Judah waited with great anticipation, as did Jacob—for the news that Tamar was with child, but it did not happen. After two years, there still were no children, and Tamar's lovely face was often red from weeping, which grieved Er much. He begged his father to intercede with Jehovah on her behalf. "I have never really believed those stories Grandfather tells, but maybe Jehovah is as real and powerful as he says. If He sends me a son, I will believe in Him," he stated.

Judah talked with his father. "I know that for years Aunt Rachel had no children, and that you besought Jehovah for her, so that she finally bore Joseph, and later Benji. I also know that Grandfather Isaac was childless for twenty years, also that he was himself given to his father Abraham in answer to his prayers. You talk with Jehovah when you sacrifice. He seems so real to you, as if you are in His very presence. Is it not true?"

Jacob stood tall and straight, his eyes alive, his lips smiling, thoughtfully rubbing his graying head. "It is true that, in a way, He is always present with me now, since He wrestled with me as an angel at the brook, Jabbok, when I returned to this land. It was then He gave me the new name, Israel, and said as a prince I had power with God and prevailed. But when I have sacrificed perfect animals to Him, He seems more real and close to me, and I know He hears me when I talk to Him. Sometimes He speaks to me in return."

Judah said, "I hope that someday Jehovah will meet me and be as real. But now He isn't, and Er would have me ask Him to give children to him and Tamar. My father, will you not beseech Jehovah in my stead?"

Jacob sat on the ground, tucked his long legs under him, resting an elbow on each knee. Judah marveled that his father was still so agile, so lean and strong. He squatted in front of Jacob, waiting for his answer.

Jacob sat with his head down for some moments, as if pondering an answer. At last he raised his head and looked at Judah, speaking slowly. "Er and Onan are my eldest grandsons, except for Dinah's son, Shechem. I dangled them on my knees and doted on them much. From the first I have watched for signs that one of them should have the quiet thoughtfulness to appreciate the birthright and blessing, should they pass to you. Neither has ever shown the quiet nature nor seemed to care for the stories of our tribe or for any knowledge of Jehovah. They have been evil, but I pray they will become better as they grow older, as you and your brothers have."

Judah winced at the reminder of his younger days, and Jacob paused a moment, then went on, "I myself have repented much of my deception of my father and my Uncle Laban—though Jehovah knows my uncle deserved it—and certainly I have grown closer to Jehovah through the years. Perhaps it will be thus with Er and Onan. I see that Er is less restless since he married; it may be that if he has sons he will think more of Jehovah and His ways. That he even asked you to intercede with Jehovah for him is good. Yes. I will make a special sacrifice soon and you and I together will pray for sons for Er and Tamar."

"Thank you, my father. And we will also ask Him to help Onan to be a better person, for he grows more unruly everyday. He goes more often into Hebron and taunts Er that his wife will not let him go anymore. He seems to hate Tamar and is rude to her at every turn. He makes fun of them both because they have no children, and he says Er is not really a man. 'If I had her,' he sometimes taunts Er, 'she'd be with child soon enough.' Of course Er will not take that and they have some bloody fights. There is little peace under my roof. If our little Shelah were not such a good son, Lala and I would have no joy at all."

Jacob listened in silence, his head lowered, his gnarled hands twirling a blade of grass. He asked, "Does Onan never think of taking a wife? He is old enough to do so and marriage might settle him some, as it has Er."

Judah answered, "He has an eye for all the wenches in the tribe, probably sleeps with some of them when he's not with the whores in Hebron. But he has not really cared about any girl, unless—well, unless it would be Tamar."

Jacob's head came up and he looked sharply at his son as he continued, "I used to notice the way he looked at her when she first came, when he thought no one was seeing him. It seemed to me to be the same look of love and longing that Er had. I was afraid he would force her if he ever got her alone. If he ever tried, she must have disdained his advances, and so he gradually seemed to grow to hate her."

Judah stopped, his brow furrowed, his dark eyes pained. "It may be as you say," agreed Jacob. "I too seem to recall how Onan looked at Tamar at first. I supposed I read too much into his looks and I have not thought of it in a long time. It could be that he pretends to hate her because Er got her first."

Jacob got to his feet, looking at his son with a smile that revealed still white, even teeth. Judah thought, *My father is still a handsome man. Small wonder my mother's face still lights up like a girl's when she looks at him.* "Perhaps," he said, "your son, Shelah, will continue to grow good and be an upstanding man. He may be the one to appreciate the blessing and birthright. May Jehovah help us to choose the right one, the one He wants to carry on the Godly line."

Judah said, "May it be as you say, Father. It was good to talk with you."

"Yes, my son," Jacob answered, "and now I should see

165

about the flocks in the west pasture. Will you ride with me?"

"Yes I will," returned Judah, and they walked back to the shelters to find their mounts.

Two days later, they offered seven perfect lambs and made their prayers to Jehovah, just after sunset at the usual altar. After the evening meal, Judah asked Er to work with him, told him of the prayers they had offered for him and Tamar, and even Onan. "Jehovah seemed more real and closer to me than ever before as we sacrificed and prayed for you. How I wish He could be a real presence to you and Onan."

Er's heart had lifted as his father spoke, but he only shrugged off the last suggestion, then answered, "Thank you, my father, and please thank Grandfather for me. Now I shall anxiously wait to see if Jehovah really hears and answers your prayers for us."

"My son," returned Judah, "it is a matter of faith. Remember Grandfather Abraham had faith; so did Grandfather Isaac—for twenty years, before his sons were born."

"I am not good at waiting," said Er, smiling wryly as he turned away.

"Er," commanded his father kindly, "listen to me. You and Onan have said you would not believe in a God you could not see. But, my son, faith sees with an inner eye. You believe and then you know. You have not tried to please Jehovah by doing what your grandfather and I have told you is right. But since you married, you have not run to the evil as you did before, and now you must be at least trying to believe or you would not have asked us to pray.

My son, I beseech you to believe that Jehovah is real, that He will bring punishment on those who do evil, unless they repent. I know, because I did a great evil in my youth, which I cannot tell you of, and I have been punished much, not openly—except in the evil you and Onan have done—but in my heart. That punishment has made me sorry for the evil, and I have repented before Jehovah. I know He has put away my evil, that He will not take my life. Maybe your punishment for evil is that you have no sons. I beg you to repent, to believe that Jehovah is real and to worship Him as the one, true God of heaven and earth, lest death be your further punishment."

Er listened in silence; his head was down, his face was surly, but he was clearly ashamed.

Judah continued, "You are the older, Er. Perhaps if you let Jehovah be real to you and tried to please Him, then Onan would follow. When be taunts you, maybe you could just ignore him. Then Onan might finally leave you alone."

"I will try, Father," promised Er, raising his head before he walked away. Judah thought, *Oh, how I love these handsome sons, so like their mother, though they are wayward. Jehovah, turn them from evil, spare them, give Er a son. I beg of You! I so want one of my sons to carry the line to bless the world.*

The months passed swiftly. They were busy months for Jacob's family. Judah and Jacob waited expectantly for news that Tamar was with child. Er waited too, but after he loved Tamar even more and renewed his efforts for a child, he began to doubt more than ever a God he could not see. He began to think, *My mother has told us about the gods of her people, little gods of wood and of stone, carved in the likeness of an animal, a bird, or a woman great with child, even statues of Astarte, goddess of fertility. She says these gods are pleased with you and bless you with children even if you do things my father's people think are wrong. They just want you to bow down to them and bring a gift for their priests, she says. I especially like the rites she says belong to Astarte, where one uses the temple prostitutes as one wishes during the festivals to her. She says if I joined in the rites or even had a carved likeness of the goddess, then Tamar would bear children. Even Tamar believes this, but my father and grandfather would be angry if I brought an idol here. Anyway, I have not wanted a prostitute since I've had Tamar. So what should I do? I suppose I will just wait a year or two and see if Jehovah answers prayers. If He doesn't, then I'll just have to see what Astarte can do. I certainly won't wait twenty years as my great-grandfather Isaac did! But I will try not to fight with Onan, as I promised my father. Besides, I may someday need him to go with me to a festival to Astarte. In two years, if Tamar doesn't have a child, I'll know Jehovah is not real, that He can't send answers. I'll also know He can't punish either, no matter what my father says.*

True to his promise, Er got along better with his brother, and both of them began to be more dependable, so Judah gave them more responsibility over the crops and the harvesting. Onan still went sometimes to Hebron, and taunted Er because he would not go with him. Er simply ignored him, kept loving Tamar and counting the months. He knew his father also counted the months, and his grandfather as well, for sometimes they both urged him to remember how long Abraham and Isaac and even Jacob had waited, and not to lose heart.

"Jehovah finally sent them sons to carry on the line, my son, and He may send you a son to carry on the line also," encouraged Jacob.

Er still thought that he would wait only two years, not twenty or more. Besides, a son for the line didn't interest him too much. He wanted a son, or even a daughter, to stop Tamar's tears and to make her happy.

When a year had passed since the special sacrifice, Judah took note that almost fifty children had been born to his brothers, their sons and grandsons, and to his father's servants. *Why not some to me or my son?* he wondered, feeling very discouraged. He asked his father to have another special sacrifice to beseech Jehovah once more on Er's behalf. "We must also thank Him that Er and Onan are not so evil and do not fight as much, that both have become more dependable," he said.

Jacob agreed and so once more they sacrificed and prayed, feeling again the presence of Jehovah. And they hoped each month for good news from Tamar. Er renewed his hopes also. When the rains came, and later, the cold, he had more time with her, and with every passing day, he was sure he loved her more.

This season of the year was also cherished by Leah. Jacob stayed with her in their room more often, talking to her, helping with the thread for the small loom she kept there, keeping the fire burning cheerfully. Sometimes he brought his basket-weaving there in order to work close to her. At other times, they just sat and talked, remembering things from long ago, even from Haran. Sometimes at night, she felt she belonged to Jacob and that he loved her in the way she had always longed for. They were both happy. It was only at times that Jacob sat staring into the fire in silence, tears running down his weathered face. Leah knew at such times he was remembering the two he would always love the most—his beautiful Rachel and his lost Joseph. At these times, she sighed and went on with her work, thankful that he gave her as much love as he could, that his house and his bed were hers. She was thankful also that her children and grandchildren showed their love for her in so many ways, that the family prospered, that her once wicked, wayward sons had come to really worship Jehovah and to be good men. Surely Jehovah had blessed her above all women, and she would no longer grieve that someone else would always hold a part of her husband's love.

Judah also had more time inside with his still-beautiful Lala, who made herself always lovely and desirable for him. Her dark tresses were kept clean and shining, her body was always scented with the deaxylon flower he remembered from his childhood in Haran, an aroma his mother always had. He bought the perfume for both of them from the Haran caravans that occasionally passed, going into Egypt. He also bought for Lala beautiful, rich robes with embroidery and jewels, gold and silver rings and earrings, necklaces and bracelets, sparkling combs for her hair, and fine sandals for her feet.

It pleased Judah that she always looked beautiful, yet still kept the household with many servants running smoothly, spun and wove and prepared food for current needs as well as for the winter seasons. She and Er's Tamar loved each other dearly. They often chattered and laughed like girls as they worked together. Judah always watched them with pleasure.

Now that Er and Onan got along so much better, and that Shelah continued to be a fine, obedient lad, Judah would have been completely happy, if it had not been for Tamar's barrenness, his sons' lack of real belief in, and obedience to, Jehovah, and his own sorrow at times for what he and his brothers had done to Joseph. If only he could bring Joseph back and could tell his father the truth, how relieved he would be. But he knew he couldn't do this, and he knew his father would grieve for Joseph forever. He felt Jehovah had forgiven him for his part in the great wrong, but he could not forgive himself, nor could he forget what he had done. And as he grieved for his own wayward sons, he knew he was paying for his sin.

This time of the winter rain was also a time for Er to be with Tamar more. Er thought he had never loved her so much and could not understand how, month after month, she could fail to be with child. *Why did Jehovah not remember them, if He was all-powerful and could do anything, as his father and grandfather said?*

Near the end of the rainy season, Judah's friend Hirah, the Adullamite, came for a visit. He brought with him Lala's sister and her husband, and so there was a joyous celebration in Judah's household for a week. There was no work, except tending the animals for the men and cooking for the women. Even Jacob's household did less work, and he and Leah visited on several nights. One night Judah gave a big feast for the whole tribe, for the weather was pleasant and they so seldom saw visitors. Then on the last night before they returned home, Jacob and Leah gave another feast, their first since the harvest festival and sacrifice about four months earlier. There was music and dancing and singing, and the children laughed, shouted, and played, much as Judah remembered the children doing when he first visited Hirah so long ago. Hirah, exuberant as always, enjoyed the festivities more than anyone. It was as if the tribe was gathering strength for the busy months to follow, and the visitors were getting fortified for the long journey home.

After they had gone, it rained only once more before the planting season was upon them, along with the care of the many animals, both newborn and old ones. Everyone was busy from morning until night, Tamar and Lala and Leah especially, for they were starting a new garden near the houses and they put out many flowers and shrubs at each place. Still, sometimes when Er came at nightfall, he knew Tamar had been weeping, and his own anxiety, frustration, and impatience at her childlessness deepened. Strangely enough, it was she who would comfort him. "Do not trouble about my tears," she often said. "You hurt as I do, and we have waited long, but we will keep hoping. Perhaps one day your father's Jehovah will look with favor upon us."

But as the months wore on, Er's disappointment began to turn to cynicism, and then to bitterness, as he remembered that in a few months the two years he had set would have passed. *Either Jehovah does not exist or He has no power, or He does not care,* he thought. *I don't want to get caught up with the Astarte worship, but if it would bring us a child, I would do so. I will wait until the two years are up; then if no child is conceived, I will ask Onan to go with me, even if he taunts me.*

The summer passed, the tribe prospered and increased that year as always. Jacob and Judah rejoiced in their good fortune and spoke of it as a sign of Jehovah's blessings. But Er's bitterness increased. *If he can so prosper a whole tribe, why does He not cause Tamar to have one child? The others have so many, why can we not have even one?*

Just before the time for the rains to start, he approached Onan about the Astarte festival. Onan laughed at him for needing anyone to help him make a child, but when Er ignored his laughter, he said he would go with him, and asked when. Er remembered that their mother had once said the festival came in the spring, when new life was beginning in the earth. He also remembered her saying the ones she had been to as a girl were held at Shireh, a city much larger than her own Adullamite village and a long way to the northeast.

Onan said they should go to Timnath before the rains came, and find out from the shopkeepers there just how far away the city was, and when the festival was held. Er agreed.

One evening a week later, Er told Tamar that he was going for a night with Onan in Hebron and she should not

171

look for him before midmorning. "Don't ask questions," he commanded sternly as she started to speak, "and tell my father, if he asks, only that we have business there."

Tamar's eyes filled with tears at his unaccustomed brusqueness as she turned away. She thought, *There can be only one reason Er would go—he is tired of me and will find another woman.* She cried herself to sleep.

When Judah asked for Er in the morning, Tamar told him what Er had said. He silently came to the same conclusion she had reached as to why he had gone to Hebron. When he told his father, he suggested that they offer a sacrifice and talk to Jehovah about both sons that very evening.

Sometime before midday, the brothers returned, tired, sleepy, and disagreeable. Tamar said nothing, her face showing signs of weeping, but Er gave no word of caring. His father came up as they went into the house, but he asked no questions.

After sleeping until mid-afternoon, Er and Onan returned to their flocks, then came back as usual at nightfall. Er ate what Tamar had prepared for him, talking with her as usual. Then he went to bed early and was soon asleep, but Tamar wept far into the night, lying beside him in the darkness.

Life went on for Jacob's tribe as usual during the rainy season, and for Er and Tamar as well. He worked with the animals some, helped Tamar with her weaving when the weather kept him inside, loved her at night, and still hoped for a child. He never did tell her that his and Onan's trip had been to her own city to find out about the festival to Astarte in the spring.

But when the appointed time came, they abruptly left their work and Er told Tamar they would return in two or three days. They left when their father was not around, dressed in their finest clothes, their mounts in their costliest trappings. Er held Tamar close, kissed her as tears ran down her face. "Don't weep," he said gently. "It will be all right. I have to go."

10

Judah's Wayward Sons

And Er, Judah's firstborn, was wicked in the sight of the Lord, and the Lord slew him.

(Genesis 38:7)

After four days, the brothers returned, took up their regular tasks, working even harder since it was the busy season. Neither of them had told Tamar or their father about where they had gone. Onan confided to a trusted servant about it once but swore the man to secrecy. He had enjoyed the excitement and uniqueness of the festival immensely and had to share it with someone, especially about the orgies with the temple prostitutes.

Not so with Er. Er found even the festivities too wild and bizarre to ever talk about them much, even with Onan. And the experiences with the prostitutes were distasteful to him. He certainly would not have participated had that not been the reason for going, with the hope that the worship and activities in the name of the fertility goddess would bring the desired child that Jehovah did not send.

Er loved Tamar with renewed fervor and was sure that within a few months she would conceive. He would not go into Hebron with Onan, though his brother taunted him for needing no more than one woman.

Jacob worried more and more as Onan went often to Hebron, and it still bothered both him and Jacob that Tamar had not gotten pregnant. They often talked to Jehovah about the boys, even when they did not perform a sacrifice. They were sure that He heard, and they believed He would one day answer.

That year, as in every year, there were weddings in the tribe. Two sons of Issachar married descendants of Hamor's servants, and a daughter of Gad married the son of Jacob's chief servant, Ziph. Several servants married among themselves.

Jacob held a great feast in the courtyard to celebrate the weddings. He sacrificed many animals and sought Jehovah's blessings upon all, asking that the newly married couples and all others be fruitful. Judah knew his father meant Er and Tamar when he said, "All others." He noticed that the two sat together, apart from the others, and did not join in the merry-making that followed the sacrifice. He also noticed that the tribe had grown so large that there was no more room for the children to play in the courtyard as they once had. *How Jehovah has blessed us,* he thought. He took note of how his brothers had aged since the first feast was held when the house was new. *Why, Simeon and Levi look as old as our father,* he mused. *And Reuben looks old enough to be the father of his young wife, the grandfather of his two sons and his daughters!*

Judah noticed also that his mother sat still on her mat while most of the women helped with the serving. *How frail and gray she looks, though she still holds herself tall and straight; she still glows when she looks at my father!* He looked at his own Lala, as she helped with the food. His heart skipped a beat as always and he knew that later this night he would make passionate love to her.

Pulling his thoughts away from her, he looked for Onan. He was nowhere to be seen. *Is he off with some servant maid?* He couldn't tell who was missing. *Has he gone into the city, deliberately missing the wedding feast? Could it be true, as my father and I once thought, that Onan loves Tamar, cannot bear to see her with Er, cannot bear anything to do with weddings, if he can't have her?*

Judah tried to think how he himself would have felt if one of his own brothers had married Lala. Then he could know how Onan felt if he did love Tamar. *Why else would he brush off all suggestions for marriage to anyone in the tribe, or even to a heathen? O Jehovah, if only I could have a grandson through whom the line would pass, surely my father would give me the blessing and the birthright! And if I never have one? But I won't think of that! Surely Jehovah will give me a grandson eventually! Will my father still be alive if I must wait for Shelah to give me grandsons? What if my father should relent and give the blessing and birthright to his first-born, Reuben, after all?* These disturbing thoughts marred the feast for him.

The heat of summer gave way to cooler weather and shorter days. Soon preparations for the rains and winter began in earnest, and all were busy from morning till night. There were so many more animals and people to care for now, and Jehovah had blessed the land with bountiful harvests: late grains, grasses, fruits, vegetables, and nuts.

Despite all the work, Onan still went to Hebron often, and now sometimes persuaded Er to go with him, leaving Tamar to weep alone. Judah also still grieved over her childless state, and worried lest harm would come to his sons in the city. He said nothing, however, knowing that forbidding their going would do no good.

Once Onan came home late, alone, and Judah asked where his brother was. He answered sulkily, "I do not know. Am I his keeper?" Then he stalked into his room.

Judah was so upset that he went to wake his father. Could Onan have left him in the city purposely, perhaps wounded—or dead? Should we go search for him?

Jacob, his eyes heavy with sleep, threw up his hands in a hopeless gesture. "My son, who can know what those two have done? If we went into the city, we likely could not find him before day. Let us talk to Jehovah about them for a while and if Er is not in by daybreak, then we will leave to search for him."

175

He quickly dressed and they went in darkness back to Judah's home, where they alternately sat on the stoop or walked to and fro in the yard, each beseeching Jehovah to bring Er safely home and to change the waywardness of both sons. Between their prayers, they were mindful of Lala and Tamar weeping together in Tamar's room.

Just before daybreak, as they had started to wake servants and get their mounts, they heard slow hoofbeats. Presently Er rode into the yard, swaying in the saddle. Judah ran to his son and helped him dismount. Just then, Tamar ran out with a lamp, saw Er's bloody robe, screamed and fainted. Her handmaid and Lala came, followed by two male servants. The women took care of Tamar, while the men dragged the bleeding Er, now unconscious, to his room. Jacob charged a young servant to run to his home and bring his faithful old servant, Ziph, who would know what to do.

Soon Judah's household was up and in noisy turmoil all except Onan, who refused to leave his room. Er was still unconscious from loss of blood. His face and body were bruised and filthy, and blood still oozed from the deep gash in his shoulder. When Ziph came, he soon cleansed the wound and stopped the blood. Tamar and Lala, weeping, washed his bruised face, and presently his swollen lips moved faintly, a groan escaping them, as Tamar tried to clean the dried blood from a long gash over his badly swollen, purple eye. Ziph gently brushed the women away, telling them to bring hot gruel. He slapped Er's cheeks briskly, and the other eye opened. Judah breathed his relief and piled cushions under his son's head and good shoulder. When the gruel was brought, old Ziph urged it through Er's bruised lips. When it was all gone, the cushions were removed and Er's head was eased down upon the pillow. At Ziph's suggestion, Judah put everyone else out of the room, and soon Er was asleep. The sun was rising, and the household went quietly to their accustomed duties, helped by Lala, while Tamar wept silently outside the door of the bedroom she shared with Er.

After two weeks under Ziph's care, Er shakily left his

room, though he was very pale and weak. Judah, Jacob, and Tamar were never able to get him to talk about what had happened to him. But much later, Judah heard him and Onan arguing loudly as they tended the animals. He came upon them just in time to hear Er ask angrily, "It was wrong for you to pick that fight with those drunken ruffians and then ride away and leave me to settle it! I ought to kill you for that! If it ever happens again, I <u>will</u> kill you!"

Onan laughed, "<u>If</u> you live!" he taunted. Just then they saw Judah and fell silent.

Judah thought, *So Onan does want his brother dead! How can he? It could only be because he wants Tamar for his own. O Jehovah, have mercy on my wicked sons!*

When the rains came and winter really set in, Er grew strong again, but did not return again to Hebron with Onan. Instead, he stayed with Tamar every night, hoping against hope that the orgy at the Astarte Festival might yet have the desired effect. But month after month, he was disappointed and she cried more than ever.

As spring approached, he wondered whether he should not go to this year's festival. But when he asked Onan about going with him, he said, "If one time didn't bring sons, none will. I will not go again."

Er did not press him, but he did not understand his refusal. *He always gets into the worst Hebron has to offer, and the festival is so much worse. Why is he refusing to go?*

The passing of time had dimmed his memory, and Er thought now that maybe he had been mistaken in thinking that Onan had left him on purpose for the drunken men to beat or kill him. After all, why should Onan want his own brother dead? Of course it would give Onan, as second son, the inheritance, and if their father received the blessing and birthright, they would pass to him also. But Onan had always scoffed at any of it. *Still, why else could he want me dead? I know we have always fought, but in later years I thought we were closer. Why would he want me dead?*

Er was surprised when sometime later Onan asked him to go into Hebron with him. At first he refused, reminding

Onan he had refused to go to the festival with him.

"You know I have no reason to go to the festival, as you do," retorted Onan. "I have no wife, barren or otherwise, nor do I want one. Come into Hebron and meet a beautiful woman who will teach you what you never knew before. Perhaps she can even teach you how to give Tamar sons."

Er turned away at first, still contemplating going to the festival again. But Onan pressed him to go into Hebron to this woman—he even promised to go to the festival with Er—that is, if he still wanted to go afterwards. Finally Er consented. What could one trip hurt? Surely his father's Jehovah did not know nor care what he did or He would have given him and Tamar a child after his father and grandfather had sacrificed for him.

So on a clear, early spring night, the brothers rode into Hebron, dressed in their finest raiment, Er somewhat eagerly anticipating what Onan had promised would be a night to remember.

It was. And it was only one of many. The red-haired beauty Onan took Er to did indeed teach him many things, and between nights with her and nights with Tamar, he was sure Tamar would soon be with child. He forgot all about the festival.

Jacob and Judah grew more and more concerned about the frequent trips to Hebron, about the later and later hours at which the boys came home, about Tamar's growing unhappiness. They sacrificed to Jehovah and sought Him nightly to turn both brothers away from their wildness and to bless Er and Tamar with a son. Judah, for the first time, voiced his own feelings to Jehovah, weeping. Both he and Jacob felt the warm presence of Jehovah in a way Judah never had before, as if a glow were upon them. For the first time, Judah knew, really knew, his father's God was real, that He was now his own God, too. Over and over, in the weeks ahead, he voiced in his heart his great desire for his wayward sons to know Him, so the line could pass through one of them.

Judah noticed his sons seemed to be getting along better

together, and he was thankful. Perhaps it was a good sign. But he also noticed that they were losing weight, that the color of Er's skin was changing, that neither seemed interested in their animals as before. And neither of them would talk much with him; indeed, they almost always averted their eyes when he looked at them. He was aware that Tamar's eyes were constantly red and swollen, that he and Lala heard her weeping more and more on the nights when Er was gone, and sometimes even during the day. But she would not talk to her mother-in-law about her unhappiness, though they worked often together. Er looked worse as the weeks passed and Judah and Lala worried.

Then one morning the brothers came home before daybreak, with Er so ill that Onan woke the household trying to get him inside and to bed. Judah pulled on a robe and ran, his heart in his throat for fear Er had been beaten or stabbed again.

He found him deathly pale, perspiration dripping from his face. Onan and Tamar were undressing him and getting him into bed. Judah hurried a servant to bring old Huldah, who, like Ziph, usually knew what to do when any of the tribe was ill.

Lala dressed hastily. She stood weeping, barefoot, with her robe awry, as Tamar washed Er's pale face, and smoothed his damp, black hair. Tamar was weeping also. Judah tried to get some idea of what was wrong from Onan, since Er was in too much pain to talk and could only lie there groaning.

Onan beckoned his father to follow him outside. There he told him they had been going to whores in Hebron, that Er's had been giving him a drink made from mandrake roots and other things as an aphrodisiac, promising him that the drink, and what she taught him, would surely help him to get Tamar with child. On this night she must have given him too much or had put something else, maybe poison, into it. At any rate, Er had stumbled out of her room, vomiting and calling for Onan some two hours ago. He got him on his beast and they came as fast as Er's vomiting would permit.

Fear and disgust tore at Judah's insides as he listened, and he lashed out at Onan, blaming him for enticing his brother to evil. Onan became very angry, denying it, cursing, and finally telling his father of their trip to the Astarte Festival. He stressed that it was Er who had persuaded him to go.

Judah's heart froze at this awful news, for he knew such wickedness would bring Jehovah's wrath upon both his sons. *No doubt even now His anger has been turned in punishment upon Er,* he thought. "O Jehovah, have mercy upon him, on us all!" he prayed. *Oh, my father, I need you here to talk to Jehovah also.* He called loudly to a servant and sent him running for his father, just as another servant came with Huldah, almost dragging her in his haste, carrying her bag of herbs himself. Judah took her arm, speaking kindly and beseechingly to her as he led her up the steps into the house. Old Ziph hurried along behind them.

Inside, Er was retching again. Tamar was wiping his face and weeping. Huldah called for water. She mixed brown powder in a cup of water, and made Er drink when he had finally stopped retching. Soon Er seemed to sleep, while Tamar continued to wipe his face. His mother, weeping, held his hand on the other side of the bed. Judah stood helplessly looking on, silently imploring Jehovah to forgive his sons and spare Er's life. He went to the door as his father and mother came in, noticing a faint brightening of the sky that heralded the dawn.

Just as they reached the sickroom, the awful retching began again, and it seemed the whole cup of brown liquid came gushing back at once, so that the covers and Er were drenched. Er began to moan and gasp for breath. Huldah came from the cooking room with a cupful of some other brew. When Er was quiet enough, Judah held him up off the pillows and he drank it slowly, before he lay back, moaning again. Judah joined his father at the open window, and they watched the light stream over the eastern horizon, both silently beseeching Jehovah's help. Presently they both fell on their knees as Jacob spoke aloud to his God, while Judah wept. Huldah and Ziph continued to attend to the retching man.

In spite of everything they did, Er grew steadily worse. He seemed to be unconscious, but he continued to moan and retch. Before the sun had reached its zenith, he died in Tamar's arms, as Judah and Lala, Jacob and Leah watched in helpless horror.

11

Mourning and a Wedding

And Judah said unto Onan, Go in unto thy brother's wife,
and marry her, and raise up seed to thy brother.

(Genesis 38:8)

Jacob's tribe, and especially Judah's household, mourned Er over a period of many days. It was a time of such utter desolation for Tamar and Lala that they clung together, weeping day after day. And at night Tamar wept alone, while Judah and Lala mourned in their room. Often in the dead of night, Judah would go out and look up at the silent heavens and cry out to Jehovah for some surcease from the agony he and Lala and Tamar know. And over and over he would ask, "Jehovah, why did You not have mercy and forgive Er? I know he did a great wrong by worshiping the heathen goddess and engaging in the heathen orgies. But he was young, and he so wanted a son. Perhaps if You had let him live, he would have repented and really found You, as I have."

Judah also endured again great remorse for the wrong he and his brothers had done to Joseph and for the lie they had caused their father to believe. He constantly blamed himself for the sorrows of his family. He grieved more than ever for Jacob's grief, for he knew now from experience what Jacob had lived through these many years. Judah's heart

183

broke repeatedly when he remembered, and he repented in bitter tears, not only for what they had done to Jacob, but because they had sinned against Jehovah, who had now become very real to him.

Of course, Er's sin and tragic, terrible death rekindled Jacob's grief over his lost Joseph, and he also hurt for Judah, Lala, and Tamar. His heart broke for Leah also, for she had loved her wayward grandchild as dearly as he.

Er's death caused Dinah to mourn the loss of her beloved Shechem all over again, though she loved her second husband very much. Through the years, as the young Shechem grew up, she had kept her grief and loneliness hidden in her heart. And though she was no longer lonely since she had married again, still she had never stopped grieving for the horror Shechem and his people had suffered at the hands of her brothers. Now the grief and anger slipped from their hiding place and leaped out at her.

Reuben and Benjamin mourned for Judah, for they were the closest of all the brothers. Reuben had long since forgiven him for his part in Reuben's shame with Bilhah and the loss of the blessing and birthright, for Reuben was ever of a simple, forgiving nature and a cheerful outlook.

Even the servants mourned and seemed to walk softly as they carried on their work in silence. Only Onan seemed not to care; indeed, he seemed not to miss his brother at all. Actually, he seemed to be lighter of heart than before. After the burial and the first few days of mourning he went back to Hebron regularly. He took main charge in the caring for the animals of both Er and Judah. Once or twice Judah tried to reason with him, even with tears, to tell him he might meet Er's fate if he continued to ignore Jehovah, but he only scoffed and left his father to weep alone.

Weeks later, the tribe as a whole gradually took up the usual tasks, as harvest season began and garden work needed attending. Even Tamar and Lala did the accustomed household jobs again, though they often wept as they worked. Judah came to terms with what he was as he experienced and remembered Jehovah's punishment, both for the wrongs of his sons and himself. He was finally able to contain his grief and to comfort his wife and Tamar. He became ever more thoughtful of his father, was closer to him than before. They talked of the circumstances of Er's death, of Onan's continued waywardness and rebellion.

Jacob could even pour out his grief at the loss of Joseph, now that he knew Judah could understand. They talked of the ways of Jehovah to men. He and Judah were together on all the work and plans for the tribe everyday. They also spoke of Tamar's continued weeping, her loss of weight, her grief-stricken countenance. They wondered when she would come to terms with her grief, and when or whether Onan would accept her as his wife and raise up children to his brother, as their custom was.

As if to make up for the loss of Er, and the grief, everything went extremely well with all the crops and animals that season. The rains had come at the right times and in abundance; warm days came early, summer heat and drought were less severe. More and stronger young were born to the animals with fewer dying. Jacob could not help but remember how Jehovah had thus blessed him long ago after his father-in-law, Laban, had so oppressed him. He and Judah took note of their blessings now, spoke of them to all their people and sacrificed to and praised Jehovah more than ever. Only Lala and Tamar could not praise, but still wept.

The death and its accompanying grief affected Benjamin very deeply. He often sought his father when he was alone and talked with him about it all, about the questions of life, about Jehovah's ways. For although he already had two sons, he still seemed child-like, still needed his father, still needed someone to see that he kept up his work and tended to his responsibilities. Since Reuben was now too busy to bother with him as he always had, it was usually Judah who kept him going, as well as seeing to their father's business more and more. Perhaps Judah's care of Benji was one reason his loss bothered the younger son so. Staying even closer to his father seemed to steady him at this time and it gave comfort to Jacob. Seeing this, Judah had the servants do much of

Benji's work, but he would not let him shirk all of his responsibilities, lest he would become even more child-like and dependent.

Many months after the tragedy, as the harvest season drew to a close and the days became shorter, Tamar seemed to suddenly accept her loss and come to terms with her widowhood. Her countenance grew pleasant again, and her formerly red, puffy eyes became clear and bright. Again she laughed at the antics of the children or the young animals, and she sang often at her work. She ate with enjoyment, often now with Judah and Lala, and soon returned to her plump beauty.

Judah and his father talked of the change in Tamar and thanked Jehovah that their prayers for her had been answered. They also began to wonder whether it was time to offer her to Onan as his wife. Of course, they must first see if he would be willing to marry her. Judah especially dreaded talking to him.

Before another month had passed, things had been put in readiness for the onset of the rainy season and the whole tribe settled down to a slower pace. It was the time of year for the big harvest feast and sacrifice. Jacob and Judah agreed that a feast would not be fitting during this year of Er's death, but certainly they must sacrifice in praise and thanksgiving to Jehovah for His extra blessings upon them.

They planned a larger sacrifice than ever, and the day before, Judah and his father went together to the field where Onan tended the sheep. With some apprehension they approached him and asked that he come to the sacrifice, turn from his rebellion, repent of his waywardness, and worship Jehovah. As they expected, he tossed his handsome head and scoffed at them for even believing in a God that they could not see.

"And even if He exists, how can you worship a God who would kill Er because he tried to find a way to help Tamar conceive? Who could care for a God like that?" His lips curled in a sneer. "I cannot, and I will not come to the sacrifice." There was bitterness in his voice and on his face as he turned away.

"Very well," returned his father, "but there is another matter we must talk to you about." Onan still would not look at them.

Jacob said, placatingly, "My son, you know it is the custom in our tribe that a man shall marry his brother's childless widow and raise up children to his brother." Jacob waited.

Onan turned and looked at his grandfather sharply, almost in surprise. Both Jacob and Judah wondered at his look, for they knew he was aware of the custom, and had thought he would expect them to bring it up.

After a moment, Jacob continued, "It is time you took Tamar as your wife to perform this duty for your brother."

A dull red suffused Onan's tanned face and he turned away.

Judah and his father looked at each other for a moment; Judah spoke, "Tamar is still young and beautiful. Surely she cannot be distasteful to you, and it is time you gave up this going to Hebron and settled down. Surely you can see you will sooner or later end up as your brother did if you do not."

Judah's voice was pleading, and tears fell from his eyes. Jacob added his own encouragement. "Turn away from the evil, my son; turn to Jehovah and fulfill your duty to your brother while there is yet time."

Onan remained silent; he was still turned away from them. They waited, each in his own heart asking Jehovah to bring Onan to repentance.

At last Onan turned to face them, saying slowly, "I will consider what you have asked."

"It is good," returned Judah, as he took his father's arm and turned him away. They walked with bowed heads back toward their houses.

At the sacrifice late the next afternoon, Jacob, graying now, but still tall, straight, and majestic, held up his hands in blessing. Leah, standing close, remembered a long-ago sacrifice in Haran, when he had stood and blessed his then-much-smaller family, when her heart had ached with love and admiration for him as she saw it was Rachel he looked upon. Now her aged heart still skipped a beat as he looked first at her and then on toward the great throng that their tribe had become.

Jacob spoke in his strong voice as he raised his eyes heavenward in praise and reverence to Jehovah. "Our God, the only true God, we thank You from our hearts for all the blessings You have given us this year: for the rains and the seasons that have brought great harvests; for the health and peace we have known; for those children added to our number; for the strength we have had to bear the loss of those that have been taken from us. Please continue to give comfort to our hearts and to bless us for another year."

Some of the people, especially Lala and Tamar, wept quietly. Jacob continued to speak to Jehovah, beseeching him for help and pardon. Judah looked for Onan once again, and there he was—at the side of the crowd, not far from his mother and Leah and Tamar. Judah breathed a silent *Thank You* to Jehovah.

When Jacob ended his prayer, the sacrifice proceeded as was usual. The people watched in silent awe until the last animal was placed upon the altar. Then as smoke and the odor of burning flesh filled the still, now chilly air, they fell to their knees, each confessing his sins and worshiping Jehovah in his own way, some with words and tears, some in awed silence.

After a while, Jacob spoke again and raised his hands. When the people rose to their feet, he blessed them and bade them to return to their dwellings. Those farthest away began to leave and the others followed. Last of all, Jacob's own family left; he and Judah joined Leah, Lala, and Tamar; then they too went home. Judah looked for Onan; he had not seen him leave, but he was nowhere to be seen.

Two days later the heavy rains began. Jacob rejoiced that the latest sheepfolds and stalls were completed, and the animals were safe and dry. The people could stay indoors, each family to itself for the most part. It was a time Leah loved, for Jacob could be with her, helping her with the many household tasks in the way he had done when he had first come to her father's family in far-off Haran. Though it was her sister Rachel he had loved, still Leah loved to remember him as he was then, young and strong and handsome. How graciously he had helped with the women's work, how adept he was at everything, how much he had taught them all! And he still loved to help even now—helping her cook his favorite foods, spinning, even weaving at her loom sometimes. How happy she was that he finally loved her, now that Rachel was gone, how she loved to have him with her at night, unhurried and rested. She thanked Jehovah for him, for her family, for the plenty they enjoyed. How good it was to have Dinah and her family still under their own roof, as well as Zebulun and Issachar with their families—and, of course, Benji. Jacob would never let him move away to a house of his own. And what a joy his two little sons were to her and Jacob! Oh, life was good!

At Judah's home, the family and servants were busy too—the women were cooking the daily food, sorting and storing late nuts, spinning, weaving, sewing, churning butter, making cheese; the men were mending harnesses, sorting seeds, and removing chaff, building furniture, making pottery. Even Onan stayed busy and didn't go to Hebron. He helped his father to tan the animal skins and make them into bags and water and wine skins. The servant Ziba was teaching him to make sandals for the family. Young Shelah was learning too.

Tamar helped Lala and played with Benji's children much of the time. Onan saw her only at mealtimes, but he was never rude to her now as he once was. She and Lala seldom joined in the conversations he and Judah had at the table, unless they were spoken to. Once Tamar looked up unexpectedly, and Onan's eyes were upon her in the old way Er had looked at her. She looked away quickly, as her own eyes filled with tears for the eyes she would never see again. In the night, she wondered about Onan's look, and cried herself to sleep for the first time in weeks.

Two days later, when the rain came in sheets and the wind tore at the bare branches of the tamarinds, Onan and two servants came into the house before Judah did. The servants went to their quarters, while Onan, sodden and cold, went into the cooking room where a fire blazed on the huge hearth. He went to stand in front of it, rubbing his numb hands, his wet clothes soon steaming. Two maids were preparing food in one corner, but they paid no heed to him. After a moment, Tamar rushed in, her arms full of cooking pots, and went directly to a table and began to busy herself with the food they contained, her back to Onan. He stood watching her, and therefore, did not see Judah come to the door and stand looking in.

Judah saw the look of longing in his son's eyes. He thought, *Why, he does care for Tamar. Perhaps he always has, as my father and I thought at the beginning. To hide his feelings, he has pretended to despise her. This could be why he has been so wayward, has gone to Hebron so often. I shall surely ask him again soon if he will marry Tamar and raise up sons to his brother.* He slipped away, cold and wet though he was, went to change clothes in his own room.

When Tamar finally turned and saw Onan, he pretended to be watching the servants, but she had gotten a glimpse of his look first. She blushed as she pulled her veil down and went on with her work, but her heart beat faster. Onan left without speaking to her.

Two days later when Judah again urged him to marry Tamar, Onan said, without anger or impatience, "If it is your wish, and you think the time is right, I will do it. Only see how she feels about it first."

"It is good, my son," returned Judah, with a pleased smile. "I will speak to her tomorrow."

Tamar wept when Judah asked her, but she consented, nevertheless. So it came about that Onan married his brother's widow two months later with a quiet ceremony and celebration at her request. Judah and Lala rejoiced that the two seemed happy together; Jacob and Judah were sure Onan would cease his wild ways now and raise up sons to his brother. They felt better about their family than they had in many years, gave thanks to Jehovah, and asked Him to send sons to Tamar.

12

A Happy Spring

One mid-morning after the spring planting was finished, Jacob came in from tending the animals, shedding his light, outer garment as he reached their room. Leah looked up from her spinning; pleasure shone on her still unlined face as it always did when she saw her beloved. Her eyes questioned him.

"Wife," he began, "it is too warm and beautiful outside to be in here. Come, let us walk to the far spring. The poppies should be opening and perhaps some early lilies."

"Yes," agreed Leah. Gladness was in her voice as her heart sang at the thought of his wanting her with him. "I'll get a light shawl." She pulled a lovely blue one from a chest, threw it around her shoulders, as the faint scent of deaxylon surrounded her. Jacob was already calling a maidservant for bread, cheese, and goat's milk to take along. As an afterthought, he sent another servant to Judah's home to ask if he and Lala, and Tamar and Onan would like to follow later. "Tell them to bring food along if they want to come, and we'll meet near the spring," he instructed the servant.

Soon Jacob was swinging a goatskin bag over his shoulder and Leah was walking tall and proud beside him. They noted the grass greening in patches underfoot, and pale leaf buds were swelling on the tamarinds and myrtles.

Jacob commented, "It seems that spring has come since yesterday, the quickest I ever remember. That means the spring crops will be up in a fortnight, and this foretells a good harvest this year."

Leah breathed the fresh, warm air with delight. "So good after a sad winter," she said. "Smell the fresh-planted earth."

"Judah started the east field yesterday and Levi and Simeon finished after sundown," Jacob added. "They are over there now, checking to see if they covered the seeds properly. See them?"

Leah squinted her ever-weak, dark eyes, shading them with her hand against the bright sun. "Yes," she nodded, "I see them now. Always together, those two."

"Just hope they're not plotting some mischief," replied Jacob with a grimace. Leah was silent, reminded once again that Jacob had never forgiven them for the evil they had wrought in the matter of Prince Hamor, of the hurt they had caused Dinah. *At least they have families now and have prospered, along with the rest. Surely they have repented of the evil and Jehovah has forgiven them, even if Jacob and Dinah cannot. How glad I am that Dinah is happy now with her husband and her handsome, almost-grown Shechem, so like his father. How beautiful she still is, and how Joel adores her! Jehovah be praised!*

Jacob broke her thoughts as he reached for her hand to help her over the rough stones and slippery needles under a bent old pine that towered over the beaten path.

Then they were walking arm in arm, aware of each other's nearness like young lovers, and laughing as they swung leisurely along, reveling in the bright warmth and beauty around them.

As the path veered to the southeast, Jacob pulled Leah to their right. "Come," He urged, "let's climb that rocky hill. From there we can get a look at the Salt Sea on a bright day like this. Remember?"

Leah nodded, laughing, and they scrambled up, Jacob half pulling his wife over some of the craggy rocks and tough terrain. Part of the way up, they were obliged to sit down to rest on a wide, flat rock, gasping for breath and laughing at themselves.

"The last time we came here we didn't have to rest," Jacob mused when he could speak. "We must be getting old."

"You will never be old to me, Jacob," declared Leah, smiling up at him as she leaned against his encircling arm.

"Nor you to me," he responded, kissing the tip of her nose. They rested awhile longer, her head against his chest. Then as he helped her to her feet, they spotted the four figures nearing the foot of the hill. They waved and continued their climb.

At the top was a broad outcrop of chalky rock that fell away on the far side in nearly vertical cliffs. With not even a mist to obstruct the view, they stood looking out at the far gray waters and on to the cliffs rising up from the sea, then on to the dark mountains beyond. Farther south, they saw a beautiful green plain reaching almost to the sea's edge. Farther west, the tree-covered slopes stretched to the never-ending brownish desert. Toward the northeast, there were lower mountains falling gently to the plains and on to the valleys that reached the sea. Awed, they looked long in silence.

At last Jacob spoke. "It is a beautiful land Jehovah promised to Grandfather Abraham's descendants, the line through which He would bless the whole world. Do you remember that means us and our children—at least one of them—and his children's children?"

Jacob looked hard at Leah, then went on, "How shall I know which one, so I can give to him the blessing and birthright, as they were passed on to me by my father, Isaac? It bothers me so much, for I am growing old, even though you say I am not old to you."

"Jacob—Israel, Prince of God, did not Jehovah so name you when you wrestled with the angel at the brook Jabbok? You will know when the time comes. He will show you." Leah spoke with surety, and Jacob squeezed her hand as he smiled down at her. "I hope you are right."

Leah's smile spoke of more happiness than she had known in a long time.

They walked around the rocks to the other side of the hilltop, then stood looking at the spring below. The tops of the trees around it reached halfway up to them. Without speaking a word, because each was occupied with his own thoughts and joy, they descended along the way they had climbed. When they met the four younger people halfway down, they exchanged pleasantries with them, assuring them of the marvelous view they would get of the Salt Sea when they reached the top. They promised to see them near the spring later, then continued their descent, found the path, followed it around the hill and on to the spring.

The water bubbled up from somewhere deep under the hill into a round, clear pool and spilled over. It gurgled and murmured over small rocks and finally splashed onto huge rocks far below, its spray forming small rainbows where the sun filtered through the trees. There was a level, open space on one side, and new grass showed fresh and green through old tufts, with wild pink crocuses and tiny white daisies peeping bravely out here and there. Near the pool's edge, purple violets rose from heart-shaped, deep green foliage.

Little sounds of delight escaped from Leah's lips as she discovered each new blossom and smelled its distinctive fragrance. Jacob smiled at her delight, feeling pleased that he had brought her here.

Why, she's beautiful, he thought, *much more so than when she was younger. How straight and slender she is still, how shapely her full breasts! How clear her skin is, how heavy her bright, curling hair, its slight gray shining in the sun!* Tenderness and desire stirred within him and he smiled when she picked a violet for him to smell. He dutifully sniffed the flower, then pulled her gently to him, kissed her rosy lips, held her away, searching for a promise in her eyes. Finding it, he kissed her again, hungrily, and crushed her to him. As always, she responded, pressing her body to his, as he kissed her eyes, her forehead, her lips, her neck.

Just then they heard Lala's merry laughter, looked around, saw her and Judah coming toward them, followed by Onan and Tamar. Jacob smiled into Leah's eyes again. "Tonight?" he said.

It was both a question and a promise, and Leah whispered, "Yes, oh, yes," with her lips and her eyes.

While the others admired the spring and the flowers, Leah and Jacob arranged the food they had all brought on a flat rock some distance away. Sometime later they all gathered around and Jacob, raising his eyes heavenward, gave thanks to Jehovah for all His wonderful blessings to them—for this food, for this remarkable land He had promised to their descendants, for the line that would one day bless the world.

After they had eaten, they scrambled down, two by two, over the rocks and fallen branches to the flat open space below. They found ferns and lilies and wild daffodils growing between the rocks where moisture from the spring overflow had seeped. The women could not resist digging some of them up to carry home.

Jacob pretended to grumble when he was pressed into service, "Oh, you women and your flowers!"

"But it was your idea to come and see them," Leah mischievously reminded him, her eyes twinkling.

The children laughed while Jacob conceded, "So I did," and he laughed with them.

They all dug as many plants as they could carry and climbed, pushing and sliding, back to the spring. There they put what they had gathered into the three food bags. Then, one by one, they knelt on their hands and knees to drink from the pool. The men rinsed their waterskins that had held their goat's milk, and refilled them from the cool spring, while the women gathered violets to take home.

The children decided to climb the hill for one more look at the Salt Sea, but Leah and Jacob chose to save their strength for the long walk home. They stood silent for a while after the others left, listening to the murmur of the water, drinking in the mingled fragrance of the flowers, watching the birds that had not been there earlier in the day. Jacob held Leah's hand as they took a last, lingering look, then he took their flower-filled bag, and gave Leah the waterskin and her shawl. They went silently up the narrow, rocky path around the hill.

On the way home they had much to talk about. They did not hurry. The air was chilly, and the sun was low on the horizon long before they came in sight of the houses. Leah had given Jacob the waterskin to hold sometime before, while she put the shawl around her, glad for the extra warmth.

When they reached their own door, they laid down the bags, turned, and holding hands, looked again toward the far spring. It was as if each were storing memories of the day. Far in the distance, against the glow left by the setting sun, they could make out the dark figures of their children. Leah turned to Jacob. "It was a wonderful day," she said. "Thank you for taking me." Jacob's hands were gentle on her shoulders as he looked into his wife's eyes. The promise was still there, and he smiled. They both knew they would never forget this day—nor the night to come.

13

Onan Dies; Tamar Goes Home

And Onan knew that the seed should not be his; and it came to pass, when he went in unto his brother's wife, that he spilled it on the ground, lest he should give seed to his brother. And the thing which he did displeased the Lord: wherefore he slew him also. Then said Judah to Tamar his daughter-in-law, Remain a widow in thy father's house, till Shelah my son be grown: for he said, Lest peradventure he die also, as his brethren did. And Tamar went and dwelt in her father's house.

(Genesis 38:9-11)

Two years passed and Tamar did not conceive. Both Judah and Jacob were disappointed, and Judah noted that Tamar's eyes were again red and swollen at times. Onan seemed happy, and it was obvious that he loved Tamar very much. Why would Jehovah not answer, when both Judah and Jacob beseeched Him often on Tamar's behalf? More grandchildren came into the families of the other brothers, including two more sons to Benjamin. Harvests were bountiful season after season, flocks and herd increased steadily. Gold and silver abounded so much that the tithe urns overflowed.

Judah felt that in everything, except the matter of grandchildren, he was more blessed than any of the others.

He praised and thanked Jehovah for His blessing continually and both he and Jacob made regular sacrifices. They went more often into Hebron and distributed a portion of their abundance to the poor.

O Jehovah, Judah often thought, *You have blessed me beyond measure, yet You withhold the one thing that would influence my father to give me the birthright and blessing! Why? Why?*

Jacob pondered his decision more earnestly, as to which son should receive blessing and birthright. Which son would be Jehovah's choice through whom the line would pass to bless the world, as Jehovah had promised Grandfather Abraham? Surely the choice was between Judah and Benjamin. None of the others seem to care. *Reuben knows he forfeited his claim in the affair with Bilhah. Simeon and Levi know they could not be trusted after their massacre of Prince Hamor's men. Surely the sons of the handmaids have no prior claim! If only Joseph had lived! O Jehovah, why? Why? He was the sensitive one, the one who understood about the line and would have treasured everything, the firstborn of my great love, my Rachel. Of course, Benji is my youngest, just as I am my father's. But somehow he doesn't seem responsible; he is still like a child, cannot even take care of his animals and business without the help of Judah or Reuben. Now I hold him too close; I've been too light on him. He does understand about the line, however, for I have talked of it to him more than I have to the others, since he is with me much. What a blessing he is to me in my old age! Jehovah be praised that he was left to me after Joseph was taken. But I know he does not have the judgment to manage either birthright or blessing. So, only Judah seems to be left. He is the logical one, and he wants everything, grasps what it all means. He also manages well, taking much of the burden of the tribe for me. But his sons have produced no sons; Er is dead, and it seems now that Tamar will not bear for Onan anymore than she did for Er. I seem to sense this. Why, Jehovah, why? And Shelah is just a boy. It will be years before he can have a son. If my time to die comes soon, what shall I do? O Jehovah, help me! Please give Tamar a son as You gave Joseph to Rachel for me.*

It seemed as if the rains were earlier and heavier than ever before. Jacob's tribe had not gotten quite all the late harvest in, and the animals had not been brought to shelter when the first deluge came. Sudden, big, heavy thunderheads appeared late one day and before sunset the rain came in heavy, gusting sheets. All night it poured down, and dug jagged wadis in the hills and filled the valleys with roaring torrents. Lesser rains came every day for weeks.

It seemed to Jacob that his family, indeed, even the whole tribe, never really got their households and animals organized during the whole winter. There was more unrest and strife than he could remember. Then Simeon's youngest daughter, Mahria, gave birth to a stillborn son, her first child. She and her husband, a grandson of Prince Hamor, were devastated and the tribe spent many days in mourning. Scarcely had they gotten over this tragedy when a worse thing came—the three-year-old son of one of the servants drowned in a hole that had been dug earlier for watering the donkeys. Somehow the child wandered away from its mother's usually watchful eyes. The tribe went into mourning again. Both Jacob and Judah sought Jehovah's answer as to why, even as they begged for comfort for the distraught parents. Could there be some evil going on in their midst that they didn't know about that so displeased Jehovah that He would punish them in this way? They tried to think what might be amiss and talked about it much with each other and with Benjamin. All they could think of was the earlier waywardness of Er and Onan. But Benjamin said, "No, Jehovah would <u>not</u> bring evil upon others for their wrongs. Besides, Er paid for his wrong with his life, we think. And Onan is no longer wicked."

Jacob was pleased that his youngest son had spoken with such insight into Jehovah's ways to men, when he usually did not speak out at all. "You are right, my son." he assured him. "Perhaps we should not try to find out why He does everything. We should just trust that He does all things well. Still, I wish Jehovah would speak to me again, as He has in times past. It has been many years since He renewed to me the promise that this land will belong to my descendants, who will be as numberless as the sand of the sea."

There was some joy in that terrible winter: Jacob and Leah were happy to be together so much while it was too cold and rainy for much outside work to be done. It was the same with Judah and Lala. He was able to comfort her over the loss of Er, and he stopped worrying so much about his own past sin against Joseph, and Er and Onan's waywardness and the possible punishment on the tribe. He and Lala were happier together than they had been since Er's death. They rejoiced in their son Shelah, who was a good, obedient boy. And they took pleasure in the evident love of Onan and Tamar, renewing their hopes that Tamar would conceive.

Also Benji and his wife were expecting another child in the spring, and that brought special joy to Jacob and Leah, as well as to the young couple themselves.

As spring drew on, the weather warmed quickly and the crops were planted early, with hopes of a bountiful harvest after so much winter rain. Jacob and Judah walked in the planted fields on a late afternoon, and thanked Jehovah for some blessings from the hard winter, for the great increase in their animals that had already begun. They also made plans for their yearly trip to the far spring. Each returned home rejoicing in their Jehovah and His favor upon them.

But the trip for this year was not to be. Indeed, the day they had planned for it was to be one of the worst that Jacob's tribe had known. Tamar awakened Judah's household with her screams at daybreak. Judah, snatching an outer garment, ran into the room she shared with Onan. He found her fallen across Onan's body on the bed. She was alternately shrieking, "He's dead, he's dead!" and calling his name in a pitiful wail.

Judah pushed her away and found that his son was indeed dead. By then Lala and Shelah, along with most of the servants, had crowded into the room or gathered near the door. Judah turned from the bed, forced the now-screaming Lala away and onto a couch in the corner.

"He is dead. Onan is dead!" he told her as tears rolled down his grief-stricken face. To the servants he spoke the tragic words more loudly, over her screams and those of Tamar. The servants began to wail and he said, "Go now about your morning's work. We need only Zerah and Loda here." The servants left slowly, still wailing.

Tamar's handmaid was trying to calm her mistress, and old Maida, Lala's maid, had just hobbled in and was bent over Lala, along with young Shelah. Their eyes questioned Judah as the other servants left. He said simply, "Stay."

It was harder for Tamar and Judah's family to get over Onan's death than it had been for them to get over Er's. It was months before Judah and Jacob decided Tamar would literally weep herself to death if she did not get away from everything that reminded her of Onan. They insisted that she go back to her father's house; perhaps her own people could comfort her, and a change of surroundings would help her to forget the sorrow she had known here. Both Judah and Jacob gave her the assurance that when Shelah was grown they would send for her and she would become his wife. In her state of misery, they doubted whether she understood the promise, but at least she consented to go to her father in Timnath.

It took three days to get Tamar's possessions and clothes packed for the journey. She herself seemed scarcely aware of what she should take, and it was her maid and Lala's who took care of it all. Lala and Judah wanted her to have all the things Er and Onan had given her—the furniture, jewels, clothes, perfumes, dishes, the dowry her father had given her—everything.

When all was ready by mid-afternoon of the third day, Tamar took Lala's hand and asked, "My mother, will you walk with me in the woods and fields for a last look at the places I have loved here?"

"Of course I will." answered Lala, kissing her. The eyes of both misted as they found light shawls. They left the house silently, went along the path through the nearby field that led to the deep woods. Tamar seemed lost in thought, but she was aware of every foot of ground they covered, of the sun on the far horizon, of the clumps of bronze tamarinds and pale green oaks against the darker green of gnarled olives and pines. Lala said nothing, just walked beside her.

When they reached the edge of the deep woods, Tamar took her hand. "Let us go into the woods as far as the stone bench—you remember?"

Lala nodded; they reached the narrow path and followed it until they came to the bench. Tamar pulled her mother-in-law down beside her. Brokenly she said, as her tears started afresh, "Onan and I came here often when his work was done and the sun was setting. We talked of many things—of the children we might have had, if they would not have had to belong to his brother Er. How Onan hated the custom, hated being the younger brother, the second one to have me, when he had wanted to be the first, from the moment Er brought me here."

Lala was taken aback. She cried out. "Tamar, you don't know what you are saying. You have grieved until you are not yourself!"

"No, it is true," avowed Tamar, weeping. After a while she went on, almost as if musing to herself, "Sometimes he lay with me here—so good in the quiet coolness. And yet, even here, he never would leave his seed in me; he always spilled it on the ground. I begged him. I told him a child would be his own as well as his brother's. But he never listened! Much as he loved me, he never once left his seed in me. Even the morning he—he—went away from us, I had begged, but he cursed the custom and refused."

She seemed now to remember that Lala was there, weeping with her. "Oh, my mother," she cried out piteously, "do you think Jehovah was finally so displeased that He would not let Onan live?"

She searched Lala's tearful face with the question showing in her eyes, dark with pain. Lala gathered the girl in her arms, and they wept together as they had often done in the past months.

Tamar persisted, "Would Jehovah do that? Would He?"

Slowly Lala answered, "I don't know. Judah would know. His father would know." She held the girl away, looking deeply into her eyes.

"Tamar, is what you say true? Why did you not tell me this before?" she asked.

"Onan forbade me. And after he was gone, I could not talk about it—not until now, when I am going away from it all."

She saw Lala's agitation, and went on, "I am sorry if I have hurt you, my mother, I know you—all of you—have thought it was my fault your sons had no children. Not Er, not Onan. But it is not me. I feel it deep within me—I know I can bear children. Something was just wrong with Er, though he tried. Oh, how he tried! How he wanted a son! But Onan, well, he simply would not raise up children to his brother."

She was weeping again, but went on, "And so I am left, bereft of both husbands and with no children. And now I am going back to my father's house—to years of waiting for Shelah to grow up. And even then, will I ever be given to him? Will not you and my father-in-law feel that he would die with me, even as his brothers have? But I tell you, it is not me, it is not!" She broke into weeping afresh and Lala held her close again, trying to comfort her.

"Hush, my dear, hush now. Of course we don't blame you. Of course you have not caused the death of our sons. And Shelah shall have you when he is grown and you will come back to us. You will bear grandsons for us. But it is best that you go back to your father's house to forget some of the sorrow and be comforted. There now, stop weeping. We must go. See, it is getting dark here; the sun is going down."

She stood and pulled the shaking girl to her feet, while she dried her tears on her shawl. Tamar took a last look around this place she loved. They walked slowly, hand in hand, out of the woods and into the sun's last shining rays.

Tamar faced the west. "How I wish I could go to the far spring once more! How I wanted to go with Onan once more in the springtime. Perhaps if we had gone once more, he would have loved me and left his seed within me. Perhaps Jehovah would not have taken him!" Again she seemed to have forgotten Lala's presence, as if she was musing to herself. This time, however, she did not weep. She stood looking into the sunset, and presently took Lala's hand and they walked silently, resolutely, back to the house.

The next morning Tamar was sent away with all her possessions and many gifts. She was weeping profusely. Lala, Leah, and the servants wept, and Judah and Jacob were sad, though they knew it was best for her. For Lala, it was the loss of the only daughter she had ever had, and she would miss her even more than she missed her sons.

14

Tragedy Strikes Again

And in process of time the daughter of Shuah Judah's wife died. . . .

(Genesis 38:12)

Jacob and Leah sat in the courtyard, with the late afternoon sun streaming over the house upon them. They watched the younger of their tribe as they played hide-and-seek among the shrubs and stones. Their sons and the older children talked and laughed together some distance away. Even Judah and Benji sat with the younger ones today, though usually they sat with Jacob and Leah. It was a family gathering to mark the end of early harvest.

Jacob, holding Leah's hand as she leaned against him, spoke softly, "It is a good family Jehovah has given us. Look at the beautiful children!"

"Yes," agreed Leah, "and He adds to them every year. It is as if He is making up for the loss of Er and Onan and the infants we lost." She was thoughtful awhile, then continued, "Has it really been more than three years since Onan died and Tamar went away?"

"It has," confirmed Jacob, and he glanced toward his grandson, Shelah, standing tall beside his father. "See how Shelah has grown?"

Leah nodded, knowing what his thoughts were. "Does Judah go to see about Tamar still?" she asked.

"Not since this season last year, I think. It is time he brought her back and gave her to Shelah, for he is grown now."

"Yes. I know," Leah said. "I also know he is taken with Levi's youngest, Tirzah. See how he cannot take his eyes off her? And no wonder; she is indeed beautiful. Look at those black curls! She reminds me of Dinah at that age."

"So was Tamar beautiful before she lost Onan," Jacob commented. "No doubt she is again by now."

"But she is so much older than Shelah," protested Leah. "He would think of her as an older sister, not a wife."

"Nevertheless," Jacob persisted, "it is only right she be given to him so that he can raise up seed to his brothers, if she has waited. Judah promised her that when he sent her back to her father. Her own people will uphold that and we want no enmity with them."

Leah was silent, still observing the way Shelah looked at Tirzah—*the same way Jacob used to look at Rachel,* she thought. *The way I would have given my soul to have him look at me.* She turned to face him now. *Still handsome, only a little gray, still strong and straight. Oh, how I love this man—how I have always loved him!* As always, her heart beat faster beneath her still-beautiful bosom. She sighed, thanking Jehovah that he was hers now, that he loved her, at least some.

She asked, "Could Shelah not have them both?"

Jacob looked at her sharply—and long, remembering. "Think what trouble that caused us," he said.

"But look at our family now, at us also," she smiled at him adoringly, "and see that it has been good."

Jacob smiled at her and squeezed the brown, still-soft hand he held. "I will talk to Judah tomorrow," he promised.

The late harvest was gathered in, the fruits were dried for the winter, the nuts and oils were stored away. Judah, Jacob, and Benjamin sat on the stone stoop at the front of Jacob's house, awaiting the call for the coming meal. Shelah and Benjamin's oldest child sprawled on the dry grass nearby.

"Before another month has passed, the planting season will be upon us," remarked Jacob, "and there will be no time then for repairs and more building."

"So we should get started on these tomorrow?" asked Judah.

Jacob nodded and continued, "And we should also prepare for the sacrifice and feast soon. When is the next full moon?"

Benjamin spoke. "I think in eight or ten days, my father."

"We'll set it for then," returned Jacob. "We have much to thank Jehovah for this year. Good crops, many animals, no bad injuries, no deaths, except two or three infants lost among the servants."

"It is true," agreed Judah, "but it seems the crops, especially the early ones, have not been too great for many years. And I'm almost sure our animals have not increased as usual, especially the sheep. Does it not seem so to you?"

Jacob rubbed his graying chin, thinking back to the spring wheat and barley harvest, and then considering the grapes, olives, and small fruits. "You could be right," he conceded. "It might be well to check the records and take stock of what is stored. What do you think, Benoni?"

"It would be well, father," answered Jacob's youngest, pleased his father had used his pet name. "Certainly we can count the animals. Shall I tell the shepherds to begin tomorrow?"

Jacob looked at Judah, who nodded thoughtfully. "It should be done, then we will know."

Judah was concerned and his thoughts wandered as his brow creased. Soon after the family gathering, his father approached him on the matter of bringing Tamar back for Shelah. Judah had put him off as tactfully as he could, not wanting to flatly refuse. Jacob had then asked if he were aware of Shelah's feelings for Tirzah, and voiced Leah's wishes.

Judah had brushed it off lightly. "Probably a boyish

dream," he said. "He is not old enough to be really caring for Tirzah or any other girl."

Jacob persisted, "He is a year older than Er was when you could not put him off about getting Tamar. Have you forgotten?"

After a moment's thought, Judah had answered, "So he is, so he is. But he has given no hint about caring for Tirzah."

"Perhaps you have failed to notice. Watch when he is around her next. Your mother knows about these things. As for Tamar, it is only right that she be given to him if she has waited." This last was a question and Judah reluctantly admitted. "When I was last at her father's house, she was waiting—she asked about all of you—and about Shelah."

Judah was remembering all this now. *Could it be Jehovah was displeased and was withholding great harvests because of Judah's determination not to risk giving Tamar to his last son? No, no, surely not! Surely Jehovah did not expect his last son!*

Judah came back to the present with a *no* on his lips. His father's and Benji's eyes were upon him, and those of the boys as well.

"What is it, my son?" asked Jacob, though he was sure he knew what Judah had been thinking.

"It is nothing," answered Judah, abashed. "My thoughts were somewhere else."

Presently Shelah and Belah, jostling one another, ambled toward the back, mumbling about what was holding up the call to eat.

Jacob again brought up the matter of Tamar's being given to Shelah and Benjamin spoke out. "Indeed, Shelah is grown in size. See how he towers over my Belah? And he is four years older. Already Belah has an eye for the girls, especially Prince Hamor's granddaughter, Admah. Surely Shelah is old enough to want a wife—or two."

Judah frowned but said no more, and was relieved when the call came for the evening meal, to which his mother had invited his family. The three went inside.

When reports were in on the number of animals, and the amount of stored goods, they showed they had not had their usual increase.

"It isn't that we don't have enough," said Jacob. "It is just that Jehovah may be showing His displeasure at something we've done—or left undone. How I wish He would speak to me again— it's been a long time, not since just before Joseph left us."

Since he still grieved for his loss, he had great compassion for Judah in his loss, but he knew his son was wrong in not keeping his promise to Tamar.

He was sure this was displeasing to Jehovah. Now he said to Judah, "If only Er or Onan had had a son. I would have given you the birthright and the blessing."

Judah's heart leaped; it was the first time his father had spoken these words to him.

Jacob went on, "They cannot go to any of the others except Benjamin. And, as you know, he is not really responsible, hasn't grown up in many ways. And he will not have grandsons for many years. I have waited long enough. What if Jehovah should take me before I settle the matter? Bring Tamar back and give her to Shelah, as you promised, and I can settle the matter within the year. Then Jehovah will be pleased and we will prosper much again."

Judah wanted nothing more than this, but somehow he could not bring himself to risk his one remaining son with Tamar. He and Lala had talked of it even last night; she was as reluctant as he was, though she had loved Tamar dearly and had missed her much.

Judah spoke, "I cannot do it, father—not yet anyway, much as I want the blessing and birthright. We must wait a while longer. There's really no hurry. Let Shelah ask for a wife first!"

Jacob did not press the matter. "Very well, my son." he returned. "But do not wait too long. I am getting old. Who knows what will happen?"

Another year passed, and when they took stock, their increase in everything was smaller than the last. Jacob was greatly disturbed, for he sensed that Jehovah was withholding His blessings because of some wrongdoing among the tribe. Though he watched closely, he could discover nothing that was wrong except Judah's refusal to take Tamar for Shelah.

Once again, just before the feast and sacrifice, he confronted Judah.

Judah said, "I have thought much on this, my father, and I will do it soon—before planting time, unless Shelah refuses."

"Do it now. Judah. Go and find him now."

But when Judah found Shelah and talked to him, the boy refused. "You got Tamar for Er when to wanted her, my father. Then it was agreeable to Onan to take her. I think he always wanted her anyway. Now I want Tirzah. If you care about me, you will get her for me and forget about Tamar."

When Judah insisted it was the tribe's custom, he got nowhere. Shelah's mind was made up. He had never refused his father before. Judah tried to placate him.

"If I get Tirzah for you, then give her a year, and if Tamar still waits, take her also and raise up seed to your brothers. It is your duty as a male of our tribe."

After a long pause, Shelah said, "I will consider it. Only get Tirzah for me now."

In his impatience, Shelah reminded Judah of the way Er had been about Tamar. *The way I was about Lala,* he thought wryly.

So he got Tirzah for Shelah, but after a year she had still not given birth. Still Shelah refused to take Tamar. And this year's increase was even smaller. Both Judah and Jacob were alarmed.

Just as winter came, Judah's beloved Lala died. She came in from a walk in the field one day at sunset, and fell upon the floor at the top of the stone steps. When her maid found her, she could not move or speak, and her eyes were wild. All through the long night, the family watched over her. Judah rubbed her hands as he kissed her still face. At dawn, she slipped away.

Judah was bereft, but he could not cry out as the others did. He gathered the still body in his arms, kissed the beloved face, wet with his own tears, again and again. Jacob and Leah stood helplessly by, weeping bitterly. Jacob relived his own grief at Rachel's death so long ago. After a while, He sent all away but Shelah, who stood in a corner, alternately beating his breast and the wall, while Tirzah tried to comfort him. Leah took her outside, while Jacob shook his grandson roughly, firmly. "It is enough, my son. You must take your father away, so Leah and the maids can—can care for your mother's body. There is no more we can do." He finally got through to the dazed young man and he began to pull himself together. They both lifted the still-weeping Judah, laid Lala's still body gently down, then led him away.

For many weeks Judah tramped the woods and fields as if he were in a dream. He refused to go when the family laid Lala's body in the burial cave at Machpelah. Jacob had sent a message to her people, but when her brothers came, Judah could not make them welcome, could not go with them to mourn at the tomb. He could only weep and turn away from all.

It fell to Jacob and Shelah to carry on with the amenities. Jacob was amazed and pleased at how well Shelah carried on, at how capably Tirzah ran Judah's household, young as she was. At nightfall, when Judah would come from his walk alone, Leah would be there to coax him into eating some dainty she had prepared especially for him. The servants would see to his bath and clothes, Shelah would sit with him and go over the day's happenings. None of it seemed to get through to his father, but Shelah would keep patiently at it, while Judah sat silently, often with tears coursing down his lean cheeks.

After two months had passed and Judah was no better, but was only thinner and weaker, Jacob sent for his friend Hirah. When Hirah arrived, he held Judah in his arms and they wept together. But Judah could not talk even to him. He merely took his hand and led him toward the fields. As they walked, Hirah talked to Judah, going back over their long friendship and recounting the many good times they had had together. Off and on for two days they walked, with Judah still silent and weeping. At last, about mid-afternoon of the third day, they went into the same cool woods that had comforted Tamar and Lala years before. By now Hirah was talking about Lala; he was making Judah remember every detail of meeting her, of that first night when they had slipped away from the others, about their wedding. Hirah reminded Judah of how much she had loved him—so much so that she left her family and traveled so far to be his wife. Suddenly he said, "Now, my friend, were there not many good years together? Do you not have much to thank your Jehovah for?"

Suddenly Judah cried out, fell upon the ground, and beat his breast; he was writhing in agony as great sobs and screams tore him apart. Hirah watched helplessly, wishing he had not spoken so. He had never witnessed such agony, and it seemed to increase as time went on. Then gradually it subsided, and finally Judah sat up. He looked around as if he were surprised at where he was, like one waking from a dream. He looked up at Hirah.

"My friend," he said, "I'm sorry. I have not been myself since—since Lala left me."

"I understand," Hirah returned. "I think you could not face the loss and so you withdrew into yourself. Come, get up, we will sit a while yonder on that fallen log. You can talk to me about it all."

He helped Judah rise, guided him to the log, and sat with his arm around Judah's shoulders.

Presently Judah was telling him all about his life with Lala, how he loved her, how happy they had been when each son was born, how sorry he was they had no grandchildren, how hard it was when Er and then Onan were first taken from them. He was weeping again. In a broken voice, he then said, "But no matter how hard that was, she was always there to comfort, and now she is gone. How can I go on?"

"You can, my friend. Now that you have faced it, you can pick up and go on. You still have one son; you can look forward to grandchildren from him. It won't be easy, but you can go on. Your God will help, and you have your father and mother. Think of how much they need you. Take heart, dear friend; let some of your grief go. In time, it will get better. I know. Remember, I lost my wife too, and a son."

"I'm sorry, Hirah." Judah said again. "I had forgotten everybody's grief but my own. How Shelah must be sorrowing for his mother; how worried he must to about me."

"Indeed he is," returned Hirah. "Shall we go and let them all know you have come out of a bad dream?" He rose and helped Judah up; they walked out of the woods and reached the house by nightfall. It was a still-grieving, but different, father who greeted his son, and who now took charge to become a good host to his friend, a master to his household.

Hirah stayed for another week. They talked of days gone by, and they made future plans. Judah began to enjoy his food again, was able to talk with his father and Shelah about the work. Sometime he even smiled again, and once or twice Hirah was able to make him laugh by recounting some of their experiences in younger years.

It was with reluctance and tears that the two friends parted when time forced Hirah to return to his own affairs.

15

Judah's Indiscretion

And Judah was comforted, and went up unto his sheep-shearers to Timnath, he and his friend Hirah, the Adullamite. And it was told Tamar. . . . And she put her widow's garments off from her, and covered her with a veil, and wrapped herself, and sat in an open place, which is by the way to Timnath. . . .

(Genesis 38:12-14)

When Judah saw her, he thought her to be a harlot. . . .

(Genesis 38:15)

And he turned in unto her by the way. . . .

(Genesis 38:16)

And it came to pass about three months after, that it was told Judah, saying, Tamar thy daughter in law hath played the harlot; and also, behold, she is with child of whoredom. . . .

(Genesis 38:24)

By the man, whose these are, am I with child. . . .

(Genesis 38:25)

And Judah acknowledged them. . . . And he knew her again no more.

(Genesis 38:26)

It took Judah a long time to come to terms with his grief, even after he came to himself. For weeks he walked the fields after sunset, when his work was done. Life seemed so empty without Lala, she had been so much a part of him for so long. The only time he could think of when he had ever been without her was when Joseph had been sold, and that memory still brought such remorse that he had to put it out of his mind. Yet it kept coming back to him on his lonely walks, as he tried to discover why Jehovah had dealt so harshly with him. *Why,* he wondered, *did trouble and loss come only to me, when my brothers were as guilty as I was?*

Only Reuben, he recalled, had been distressed at their treatment of Joseph, and had wanted later to tell their father the truth. And he, Judah, had threatened him if he did. *Oh, we were a rough, wicked lot back then,* he thought and the thought made him weep. *The treachery and cruelty of Simeon and Levi to Prince Hamor—wasn't that as evil as what they had all done to Joseph?* And yet not even those two had been punished by Jehovah. Of course, their father would never really forgive them, would never have any close dealings with them, even to this day. That seemed to be their only sorrow. If Jacob could not forgive them, then Judah knew he would never forgive any of them if he ever found out about Joseph; then he would certainly not leave the blessing and birthright to Judah. Everything would go to Benjamin, whether he could handle it or not, since he was the only one who was not guilty.

And yet there were times in his own grief over the loss of Er and Onan, and now in the loss of Lala, when Judah wished he could confess to his father, when he thought it might bring relief. Of course, he had long since confessed his guilt to Jehovah, was truly sorry for the great wrong he had done before Him; he knew also that at least some of his brothers were sorry for their evil, for they spoke of it sometimes.

And Judah thought of the matter of his daughter-in-law, Tamar. *Could his loss of Lala be Jehovah's punishment?* His father had not spoken of it since Lala's death, but Judah knew he had not forgotten. He continued to try to discover whether Jehovah's displeasure was because of Joseph's treatment or of Tamar's. He could not be sure and his torment went on, so he could never be at peace.

He knew his father would soon insist again that he bring Tamar back for Shelah. He steeled himself against that time, determined he would not force Shelah to marry Tamar against his will, and he was sure the boy was still against it. Judah decided he would defy Jacob if it came to that.

The seasons came and went, and Jacob prodded Judah about Tamar; he in turn questioned Shelah, and Shelah put him off. Hirah came to visit about twice yearly, and at the end of the third year after Lala's death, Judah realized that his grief had passed, without his knowing just when. He assured Hirah that he had become whole again, had begun to find joy in the everyday occurrences of life, was almost surprised he could laugh again, and even could feel the need of a woman again.

Jacob had ceased to bring up the matter of Tamar. The facts that crops and animals decreased each year no longer bothered Judah. He had decided that, after all, it was not a punishment from Jehovah, that his father was wrong in thinking that it was. Still, sometimes, he felt a vague uneasiness.

One summer day during sheep-shearing season, as the sun was setting, Judah was returning home after penning a special flock of sheep. He chanced to look across the horizon, and there he saw, silhouetted against the red west, three swift camels. Even as he was struck with the beauty of the scene and the floating grace of the animals coming toward him, he thought suddenly that the lead figure rode like Hirah. *But why would he be coming from that direction?* Nonetheless, it was Hirah and two herdsmen.

After happy greetings, Hirah explained, "A great part of my flocks have grazed to within a few miles on the other side of Timnath, for the valley there remains green. It seemed good to bring them on to Timnath for shearing, and I could not come so close without seeing you, my friend."

"How welcome you are!" responded Judah. "It has been long since you were here. How have the months been with you?"

Well," answered Hirah, "except for the drought. I have sold many animals at a loss. It is worse with me than you have here. But, my friend, it is not all bad. I have taken a wife since I last saw you. I must tell you about it later."

"Oh, I am happy for you, Hirah!" cried Judah. "You have been alone for too long."

"Yes. But then so have you."

"Perhaps I have. But, come, you are weary and hungry. Let us go to the house at once."

And so it came about that on the next day, after Hirah had talked half the night about his beautiful, young wife, that he returned to Timnath and Judah accompanied him. This happened after he sent the herdsmen with a flock of sheep toward the city. On the trip, Judah ventured, "My friend, I found Lala when I visited you once. Do you think I could find another as beautiful as she was now?"

Hirah laughed. "My friend, I am sure of it. Indeed, I can think of two already. Your asking tells me your grief is ending. You are ready to start living again."

Once they reached the outskirts of Timnath, Hirah and his servants and Judah's two servants rode toward the sheep-shearing sheds. Judah rode on toward the city alone. To the west of the huge city gates there was a large grove of oaks, pines, and tamarinds which Judah knew well from past visits. It looked cool and inviting, so Judah suddenly decided to go there to cool down before riding through the gates.

He urged his beast forward, till he reached the ridge of the grove. When he dismounted, he saw that someone else was in the grove—a woman! She was seated on a huge stone under a spreading tamarind; her back was turned toward him. Should he mount and ride away? And then he noticed the veil over her head. That could mean—well, she could be a harlot, waiting purposefully here for any man who might come by. Judah's pulses quickened as they had when Hirah had spoken of his new wife. He thought, *It has been so long since I had a woman. Not since Lala, three years ago. Why not?*

The woman still had not turned. He secured his beast and walked toward her. He stood watching her then, as desire mounted within him. Only when he called out softly did she seem to become aware of him. She turned to face him, unafraid, but drawing her veil more closely, with only her eyes uncovered. They gazed steadily, invitingly at him.

"Who are you?" asked Judah, moving closer.

"Does it matter?" she countered in a strained voice, that seemed somehow familiar to Judah. "Come and sit beside me." She patted the rock. Judah needed no urging; his heart was racing wildly.

The woman lost no time in letting him know why she was there, and he soon asked if he might find her there about nightfall, when they would not be disturbed. She promised that she would wait for him. After a while, though filled with desire that both frightened and delighted him, Judah left, filled with fantasies he hoped would come true that evening. He would have wondered, perhaps been disturbed, had he seen the smile of triumph on her pretty face as she removed her veil and hurried after him into the city.

True to her word, the veiled woman was waiting at the edge of the grove when Judah rode up just before darkness. Before they went into the shadows of the grove, she asked what he would give her.

"A kid from the flocks," Judah promised. "You shall have it tomorrow."

She countered, "Will you give me a pledge until you give it?"

"What pledge?" he asked

"Your signets, your bracelets, your staff."

Judah laughed, handing her his staff, with its gold identification marks. "Isn't that enough?"

"Give me all," she said huskily. "They'll be returned to you."

Desire took over, and Judah stripped off his bracelets. He held them out to her with his signet. She took them and he hurried her into the darkness of the grove. Only with daybreak did he leave her, and his pledge, and ride away to the shearing shed.

He found his friend Hirah about to ride into the city to attend to business. When Judah told him of his agreement with the woman, Hirah laughed. "My friend; you are indeed getting over your grief. It is good."

"Will you take a kid as you ride by the grove and redeem my pledge?" asked Judah. Hirah nodded, still laughing. Judah called a servant to bring a choice animal and ride with Hirah to deliver it, then return immediately with his pledge. He stood watching as the two clamored around the olive trees and disappeared over the brow of the hill.

All morning Judah's thoughts strayed back to the pleasures of the night as he helped the other servant and the two herdsmen who had brought his flock. He missed his bracelets and signets, but especially his staff, as he kept looking for his servant's return.

It was almost midday before he spotted both his servant and Hirah coming over the hill at full speed, trailing clouds of dust. As he watched them approach, he was dismayed to see that his servant still carried the kid in front of him. What could have happened? Surely the harlot had waited where he told her to.

Hirah dismounted when he reached Judah. "We found no one at the grove. We rode everywhere around there, asking men we saw about her. They said there had been no harlot near the place, ever. We rode over the city also but did not see any veiled women. I'm sorry, my friend."

"I am shamed," answered Judah. "I promised her the kid." He realized the little animal was bleating, "Take it to its mother," he commanded. "She has been bleating all morning."

He said to Hirah. "I will go to the grove tonight and take an animal. Perhaps she will be there again."

Hirah's eyes twinkled. "Likely you should take two," he said. "Maybe I should go and help you."

Judah laughed, a little abashed. "As you like, my friend."

But when the two went back to the grove, each carrying

a small, distraught animal, they still found no one. They rode around and through the town, but found no woman wearing a veil, and no man who could tell them anything about a harlot at the grove.

Twice more before the shearing was done and Judah returned home, he went at night to the place and waited. He also went in daylight, but found no one. He was both puzzled and worried, ashamed at not being able to give what he promised, concerned at having lost his pledge.

The week after Judah returned home, he and two trusted servants left for a visit to Hirah, as he had promised. Judah took gifts and some of his finest clothes. Jacob had approved, and he and Leah and some of their grandchildren stood watching them ride away, their trappings shining in the morning sun.

Leah sighed and said, "Children, your Uncle Judah may bring a new wife home with him—she would be your aunt, since your Aunt Lala has died. Can some of you remember her?"

"I can, I can!" piped up several children. One said, "She was very pretty, with black hair."

Another said, "And she played with us."

An older girl added, "She taught us to make cheese and grow flowers."

Then there were questions as to how Uncle Judah would find a wife, and how she could come back with him. Leah explained as best she could, and there was great anticipation during the weeks while he was gone.

And so it was that Judah brought a second wife from Adullam, not quite as young or beautiful as Lala had been, but young enough to bear children. Her name was Banah. After performing the wedding ceremony, Jacob congratulated him. Privately he told him how happy he would be if he had sons now, so the birthright and the blessings could be secured. But he also told him, "I must entreat you again to keep your promise to Tamar. You think lightly of it, but you know Jehovah is withholding His blessings on our crops and flocks. I am sure that is the reason."

Judah made his usual excuse. "Shelah is not willing. Indeed, he refused vehemently the last time I asked him."

"Speak with him again, my son. Insist upon it," urged Jacob. Judah promised that he would do so when the excitement over the wedding had passed.

More than two months later, Judah and Benji rode up to Timnath to see if Tamar would be still willing, if Shelah would agree. Judah almost hoped her father had by now betrothed her to one of their own people, so that Judah's family would be rid of her for good. Yet he felt somehow guilty over such a hope, inasmuch as he was not sure that would restore Jehovah's full blessing on Jacob's tribe. Besides, he was still doubtful of Shelah's acceptance of Tamar.

Those thoughts occupied his mind as he and Benji rode toward Timnath's gates. He felt compelled to ride through the grove again, hoping the harlot might be there this time. He would give her money instead of a kid and get back his pledge. Then his shame would go away. He was disappointed when he still found no one.

It was quite hot as they rode through the gates. They tied their mounts to limbs of a spreading terebinth tree just inside. By chance, a friend of Judah's from sheep-shearing days—Zubah—was tying his mount also, and they greeted each other heartily. Then Zubah insisted on buying wine, bread, and cheese for them from a nearby shop. While he went for these, the two brothers rested and cooled themselves on a stone beach under a great oak.

When Zubah returned, they all ate leisurely and talked about the events that had occurred in the city since the last time Judah was there. Zubah finally asked discreetly if Hirah had ever found the harlot he had asked about at shearing time. Judah flushed under his tan as he answered negatively, shaking his head, and Benji looked at him curiously. He thought; *Why would that question bother Judah?*

Zubah lowered his voice, looked around to see that no one was near. "My friend," he asked, "have you heard that your daughter-in-law Tamar has played the harlot and is three or four months with child?"

222

Judah was so stunned that his mouth flew open, yet he could utter no words for some moments.

"Ah, my friend, I see you do not know. Forgive me for startling you with the news."

Benjamin, silently looking from one to the other, thought he detected almost a note of glee in Zubah's voice. *Perhaps he enjoys tale-bearing,* he told himself.

When Judah finally found his voice, a heavy flush of anger colored his face, and his eyes hardened. He asked, "Are you sure? This is a hard charge. You know what happens to her kind."

"No doubt about it," answered Zubah. "I saw her in her father's shop yesterday. Already her condition shows. Indeed, she seems even to flaunt it, as if she is unafraid. How long ago did she leave your home—some five years?" Judah nodded and Zubah continued, "You have another son who is grown by now?"

I have," Judah answered. "It was to see if she would be his wife that I came here today."

"I see," returned Zubah. "I am sorry I told you."

"Don't be," said Judah. "I am glad to learn this before I reach her father's place." His anger and agitation mounted as he spoke. "Played the harlot indeed!" he almost shouted. "She shall be burned!"

Benji spoke quietly, "You see our father was right when he wanted you to get her for Shelah some two years ago." Judah's look remained hard.

"She shall not shame my family and go unpunished!" He turned to Zubah. "Thank you, my friend, for the food and the news." He was rising. "We will go now. We must deal with this."

"You are welcome," returned Zubah. "May it work out to your satisfaction."

Judah and Benjamin led their mounts through the streets to the shop of Tamar's father, tied them in front and went inside.

Judah, at Benji's insistence, had calmed himself, and they greeted Tamar's father with respect. He returned their greeting, seemingly not upset nor afraid.

Judah got to the point immediately and his anger returned as he talked. "I came here today to inquire whether Tamar still wished to be married to my son, Shelah. But from a friend, I learn she is with child of whoredom. How could this happen? Once wed to each of my older sons, she has now shamed my family!" His face hardened with rage, his voice rose.

Her father calmly countered, "Why did you not send for her some three years ago before your son took another wife? You had promised her—and me. It is you who have shamed both her and me."

"Could she not wait even a few years without playing the harlot?" shouted Judah. "She is yet young, why could she not have waited a few years?"

"Perhaps," answered her father soothingly, "because she is still young. The young are hot-blooded; they do not want to wait forever, and you have given her no assurance these many years."

A pang of guilt made Judah's anger flare even more. "You know that such are to be burned, and so shall she be! I shall gather the city fathers together now and she shall be burned at sunset. Bring her forth, lest you and all you have be burned also!" He turned to leave.

"You'd best wait till you know all the facts, my friend," her father said, his voice level, yet commanding. Benjamin marveled at the man's calmness, and Judah turned to face him once more, his anger seething.

The man went toward the back of the shop, without hurry. "Tamar! Tamar!" he called through an open door. "Come here, my daughter." He waited until she came through the door, holding three articles in her hands. She walked beside him to face Judah and Benjamin. Benjamin thought, *Why, the woman is more beautiful than she ever was! Why wouldn't Shelah want to raise up sons to his brothers by her?*

She looked at them levelly, her dark eyes not flinching at Judah's angry face as he took in her heavy figure. "Why have you chosen to shame my family?" he raged at her. "Why couldn't you wait for Shelah?"

"I did," she replied calmly, meeting his eyes. "Five long years I waited." Then she held out her right hand, holding a staff toward him. Judah noticed it for the first time. His face blanched. She held out her other hand with the bracelets and signet.

"By the man whose these are, I am with child," she said clearly with no trace of fear. "Do you know whose they are?"

Judah's hands trembled as he took the staff, looked at the gold seal, then took the bracelets and signet, examining them closely. A heavy flush replaced the paleness of his face, his eyes dropped before her gaze, while Benjamin stood open-mouthed, watching.

Judah was trembling as he admitted with obvious difficulty, "They are mine. They were my pledge to a woman I thought was a harlot at the grove."

The truth suddenly hit him as he held the objects before him. "<u>You</u> were the harlot at the grove! No wonder we could never find you to redeem my pledge!" He was weeping now, his head down, his voice shaking. "It is by me you are with child?" he asked.

"It is," she answered, still calm. "It was the only way to gain my rightful place in your family. You were never going to come for me. You blamed me for your Er and Onan's deaths, you blamed me that I gave them no children. Now you can see it was not because of me."

"You have dealt deceitfully with me, my daughter-in-law. What you did was wrong. Yet you have been more righteous than I. But we did come here today to see if you still wanted to become Shelah's wife. Now I ask you to go back with us, not to be Shelah's wife, not to be mine, but as my daughter-in-law and mother-to-be of my child." He paused, looking up at her for the first time; shame and contrition evident on his face. "Will you come on those terms?"

Tamar looked at her father; there was a question in her eyes. The man nodded as he said, "It was what you wished, wasn't it?"

"It was. It is," she said to him. To Judah she said, "Yes,

I will go on those terms, if I will be treated as truly a part of the family, as if I were wife to Shelah."

"When shall I come for you, then?" asked Judah.

"Stay here tonight, and I will be ready to leave with you in the morning," answered Tamar.

16

Twins Born to Tamar

And it came to pass, in the time of her travail, that, behold, twins were in her womb.

(Genesis 38:27)

. . . therefore his name was called Pharez.

(Genesis 38:29)

. . . and his name was called Zarah.

(Genesis 38:30)

Some five and a half months after Tamar came back to Jacob's family—happy to be back, even as they were happy to have her back—her time came. It was late on a rainy, blustery, winter day that her pains began. Judah sent a servant to get the tribe's midwives and his mother. The midwives came immediately, and Leah arrived before dark, braving the bitter wind that blew black clouds across the brighter western horizon where the sun had gone down.

All through the cold, weary night Tamar's pains were regular and severe. Leah bathed her face each time they subsided, and she talked soothingly to Tamar. Sometime before daybreak, Tamar was reduced to screaming and clutching Leah's hands when the pains came.

Judah had lain all night on a couch outside Tamar's door. From time to time the midwives had reported to him of Tamar's progress. He had mixed emotions—concern over Tamar's pain and eagerness for his son—it had to be a son—a safe and healthy son. His thoughts strayed to the births of his other three. He remembered how afraid he had been, how he had suffered each pain that Lala had, how happy he had been when each had finally arrived and all was well. Could his two older ones really have grown up and then died since then? It seemed so strange, like a dream, even as his lying with Tamar nine months ago now seemed. But this anxious waiting, and now Tamar's screams, were no dream. They were very real. He jumped up and began pacing the floor. His young wife, herself with child, was wakened by the screams and came to walk beside him.

The screams came closer together, then became more agonizing as the gray sky lightened. Judah could bear them no longer. He went to their room with Banah, told her to go back to bed, then he grabbed a heavy goatskin coat. He put it on as he ran out of the house into the rain and the howling winds that lashed the pines and tamarinds almost to the ground. He roused the herdsmen to have them make the rounds to the stalls and sheepfolds, feeding the animals and securing them against the storm.

It was with dread that he returned to Tamar's screams. He found his father there, unable to bear the waiting any longer in his own house. Hanging up his dripping coat, he huddled with Jacob on the couch, as the screams became continuous. Soon a midwife opened the door, gave them the news that there were twins in Tamar's womb. One had put out a tiny hand and they had bound a scarlet thread upon it as the firstborn. But the hand had been drawn back. Soon, she assured them, the firstborn would be delivered. She closed the door then, and turned back to the screaming Tamar.

Jacob put a hand on Judah's shoulder. "Surely you will have two sons to take Er and Onan's place, my son," he said soothingly. "They will make up for the sorrow you have had.

I know Jehovah has forgiven your wrong to Tamar, and is blessing you again."

"I hope so, my father, for your sake as well as mine." They both stood up, silent, each beseeching and thanking God in his own way.

A terrible, shuddering scream tore through the closed door, and then a lusty cry. The men held their breath, waiting. Soon a midwife, who was all smiles, opened the door and announced, "A fine son, master; not the one with the scarlet thread, though. No doubt he will be born soon." She closed the door and again went back to Tamar as her screams began again, weaker than before.

Judah wondered, *Will she have the strength to bring a second child to birth? Will it be a son also? Jehovah, please let it be. Please help her.*

After what seemed an interminable amount of time to the waiting men, amid Tamar's ever-weakening screams, there came, blessedly, another lusty, angry howl. The men sighed relief and smiled as they realized the ordeal was over. The midwife came out with the confirmation that it was indeed another son, whose hand still bore the scarlet thread. "In a few minutes," she promised, "you may both come in and see them."

When Tamar was strong again she insisted on calling her firstborn Pharez and the second Zarah, because of the way they were born. To Judah and Jacob, the names seemed odd. Judah gave in, however, thinking she should at least be allowed to name her own sons since she had no husband. He himself was very proud, since he was sure his father would now give him the blessing and birthright. Surely two sons at once could secure the line, whether or not his wife gave him a son, or whether Shelah's wife gave him sons. There was great celebration in the tribe when the boys were circumcised on the eighth day.

By the time the twins were a few months old, both Jacob and Judah were partial to the precious little Pharez, while his mother and Leah favored Zarah. He was such a beautiful, good child, who seemed to be so humble. Pharez, though only a few minutes older, soon dominated his brother. Jacob remembered how his own mother had always favored him, while his father had preferred Esau, and that jealousy and trouble had resulted. Still it had all worked out, as prophesied, in Jehovah's own time. Surely this would, too. So he did not warn Judah as to what trouble parental partiality might cause.

True to his promise, Judah saw that Tamar was well-cared-for so that she did not tax her strength after the hard labor. He gave her a second handmaid to care for the twins, had special jewelry—rings, bracelets, and earrings brought from Egypt in gratitude for her having borne him two sons. Of course he was wise enough to get special things for his wife at the same time. He still thought of Tamar as his daughter-in-law, of whom he had always been fond. He had seen her as the daughter he never had. To her, he was still the kind father she had known when she married each of his sons.

As spring came, Judah and Jacob were eager to see how the harvest from the fall planting would turn out. They also watched closely to see if the animals had increased. They were not so interested in the increase itself as in the assurance of Jehovah's favor being upon them, now that Judah had at last done the right thing by Tamar.

But they were disappointed, for the increase of crops and animals was smaller than it had ever been. There was, however, an increase in the tribe's children. By midsummer both Judah and his son Shelah had children born to their wives, both girls, and the wives of three other grandsons were with child: Zebulun's Gomer, Gad's Mahlah, Naphtali's Zurah, as well as Levi's Hadiah. Also, no less than six servant families were expecting children. Jacob and Judah wondered how so many could be cared for if the crops and animals continued to fail. Ever the optimist, Benjamin pointed out to them that perhaps Jehovah was showing His approval and His blessing in terms of children instead of crops and animals. When they considered, they agreed and stopped worrying, and began to praise Jehovah and be thankful.

Another year passed pleasantly. There was rejoicing and thanksgiving at the sacrifice and festival even though the harvest was scant. Then there was a period for resting and being more at ease than Jacob could remember his tribe having experienced before. He did not have the vigor of former years; now he reminded himself that his sons were growing older and needed to let up some. After all, they were quite well off, had many servants to take care of the harder work and the animals. He noted also, with a little apprehension as well as gladness, that Leah was not working so hard either. She lay in bed longer in the mornings and sometimes rested after the midday meal. Indeed, all the households slowed to the bare essentials during the bitterest cold. Only a few industrious souls kept incessantly at the spinning, weaving, candle-making, harness-mending, and sewing.

As spring returned, the twins were walking, talking, and getting into everything. They were quite fascinated with their small half-sister, especially the quieter, more serious Zarah. Tamar and Judah's wife, Banah, became quite close friends, neither feeling threatened by the other. Shelah's wife, Tirzah, also enjoyed a friendship with Tamar and Banah, as did their children. Dinah, still young-looking and beautiful, often came with her two small grandsons and Leah to visit Judah's home. Leah reveled in the young children's antics, and Jacob came every day to see them. He was still especially taken with little Pharez, who warmed to him in return.

So the years passed gently upon Jacob's tribe. More sons and daughters were born to his grandsons. Two more sons, and then twin sons, were born to Benjamin. Both Judah and Shelah had daughters, but neither had the longed-for sons.

Judah put his hopes for the blessing and birthright upon Pharez as Jacob doted upon him increasingly. The child was so unusual in his understanding of all Jacob told him about Grandfather Abraham and Jehovah's dealings with him, and with Isaac, Jacob, and the whole tribe. He would listen for hours on end to the stories Jacob told, sitting on Jacob's knees by the fire in winter, or tramping through the fields and woods in summer. Judah also took up so much time with him that he became adept with the animals, and as he grew older, he did well with the crops as well. Everything seemed to come easily for him, as if Jehovah were even smiling on him. Jacob often thought of how much like Joseph he was, and some of the grief of his own heart was healed.

Jacob noticed one difference, however. None of the tribe's children, certainly not his brother Zarah, was jealous of Pharez nor seemed to bear any resentment that both Jacob and Judah preferred him. Zarah loved staying with his mother and Leah, and learned well the lessons they taught him. He also played much with his half-sisters. When he and Pharez were together, they got along well. Pharez always took the lead in whatever they did, and Zarah was content to follow. Watching them, both Judah and Jacob marveled at how different their relationship was from that of Er and Onan, who had forever fought and bickered. Thinking back, Jacob wished that he and his twin, Esau, could have gotten along like these two did. But there was no prophecy concerning these two, that the older should serve the younger, as there had been with him and Esau. Perhaps that made the difference.

Jacob wished that Jehovah would come to him again, as He had long ago, with definite instructions that Judah should receive the blessing and birthright and pass the chosen line down through little Pharez. He never failed to beseech Jehovah on this matter in his heart, though he never voiced his wishes to any except Judah. Yet he grew closer to Benjamin all the while, and loved the little sons Benji's wife kept bearing. He knew, however, as time went on, that Benji would never quite grow up, would never quite accept responsibility. Jacob could just not think of giving him either the birthright or the blessing, though he was Rachel's son, and for that reason he would have liked for the line to pass through him. Hadn't they long ago felt that Jehovah promised this? When Jacob thought of this, however, he remembered that Rachel had once reminded him that God's promise was to his descendants, not hers. At the time, he had considered them the same.

Jacob and Judah spoke of Benjamin sometimes, but they could not decide why he never seemed to grow up, had little confidence in himself. It certainly wasn't that he was feeble-minded; he was bright and apt enough in most things.

Jacob reasoned aloud, "It must be that we both were too protective of him when he was young and motherless." As he so reflected, tears came to his eyes, his voice broke, and Judah understood better than ever his father's grief at losing Rachel.

Recovering his composure, Jacob went on, "Then after Joseph was gone, I held on to Benji more closely than ever. Even now I think of him as a child, and never insist that he make his own decisions about his own affairs. I suppose I have never really allowed him to grow up."

The two sat thinking awhile, silently. Then Judah said, "And yet he helps you ever more with your work, he has fathered all those sons and is good with them, and firm. I suppose we'll never know exactly what has made him what he is, but it is certain that Jehovah blesses him."

Jacob nodded in agreement. "And yet I cannot feel that he is the one to carry the line, no matter how much I should want him to. I suppose that depends, my son, on what comes of your Pharez as he grows up."

"I hope he will be worthy," answered Judah wistfully.

As Judah grew older, his knowledge of Jehovah and how He had worked in the lives of His father, his grandfather Isaac, and his great-grandfather Abraham, made Him seem more real. Yet Jehovah had never spoken to him as He had to them. *Why? I try to do now whatever my father says is right and will please Jehovah. I am concerned for all my brothers and their families. I have tried to help them repent of our wrong to Joseph, just as I have. I take good care of Tamar, the mother of my sons. Surely I am forgiven for not giving her to Shelah. I hope Jehovah will speak to me someday, will assure me—and my father—that I am the one for the line to pass through. I know that I am, and that my son Pharez will grow up to be worthy.*

17

Leah Dies

In the cave that is in the field of Machpelah, which is before Mamre ... and there I buried Leah.

(Genesis 49:30-31)

The harvest continued to grow less bountiful. Likewise, the animal increases were smaller each year. Because of decreased rainfall, many streams dried up and the grass failed to sustain the flocks and herds. The herdsmen had to go even farther south to sustain the animals. Finally Judah and Jacob talked with the other sons. They all agreed they must sell many animals immediately. They, therefore, steadily sent great droves into Egypt, where the market was good.

Soon they were forced to sell some of their servants and herdsman as well, and this hurt Jacob immensely. At first, they sold only those who seemed interested in going to a new place. Jacob prayed that he would not have to sell those servants with their families who did not want to go. His heart was often heavy with this feeling of dread.

Even so, his greatest concern was for Leah, as he and all the family watched her grow weaker and thinner day by day. As time went on she developed a cough that grew steadily more severe. She was cared for tenderly by Jacob and her maids, by Dinah and Tamar, and her sons' wives. Special sacrifices were made for her by Jacob and Judah, and Jehovah's healing was sought for her benefit by all . Leah never complained; finally because of the weakness and coughing she was unable to speak at all.

Then in the later winter, she literally coughed her life away, as Jacob kissed her withered hands and the family stood by her bed, weeping.

Her wasted, beloved body was placed in the cave at Mamre, where Abraham, Sarah, Isaac, and Rebekah had been laid so long ago, where Er and Onan and Lala had been placed in recent years. The whole tribe mourned her for many days.

Jacob carried on as one in a dream for weeks. Nothing his sons nor Dinah could say or do seemed to reach him. He grew very thin, his once-black locks had now turned completely gray, and his feet shuffled when he walked. Judah despaired of his life, but could do nothing. He had moved him into his own home a few days after Leah's death, for he was certain that getting away from the place that reminded him of her absence would be best. Jacob did not resist, but it did not help his grief. At least Pharez was always around and walked with him in the fields and talked with him as his sons could not. Tamar and Judah's wife, Banah, coaxed him to eat enough to keep life in him. His old servant Ziph slept on the floor beside him, and was there to comfort him when he woke from unhappy dreams and wept in the night.

Judah tried to help his father see how they needed him to make decisions about the crops and animals, but he did not seem to understand and merely mumbled, "You can decide. It doesn't matter anyway."

Watching him shuffle off with Pharez, Judah would weep for him. *How white his hair grows, how wrinkled his skin! The proud, straight figure, how stooped it has become! This is the third loss for you, my father. I was young, but I remember how you grieved at Aunt Rachel's death, and after I lost Lala, I knew how you felt. And I, with my brothers, caused your grief over*

Joseph. O Jehovah, I know you have forgiven me, but I can never forgive myself! And now with my mother's passing, he has only Benji left of his special ones. Only Benji and my little Pharez. Perhaps the child can reach him soon. Jehovah, I pray that you will help my father in this grief. He must not die yet; he has not settled on the birthright and blessing. Still, he knows Benji cares not for them, and he knows my son does. Jehovah, show my father that the promised line to bless the world should pass through me and my son Pharez. It is so clear to me that he is the one.

Thus Judah mused and prayed while his father grew weaker, more withdrawn. And it was the child who finally reached him, as Judah had prayed he would, and as his friend Hirah had finally reached Judah in his grief at Lala's death.

One day when the heat was severe, Pharez guided his grandfather along the path to the big stone in the deep, cool woods, where Leah had once listened to Tamar and given her strength, and where Hirah had helped Judah. The child, tired and hot, sat on the rock in the coolness and pulled Jacob down beside him. The old man was weary, too, his breathing heavy, and they rested a while in silence.

Then, innocently, Pharez asked, "Grandfather, why do you not really hear me when I talk to you since Grandmother died? It seems like a part of you is not with us now. Where is it? Did it go with her?" His eyes searched Jacob's face, and Jacob really <u>saw</u> the child. His earnestness got through to Jacob's inner being as nothing had been able to since Leah's death. He could only stare into the troubled blue eyes.

The child continued, "I want <u>all</u> of you back with us. We need you. Grandmother doesn't, for she is with Jehovah now. Only the part we could <u>see</u> is in the burial cave. That is what my mother says, and when I asked my father, he said it is true. Is it, Grandfather?"

The boy's earnestness forced a part of Jacob's mind that hadn't functioned in a long time to consider his question. He was aware he was waiting for an answer. Slowly his mind fought through its dullness and he really thought on what Pharez had said.

Finally he spoke. "Your father and mother are right, my son. The part of your grandmother that still lives is with Jehovah God—somewhere in the heavens—not there in the grave with her body. As for part of me being with her, I don't know. But you are right, some part of me has been so wrapped in grief and loss and memories that it has been lost to you."

"Can't it come back?" asked Pharez again.

Jacob was weeping now, and gathered the child against him. "Perhaps it can," he answered brokenly, through his sobs, "now that you have made me aware that I've been away. It may be that Jehovah will help me. Let us ask Him, for I know He hears always. And sometimes He has talked to me in days gone by. Remember I've told you?"

"Yes," answered the boy.

Again weeping, Jacob raised his eyes heavenward, and when he could speak, he prayed. "Jehovah-God, I have been so buried in my grief that I have not even tried to turn my heart to You. I have even been angry that You have taken this last one from me. I have not thought of my children who need me, but only of my grief. Now You have used this little one to show me how selfish I have been. I ask You to forgive me, to help me come back to You and to my family and to be of help to them and to take back my responsibility for my tribe. It will not be easy. Even now there is the pull to go back to the past, to be with Leah in thought, even in the grave. I know of course she isn't there. The child has brought that back to me. You have spoken to me when I needed You in times past. Will You not speak to me again soon, to let me know for sure about the blessing and birthright and about the sore drought? Help me to know what to do. If there is evil in our tribe, turn us from it and give us help."

Pharez had watched his grandfather's face with wonder. Every word seemed to be cut into his mind, and he knew he would never forget. He knew also that the God his grandfather spoke to was real, that He lived, though he could not see Him. It was the same knowing that had come to Jacob at the time of his dream of the ladder at Bethel, when he had first met Jehovah for himself. Jacob had told this story to Pharez many times and, through Jacob's prayer, Pharez had received the same insight and recognized it. Suddenly he was awestruck, gazing at Jacob but <u>seeing</u> Jehovah.

When Jacob stopped and looked down at Pharez, saw the rapture on the child's face, he knew that something did come to him. After a moment he asked, "What is it, my son?"

Pharez looked around as if he had just awakened. He spoke with awe, "Grandfather, this place too is the house of God, just as your Bethel was, for Jehovah is here. I saw Him as you talked to Him. If we had oil we should anoint the stone, as you did. But I promise Him, as you did, that He will always be my God, and I will serve Him as you do."

Beholding the earnestness on the face of this child, his favorite grandson, it came to Jacob—as surely as if Jehovah had spoken audibly—that the line to bless the world should pass through him. Jacob again raised his eyes heavenward, and in humility said, "I thank You, Jehovah, that You have already answered a part of my prayer."

As they rose and walked slowly homeward, Jacob recounted once again for Pharez the times Jehovah had spoken to him. "There was that first time at Bethel, as I fled my brother Esau's wrath to Haran. I saw Jehovah standing above the ladder. He assured me He was the God of my fathers, and promised all this land here to me and my descendants. He said they would be as numerous as the dust of the earth, and that He would bless all the families of the earth through them. In return, I swore that He should be my God and that I would surely give the tenth of all He helped me get to Him. My son, you have seen the tithe urns. You know I have kept the promise, and Jehovah will keep His."

The child nodded solemnly and Jacob continued, "The second time was when I had been in Haran for twenty years and had been ill-treated by your grandmother's father, Laban. Jehovah told me to return to this land and promised to be with me. Soon after that an angel spoke to me in a dream. He said, '*I am the God of Bethel, where you anointed the pillar and vowed a vow to Me. Now arise, get out of Haran and return to the land of your kindred.'* I did as He told me, but when I was near this land, I became afraid of meeting with Esau, fearing that his anger toward me still burned. I sent my goods and my family over the brook, Jabbok, one night while I remained on the other side praying. A man wrestled with me until daybreak. When He could not prevail against me, He threw my thigh out of joint, but I would not let Him go till He blessed me. Then He asked, *'What is your name?'* When I answered, 'Jacob,' He said, *'You shall no more be called Jacob, but Israel, for as a prince you have power with God and with men, and have prevailed.'* And He blessed me there, and I knew it was Jehovah who had wrestled with me, that I had seen Him face to face and He had spared my life. It was a long time before my thigh healed, and you know we do not yet eat of the underside of an animal's thigh. That is why."

Again the boy was wide-eyed with wonder, though he had heard the story before. After a while, Jacob continued, "Then we settled in this land at Succoth, but soon Jehovah said to me, *'Arise, go up to Bethel and live there and erect an altar for Me,'* which I did. Later, Jehovah appeared to me there again and blessed me. He said again. *'Your name is Jacob; it shall no longer be called Jacob, but Israel shall be your name. I am God Almighty: be fruitful and multiply; a nation and company of nations shall come from you, and kings shall come from you; this same land I gave Abraham and Isaac, I will give to you and to your seed after you.'* And then Jehovah left me, and I set up a pillar of stone and poured a drink offering upon it, and called that particular place also Bethel—house of God."

They walked awhile in silence, each thinking of what Jehovah had promised, until they saw the houses in the twilight. Then Jacob said. "Soon afterward Benjamin was born and his mother died. Years later I lost Joseph. Each time it was long before I could stop grieving, and Jehovah did not come to me again. But always your grandmother was there with me, loving me, helping me to go on. Now there is no one to comfort me, no one to carry on for." Jacob wept again, and the child took his thin hand.

"But we love you, Grandfather, and we need you with us," he said earnestly.

"Yes," Jacob answered slowly, "you made me see that today. And after all the silent years, though Jehovah still didn't speak, yet He was there. I <u>knew</u> it, and you saw Him. Never forget that, my son. It means you are a favored one."

"I shall never forget, Grandfather. Do you think I will ever see Him again, that He will speak to me?"

"I do not know. Jehovah's ways to men cannot be foretold. Perhaps if you ever need Him to, He will speak to you. But now you know He <u>is</u>, and you must never doubt it nor cease to worship Him and seek to do His will."

Jacob's recovery was swift. His family could hardly believe it. That very evening when he and Pharez reached home, the change had begun. He ate and talked with the family again and slept the night without waking. In the morning he called all his sons together and let them know he was really with them again. He began to oversee his own work, his own animals again, with the help of Judah, Benjamin, and Pharez. He talked of Leah sometimes, of how he missed her, and he often wept. But in a few weeks his accustomed vigor had returned and his body grew straight and well again.

When he realized that the wells around them contained little water, and the springs and streams were failing, he and Benjamin and Pharez hunted until they found a spot that Jacob was sure would provide a well like the one he and Rachel had dug in Haran long ago, the one they called Rachel's well. The older sons could remember it and how it had given water to produce an abundant garden. They all took turns digging and soon a huge stream of clear water was gushing up. It was not close to the houses, but water from it could be carried the distance. Also, its overflow would water many animals as well as a garden large enough for the whole tribe. When it was all planned and the garden was ready to plant, Jacob called the whole tribe together near the well. He and Judah built an altar and they sacrificed several animals from their now rather-small flocks, in thanksgiving to Jehovah for the well. Jacob also asked that they be shown any wrong in the tribe and that Jehovah again bless them with rain and crops and animals. Afterwards the tribe gathered again in the courtyard at Jacob's house and had a small feast. It was not as lavish as the feasts had been when there was abundance, but the family was happy together again for the first time since Leah's death. Only Jacob was sad, but he tried to hide his loneliness. As he and Judah and Pharez walked together back to Judah's house, a few steps behind the others, they spoke of Pharez's vision and of Jehovah's presence at the time.

"My son," Jacob said to Judah, "I knew then that you are the one, through Pharez here, to carry on the line to bless the world, and so the blessing and birthright pass to you when I am gone." It was what Judah had waited so many years to hear.

"Thank you, my father," he said joyfully, "and thanks unto Jehovah, as well." Then putting his arm around Pharez's shoulders, he said, with great feeling, "May Jehovah bless you, my son."

18

Famine

Two more years passed with no rainfall. Jacob had to sell more and more animals. More money was given to the poor of Hebron, more added to the tithe urns, more added to the treasuries of each family. Another well near the houses had dried up and the garden well was not producing enough water for all the garden and household needs, certainly none for the animals.

Each family used as little grain, stored from previous years, as possible, but the supply had dwindled alarmingly. Many of the fruit and nut trees had died. There was little to store for the cold months. The tribe subsisted on the food the garden produced. They kept the few animals they had far away, bringing them home only as needed. Jacob and

Judah, and the others as well, became increasingly worried. Prayers were continuously offered to Jehovah for the removal of what seemed to be a curse on the land, but to no avail. Jehovah seemed to turn a deaf ear to them.

Through caravans that passed nearby, Jacob learned that all the surrounding lands were suffering drought as well, but there was corn in Egypt.

By late spring, Jacob's grain supply was so low that the families ate bread at only one meal daily. Jacob called his sons together. His voice was grave as he told them, "You know there is corn in Egypt. This you shall do. Go there and buy corn, all you can carry, and hurry back here, that we may eat and live. Some vegetables and fruits we still have, watered from the well, but we must have bread." He looked from one to the other to see how each would respond to his words. They all looked to Judah, standing by their father with Benjamin, and waited for him to speak.

"Will you go?" Judah asked. "It seems the only thing we can do." They nodded, and looking around at each other, Reuben spoke for them all, "Yes, we will go. We must. It is all that is left to us, lest we and our children starve." He looked at his father as he continued, "When shall we leave?"

"Early in the morning. No need to wait, for the time is short before all our grain is gone. Let each of you take two donkeys, one to ride so you can hurry, one to bring back the grain you buy. It will take less provender for them than for your camels. I will supply the money for all of you."

All were silent a while as they considered the journey. Finally Judah reminded them, "There will be much to get ready for the journey. Go now and we will meet here at daybreak to start."

They began to leave by twos and threes, talking among themselves about what they should carry. Benjamin started to leave also. Jacob put a hand on his arm.

"My son," he said, "you know I cannot let you go down with the others."

Disappointment showed on the young man's face. "Why not, Father?"

"Some mischief might befall you and I could not bear to lose you, my youngest, as I lost Joseph. It would kill me."

Benjamin did not argue, but turned away, visibly dejected.

"It will be a hard journey, my son," he said to him. "The other ten can bring back enough grain for us all. You have young children to see to, and I will need you with me to keep me company and help me if anything goes wrong here."

"Yes, my father," his youngest answered, but his head was bent and his shoulders sagged as he walked away.

And so it was that the ten went down into Egypt, accompanied by Jacob's faithful servant, Gerah, and Judah's servant, Ziba, while Jacob and Benjamin cared for things at home and waited eagerly for their return.

It took seventeen days instead of the fourteen Jacob had anticipated. The grain in all the houses was gone, and Jacob was nearly frantic, constantly watching the pathway for the return, and saying to Benji, "My son, how thankful I am to Jehovah that I did not let you go. I fear some mischief has befallen your brothers."

On the seventeenth day, just before sunset, as Benji, Judah's wife, Banah, Tamar, and the children watched with Jacob, Benjamin spied one of his brothers—he thought it was Judah— walking beside his donkey and leading one behind him.

"My father, they come! Can you not see them!" he cried. Before he finished, Pharez and Zarah were running down the pathway while the little girls, the women, and Jacob strained to see.

"Praise be to Jehovah!" exulted Jacob. "Who is leading, my son?"

"I think it is Judah, Father. Come, we will walk toward them and we can better tell as each comes into view."

They hurried forward and the women and girls followed. The other households had been watching also, and soon all were running down the pathway, calling greetings to their men.

When Pharez and Zarah reached their father, there were kisses, embraces, and excited words. Judah handed a donkey halter to each son and rushed toward his wife and Jacob and the others. Then he sank down to wait for his brothers. The other families ran past them to greet their own special ones. As Simeon's wife, Hoglah, and her children came close, Judah called to them to stop with him. Jacob and Benjamin were on the ground near him.

With hesitation, Judah began. "My father, Hoglah, you children of Simeon, you will not find Simeon with the others. He was forced to stay in Egypt for a while."

Hoglah cried out, sank to her knees before him. "Why? Why? What are you saying?"

"Don't be afraid," comforted Judah. "He will come later. It is a long story; we will tell it all to the whole tribe later, when we have eaten and rested."

By now Levi's family had met him and they all came to Judah. Levi looked forlorn without the brother he was closest to. Judah began again, "The man in charge of the grain—the one second only to Pharaoh himself—assumed we were spies. He asked all about our families. When we told him we were all sons of one man, he asked if there were other brothers. When we told him there was a younger one left at home, he spoke roughly to us and accused us again of being spies. At last, after he had kept us all in prison for three days, he chose Simeon to remain in prison until we should return with our youngest brother."

Jacob cried out at this. "No, no, I will not let Benjamin go!"

By now Simeon's wife was weeping softly and her children were crying aloud. Levi began to weep also, and his family joined in.

The other brothers and the two servants had now come with their families to join them, and there was much confusion. Jacob began to wail, "My son, my son! Oh, I am bereft of my children! Why has Jehovah done so to us?"

Judah stood up. "Stop, all of you!" he commanded. "I told you Simeon will come later. What's done is done for now. Come, we will talk about it when we have rested." He lifted Jacob up and Hoglah's children lifted her, trying to console her. Jacob walked unsteadily between Benjamin and Tamar, with Judah and his family close, while the other families went to their homes.

There could be little rejoicing in the homecoming for any of them, none at all for Simeon's family. Judah somehow felt responsible for what had happened and Jacob wept for the son he loved but was not close to, whom he had never really forgiven. He could imagine what fear and loneliness Simeon was feeling. *Why did not one of the others stay with him? Jehovah, why has this happened? I have lost so many already. Do you have some purpose to this? Are you punishing my tribe still?*

While Judah bathed and ate, Jacob and Benjamin went to Simeon's house to comfort his family. They finally convinced them that Simeon was in no great danger, that his brothers would soon return and secure his release. Jacob was thinking all the while, however, *They'll have to go without Benji. I will never risk his being taken from me!*

When they left Simeon's home, Benjamin went to his own, and Jacob returned to Judah's. When he went inside, he found Judah was already asleep, and he and Pharez and Zarah went back to sit on the stone steps, trying to figure out exactly what had happened in Egypt, and why. Pharez wanted to know what "spies" meant, and then why a ruler would think ten weary men from Hebron could be spies. They could only wonder.

Zarah asked, "Grandfather, you will let Uncle Benjamin go to Egypt, won't you? So Uncle Simeon can come home?"

"No, my son," answered Jacob. "We will have to find another way to get Simeon home."

"Maybe I could go, Grandfather. Wouldn't the ruler accept me instead of Uncle Benji?" asked Pharez.

"But I could never let you go either, and surely your father would not."

Weariness and worry finally drove the three into the house and to bed. But there was no sleep for Jacob.

On the morrow, by mid-morning, all the brothers had assembled at Judah's house. Some sat on the steps, some on the stone benches in the shade of the big terebinth tree. Their father and Judah sat in their accustomed places on the porch, with Pharez between them on the stone floor. Their women and servants had been up late grinding the grain from Egypt into flour. They all had bread for their morning meal, they were rested, and glad to be home. But sadness and worry pervaded the group. Simeon's absence cast an almost visible pall over the gathering.

"Tell me again what exactly took place when you reached Egypt, my sons," begged Jacob. Worry lines deeply etched his face.

The others waited and Judah spoke. "We came to an inn at nightfall, not far into the land. We inquired as to where the grain was sold. Only one man could understand our language. He said it was perhaps a three hour journey to where the governor, second only to Pharaoh, was selling the grain himself. We rested for the night, rose and dressed in fresh clothes, ate the food that was set before us, and left at daybreak. The land seemed strange and it was as dry and bare as our own. When we came near the city, crowds were coming from all directions. They were strangely dressed and they spoke strange languages."

Judah paused, then looked around. The others were nodding.

Levi spoke, "Some were on camels, some on donkeys, a few on wagons or carts, some on animals we did not know. Some were brown men, some black, some fair."

Reuben joined in. "I've been to Egypt before, but I never saw so many people. There must be famine in all the lands."

Now Judah continued, "When we found the big storehouses on the outskirts of the city, where the grain was being sold, we tied our donkeys and pushed through the crowds that were milling around the great porch, where the grain was weighed. There were many sweating men up there, handling the grain, but it was the governor himself, dressed in a fine purple robe and wearing a gold headdress, who was actually selling the grain. A man in good, but plain, raiment stood by him to interpret for him, taking the money and putting it into huge bags.

"We noticed that the governor kept looking at us, even before our turn to buy came. When it finally came, we bowed ourselves to the ground before him. 'Up, up!' he said roughly. 'Where do you come from?' When the interpreter spoke to us, we rose and I answered, 'From the land of Canaan.' The interpreter spoke my words to the governor. His face became hard and he spoke through the interpreter, 'You are spies, who have come to see the nakedness of the land!'

"I protested, 'No, my lord, we are here to buy food. We are all one man's sons; we are true men; your servants are not spies.'

"The governor seemed angrier than ever and repeated his same words in a loud voice, 'You are spies!' "

Levi turned to Jacob as the old man sat trembling. " So I said to the governor, 'Your servants are twelve brothers, the sons of one man in the land of Canaan; and behold, the youngest is this day with our father, and one is not.' "

Naphtali spoke up, "And so said we all, but the man said, 'No, it is even as I said to you. You are spies, and hereby you shall be proved: by the life of Pharaoh, you shall not go forth from this place except your youngest brother come here. Send one of you to fetch him, and the rest of you shall be kept in prison; so shall your words be proved, whether you tell the truth; otherwise, by the life of Pharaoh, I shall know you are spies.' "

When Naphtali paused, Gad continued the story. "We were very afraid and we protested, but the man called loudly and several men with spears and swords came and roughly dragged us off to the prison, some half a mile away. We were there for three days, all in one big room, down under the prison house. It was foul and dark, with only a few candles, and they brought us little food."

Asher said, "We thought we might die there. We didn't know what happened to our animals, but they let us keep our money. On the third day, the governor himself came down into the prison and brought us up into the outer court, where guards were all about. Then he said to us, 'This do, and live, for I fear God. If you are true men, let one of you be bound here in this upper prison, and the rest of you go and carry corn for your families. Then bring your youngest brother to me, and I shall know you are true men and not spies. So only shall you not die.' "

Dan spoke for the first time, "And this we agreed to. What else could we do?" He looked to his father for approval, as they all waited, fearful.

Jacob nodded. "Yes, it was all you could do. I see that." The sons breathed with relief, and satisfaction showed on their faces. "But I cannot let Benjamin go. Perhaps the man will change his mind, or you could take someone else."

The ten shook their heads, and Reuben said, "He will not change."

Both Issachar and Zebulun, though they had been silent, gave voice to the same surety, while the others nodded assent.

Jacob was silent as he looked around at them all, and tears began to course down his face. It was Benji who asked, "Why did the man keep Simeon?"

Dan answered, "When the governor demanded that one of us stay, he was the first to say he would. Others of us offered also, but the man chose the first, and had him bound before our eyes."

Jacob broke into loud sobs. Benji and Pharez joined him. Judah reached out his hand to console his father and his son. "My father, it will be well. You will see. Just let us return with Benjamin and we can all come back with another load of grain. What we've brought will not last long."

Jacob was adamant. "I will not be bereft of any more of my sons. I will never let Benji go!"

Pharez, child though he was, now spoke. "Could not you take me instead of Uncle Benji, Father? The man would not know I wasn't he and I would be safe with you." The men smiled at his seriousness, even Jacob, through his tears.

Judah tousled his son's hair fondly. "It is brave of you to offer, my son, but you are too young. We would never fool the governor."

Jacob spoke positively. "Nor would I ever consent to let you go from me either, my son."

All fell silent again, lost in thought, their faces troubled.

Finally Judah said, "There is something else you should know, Father. After Simeon was bound and taken away, we each gave the man our money. Then we waited in the upper prison. Food was brought to us and then the man's steward came and brought us out. Our donkeys were restored to us, each with his sack of provender refilled and the grain our money had bought. We took them and went back to the inn where we had first stopped. Levi opened his provender bag to feed his animal because it kept braying, and there, in his bag's mouth, was his money. We were very frightened. Then we each opened our own provender bags and found nothing. We did not open our grain bags until last night. Then each of us found his money in his grain bag. Is it not so, my brothers?"

"It is so," they all answered. "What can it mean?" Judah continued.

Jacob grew pale and his hands trembled. "I fear the man is up to some trick, perhaps that he may accuse you and keep your brother for a slave." He wept again.

"We will keep the rolls just as they are and take them back to him when we return. Be sure you keep them safe," Judah said to his brothers. Then he turned to Jacob. "Father, are there other questions you would ask?"

"I can think of nothing now. We will talk of it again when I have thought it over. Go now to your work before it is too hot, and then spend time with your families. You have been away long."

The brothers departed in small groups as always. Benji left with Judah last, and Pharez followed his father instead of staying with Jacob.

251

19

To Egypt a Second Time

Take also your brother, and arise, go again unto the man. . . .
If I be bereaved of my children, I am bereaved.

(Genesis 43:13-14)

. . . and Joseph said, . . . I am Joseph; doth my father yet live?
(Genesis 45:3)

And they told him, saying, Joseph is yet alive, and he is
governor over all the land of Egypt. And Jacob's heart fainted. . . .

(Genesis 45:26)

And Israel said, It is enough; Joseph my son is yet alive: I will
go and see him before I die.

(Genesis 45:28)

Days followed hot, wearying days, and always the
brothers talked of going back for Simeon. Simeon's wife and
children wept and often begged Jacob to send the brothers
back for him. Each time Jacob tried to send them back, they
reminded him it was no use without taking Benjamin. Each
time Jacob wept, but refused.

Another well failed completely and the garden well gave
less and less, so the garden did not produce enough

vegetables for the tribe, and many additional fruit trees died as well. Though the households used the grain from Egypt sparingly, it was running low again. In the late afternoons, Jacob and Pharez and Benjamin walked in the dry fields, wondering what was happening to Simeon, weeping and praying, seeking the will of Jehovah for their tribe.

The time finally came when Judah knew the grain in his house would not last another two weeks. When he questioned the others, he found it was the same. He told each one to meet in his home at mid-morning on the next day, for they must go back to Egypt for food, as well as to get Simeon. Judah, Jacob, and Pharez were again in their accustomed places on the porch as the others joined them.

Jacob was visibly upset and as he began to speak, he wept. "You have bereaved me of my children. Joseph is not," here his voice broke and Pharez took his trembling hand, weeping also. "And...Simeon is not, and now you want to take Benjamin away. I know that is why you have come. Everything is against me." He sobbed aloud and could not go on.

Reuben was the first to speak. "Father, you must let Benji go; it is the only way. Deliver him into my hand, and I will bring him safely back to you. If I do not, then you can slay my own two sons." The men looked at each other, wondering what would be their father's response.

Jacob spoke almost angrily. "That would not help; my son shall not go down with you! His brother is dead and he alone is left to me. If mischief befalls him by the way, then shall you bring my gray hairs with sorrow to my grave." He began weeping again.

Judah said, "Father, the grain is getting low; it will not last until we return even if we leave now."

"Then go again—now. Buy us more grain," pleaded Jacob.

"Now, Father, we've told you again and again that the governor told us emphatically that we should not see his face again unless we bring our brother with us. If you will send Benji with us, we will go and have food. If you will not, we will not go," said Judah positively.

Jacob asked petulantly, "Why did you deal so ill with me as to tell the man you had another brother?"

Naphtali spoke and the others assented. "The man asked us directly about our state and our kindred. He inquired, 'Is your father yet alive? Have you another brother?' How could we have known he would say, 'Bring your brother down?' " Jacob continued weeping as Pharez tried to console him. Benjamin begged his father to let him go.

Again Judah spoke, this time with authority, "Send Benji with me, and we will arise and go, that we may live and not die, nor you or our children. I will be surety for him. Of my hand you shall require him; if I do not bring him back and set him before you, then let me bear the blame forever." He paused and his father's weeping was the only sound, as the brothers looked at one another, waiting.

Judah continued, "If we had not lingered, but had taken Benji back with us weeks ago, we would surely have returned already, bringing Simeon with us."

"It is so," affirmed several brothers.

Jacob raised his gray head, dried his tears, and looked around at them all. When he spoke, it was as Israel, prince of God, not as the old, uncertain Jacob. There was no wavering, no weakness. His mind was at last made up. "If it must be so now, do this: take of the best fruits of the land in your grain bags, carry a present to the man—some balm, some choice honey, spices, and myrrh, nuts, and almonds. And take double your money in your hands, also the money that you brought back in the mouths of your sacks. Likely it was an oversight. Take also your brother,"—here the faces of all showed relief and Benji's showed pleasure,—"and go again to the man. May Jehovah, the Almighty God, give you mercy before the man, that he may send back your other brother and Benjamin. But if I lose you all, so be it. Go now, and prepare to leave when it is cool enough to travel. Come, Pharez, we shall see to the money while your father sees to the animals before the day becomes hotter." He turned to Judah. "Take Gerah and Ziba again."

The men scattered immediately to their own homes and

an hour before sunset, they were all back at Judah's house, and soon left. Jacob stood silently, watching the last animal go around the bend and out of sight, his face unhappy but calm. Benjamin's wife and small sons stood watching with him, and all were weeping. Pharez attempted to comfort both them and his grandfather. "You have done the right thing. Jehovah will care for them all, especially for Uncle Benji, so don't weep."

Jacob smiled. "It is so, my son. Come, we will walk his family to their home."

For all Jacob's determination not to worry or grieve, and for all the extra work that had to be done, with the sons and two servants gone, after the tenth day had passed, he and Pharez watched nightly for their return. They, along with Benji's wife and children, sat on Judah's porch and watched from sunset until darkness hid the path from sight. Then they would help Benji's wife, Serah, get her sleepy children home, before returning to their vigil.

On the fifteenth day, as they watched the path, a young servant came running from Zebulun's house, calling excitedly, "Master, master, men are coming from the direction of the caravan route. There are wagons and many donkeys. Could it be our people coming from that direction?"

Without taking time to consider, they all started toward the way the servant pointed. Pharez and Zarah were in the lead, Jacob close behind. Benjamin's two oldest sons followed, then the women with the smaller children.

As soon as Pharez saw the small caravan, he called out, "Grandfather, that is Father walking ahead. I know it is! And behind him are wagons drawn by such big donkeys!" He was still running, along with Zarah and Shelah, and soon they were in their father's arms.

By then all the families were running toward the caravan. The wagons stopped and Benjamin came running toward his father and family. Simeon outran him and reached his family first. Soon all the sons were reunited with their families and Jacob, and the air was filled with laughter and tears, and much praising of Jehovah.

Pharez was the first to ask about the wagons, now almost invisible in the fading light. "Where did you get the strange wagons, Father, and also the many big donkeys?"

"My son," answered Judah, a fond hand on the head of each son as they stood on either side, "it is a long story that will take long to tell. We are weary, the animals are hungry and thirsty. For now, let us just rejoice that all of us are back, safe and sound, with Benji and Simeon among us. We should each go to our homes and bathe and eat before we talk."

He turned to several servants who were standing behind the families. "Help Gerah and Ziba move the wagons closer, then unhitch the animals pulling them, and untie our donkeys. Pharez, Zarah, Shelah, you can help give them all food and water."

The sons joined their families and went to their own homes, and Judah walked with his father and family toward his. Jacob, so happy to have his sons home safely, was yet curious about the wagons. He noted the sparkle in Judah's eyes, even in the fading light, the spring in his step, the air of excitement about him. He asked, "My son, why did you take the caravan route?"

Judah answered, "With the wagons, it was easier, though it is longer and took an extra day. It was different and interesting, though. It runs through Grandfather Abraham's old city of Beersheba, and we stayed there last night. We rose long before daybreak and, except for two hours at mid-day, have been traveling hard all day."

"I know you are weary," observed Jacob, "but there is still some strange excitement about you. Can you not tell me what it is now?"

They were almost to the porch, where a lamp glowed. "Let us sit, Father," insisted Judah. He helped Jacob up the two stone steps and led him to his accustomed seat, near the lamp.

"Father, what I have to tell you is so unbelievable, so wonderful, that I don't know whether you can bear it. Still I have waited long enough. Father, your son Joseph is alive!" Jacob stared at him blankly, not taking in his words.

Judah repeated slowly, holding his father's arm, "Joseph—is—still—alive, <u>alive</u>, do you hear? He is governor of all Egypt. He is the man who sold us the grain, the one who kept Simeon."

Comprehension came into Jacob's mind, and showed in his eyes. He tried to speak but could not. Then he fainted and would have fallen forward had not Judah caught him. Judah cried out loudly, "Banah, Tamar, bring water. My father dies! Hurry!" Even by the lamplight, he could see the deathly pallor on Jacob's face. He slapped him briskly with his free hand, while with the other he kept him from falling.

The women came running. Tamar's maid carried a pitcher of water, which she splashed on Jacob's face. Jacob caught his breath sharply, and began to tremble violently. Judah watched the color come back to his face. He and Tamar and Banah laid him on the stone floor, as a maid came with a pillow and some blankets. Benji, hearing the commotion as he came from tending the animals, ran up. "What is wrong with Father?" he asked with fear in his voice.

"He fainted at the news. Here, help me get him on a blanket," said Judah, as Tamar took it from the maid and spread it on the floor. When Jacob was laid on it, she put the pillow under his head and covered him with another blanket.

Judah asked, "Father, are you better?"

Jacob's lips moved, but no sound came forth. By now several other sons and Shelah, Pharez and Zarah ran up, asking what had happened.

"When I told him Joseph is alive, he fainted. Now he shakes and cannot speak. But he will be better soon. The news is too wonderful to believe," answered Judah as he turned to Banah. "Could we get a little wine for him?"

"Of course," his wife answered, then ran to fetch it.

"Father," said Benji, "the wine will revive you and help you to stop shaking."

Reuben asked, "Shouldn't we put him on his bed?" Jacob shook his head. The tired, hungry men waited anxiously around their father, speaking in low voices, not wanting to leave till they knew he was all right.

When Banah returned, she brought a cup of wine for Jacob, and her maid brought a large bowlful for the others. While Judah held Jacob's head up, Benji took the cup to help him drink. The bowl was passed around to all the brothers. Just then, Tamar's maid came with cheese, apricots, raisins, and a little bread. Judah wondered how she had saved enough grain for the bread, and he silently blessed her. He and Benji ate their portions after Jacob had finished the wine, each sitting on the floor beside him.

"Father, do you want more wine or some of the food?" asked Benji. Jacob shook his head; his eyes remained closed.

When the food was gone, Reuben came near his father and asked, "My father, can we not put you to bed?"

Weakly Jacob answered, "No. I must hear from all of you about Joseph. Reuben, is my son still alive?"

"Aye, Father, he is alive indeed. You cannot imagine the splendor he enjoys, for he is governor of all Egypt, second only to Pharaoh himself."

Benji spoke up. "He sent you the wagons, Father, and ten donkeys laden with the good of the land."

Zebulun spoke from the steps, "And he sent also ten more female donkeys loaded with corn and bread and meat for later."

"For later?" questioned Jacob.

Judah now told his father that Joseph wanted them all to go to Egypt to live. "He commanded us to bring you and all our households down to him to live. Will it not be wonderful to see him again?"

Jacob paled at the words and he burst into tears.

Gad assured him, "He sent the wagons so that you and our families could go, along with our tithe urns and other treasures."

"The good of the land of Egypt shall be ours," added Dan. "You will go, won't you?"

"I could not make so long a trip. He must come to me," answered Jacob.

"Father, he cannot leave Egypt," said Asher. "Everything depends on him there."

Jacob was silent awhile. Then he said, "It is enough; Joseph my son is still alive. I will go and see him before I die."

The brothers breathed a sigh of relief. "There is so much more to tell you, Father," said Benji, "but we are tired and it is all too much for you. Judah and I will get you to bed, and the others can go home to rest and be with their families. You are all right, are you not?"

"My strength seems gone," said Jacob, struggling to stand. Judah and Benjamin helped him to rise and helped him inside to bed, while the others left. Assured that his father was comfortable, Benji went home to his family. Judah went to his own family, leaving Jacob's servant to care for him. Jacob, too excited to sleep at the prospect of seeing his long-lost Joseph, wept and talked far into the night, thanking Jehovah over and over that Joseph was alive, that Benji and Simeon and the others had come safely back to him.

The sun was far on its journey when Benjamin came to see about his father, after all the households had risen late. He was relieved that Jacob was not only all right but very excited. He and Judah had just finished the morning meal, relishing the dried fish and several breads and cakes Joseph had sent, and talking about Joseph.

Jacob beamed at Benji. "My son, how happy I am to have you back with me. Tell me, did Joseph look the way you remembered him?"

"Father, I was only five when he left. He did not at all fit the vague memory I had of him. His face is now brown and he has a beard—black, like his heavy hair. And, oh, the richness of his dress! None of us would have ever known him. I'm sure Judah told you it was Joseph who recognized us."

Judah said, "I suppose none of us but Benji has changed much since he went away."

"Tell me how Joseph came to be in Egypt," Jacob suddenly demanded.

Judah looked uncomfortably at Benjamin, a question in his eyes.

Benji returned his look for a long moment; then he said, with a nod, "Tell him now."

Judah began hesitantly, "Father, I have been sorry a long, long time; I have repented of the deed and paid for it over and over. My brothers and I—we sold Joseph to merchants going into Egypt."

Jacob's head jerked sharply toward Judah and his face blanched as comprehension of Judah's words came to him.

"What are you saying?" he screamed in consternation.

Judah continued, "I know it was a wicked thing to do, a grievous sin—against him, against you. But we were young then, and we hated Joseph because you loved him best. You gave him the coat of many colors; you always favored him because it was his mother, not ours, that you loved." Judah's words came slowly, painfully, his eyes averted from his father's.

As he paused, Jacob, remembering, had to admit that what he said was true. He was trembling violently; his face was ashen. Benji put out a hand to steady him. There was a long silence, then Jacob burst into sobs. Judah still could not look at his father, and was himself weeping.

Jacob struggled for composure. Finally, he said brokenly, "It is true. But one cannot control whom he loves most. You know that. You also know Laban tricked me into marrying your mother. I could not help not loving her then, but I did come to love her later. You cannot deny that."

"It is true," admitted Judah, still not facing Jacob.

The patriarch continued, "I should not have shown my favoritism for Joseph. I've known that for a long time. But how could you do such a terrible thing to him, your own brother, and to me?"

"We hated Joseph more than ever after he told us about his dream of our sheaves bowing down to his sheaf as we were binding in the field. And you even rebuked him when he told his second dream of the sun and moon and the eleven stars making obeisance to him."

"I remember," said Jacob. "It did seem arrogant that his dream suggested that his mother and I and you, his brothers,

261

should bow ourselves to him."

"But we <u>did</u>, Father; every one of his brothers, even Benji, bowed to him many times in Egypt. The dreams came true," Judah affirmed.

Jacob wept aloud again, his head bowed, Benji stroking it to comfort him. At last he recovered again. "Go on with the story."

Judah resumed, "When you sent Joseph to us when we were in Shechem with the flocks, we had already gone to Dothan. He found us there. When we saw him coming, we conspired to slay him and throw him into a pit nearby and to tell you an evil beast had devoured him. Oh, then we would see what would become of his high and mighty dreams! But Reuben said we should not kill our own flesh and blood; he said we should just throw him into the deep pit near us there in the wilderness. This we did, after we had stripped off his fine coat."

Again Jacob sobbed aloud, before asking, "How could you have been so cruel—to him and to me? I wonder why Jehovah did not strike you dead."

"So did I, later," Judah went on. "But then we left him and soon reached the caravan route. There we saw a company of Ishmaelites going into Egypt with spices and balm and myrrh. I said we should sell Joseph to them and my brothers agreed. All except Reuben, who had gone off hunting a stray lamb. We went back and drew Joseph out of the pit and sold him to the Ishmaelites. They sold him to Potiphar, a captain of Pharaoh's guard. This we learned from Joseph after he made himself known to us on this last trip." Sorrow and shame were heard in Judah's voice, and he did not lift his head as his tears fell.

Jacob and Benjamin were both sobbing loudly now. Tears were pouring down their faces, also.

"How could you? How could you?" cried Jacob. "Sell your brother for a slave! And then come bringing his bloody coat and lie to me that a beast had killed him!" Jacob was angry now as well as grief-stricken.

For the first time Judah wept aloud also. When he could speak again, he said quietly, "No, Father. We brought you the coat, dipped in a kid's blood, but it was you who said a beast devoured him."

Jacob was quieter now but his voice still held anger. "But you let me think it! You could have told me the truth!"

"Reuben wanted to tell you, but we would not let him," continued Judah. "I think you would have killed us all."

Jacob went sadly on, "You let me grieve all these years. Yet at first you pretended to comfort me! I don't think I can ever forgive you."

"Joseph has," returned Judah, with wonder in his voice. "When he made himself known to us, he said, 'Do not be grieved nor angry with yourselves, that you sold me, for it was God who sent me here to preserve life.' "

"That is so like my son," mused Jacob, and both he and Benji wept again. At last he asked, "Joseph knew you the first time you went. Why did he keep Simeon and make you take Benji to him?"

Benji answered him, as Judah wept. "Perhaps he wanted to make sure they would go back, Father. And he did want to see me, also."

Judah spoke, "He was testing us, Father, to see whether we now cared more for Benji and for you than we had cared for him, whether we had repented of our evil to him. He is wise, Father. Jehovah, through his years of suffering, has made him so." Judah paused, then went on, "And we have repented, Father. You must surely know that. Have we not tried to comfort and to take care of you and obey you these many years? Even at first, when we saw your anguish, and came to ourselves, we felt the guilt. Then as we saw you grieve year after year, and remembered how Joseph had cried and begged us not to do the evil thing to him—when all of it went over and over in our minds, we were sorry. After I lost Er and Onan, I could really know how you grieved. Many times we would have told you, but we thought it would be even harder if you knew Joseph was alive and yet did not know what had finally befallen him."

Jacob wept quietly now, and Judah and Benji were silent. Benjamin was trying to piece together the story he had heard only days before, and then only in parts. Judah was bowed in grief and shame.

After a while, Jacob seemed to have wept away some of his anguish and all of his anger. He demanded softly, "Tell me how Joseph made himself known to you."

Judah raised his head, looking at his father tearfully. He began, "When he saw us at the place where he sells the corn, he spoke to the steward of his house, and the man came to us and told us we were to dine at the governor's house. We were afraid; we thought it had to do with the money we had found in our sacks and that he would take away our animals and hold us as slaves. We talked among ourselves while the steward found servants who took our animals and money away. Then he bade us to follow him, and when we came to the governor's fine house, we told him how we had found the money in our sacks, and that we had brought it back to him this time. He said something strange that we could not understand. His very words were, 'Peace be unto you; fear not. Your God, and the God of your father, has given you treasure in your sacks; I had your money.' " He paused, "Is it not so, Benji?"

"His very words," confirmed Benjamin. "Father, do you think Jehovah did put the money in our sacks?"

"Who can tell?" answered Jacob. "Jehovah's ways are strange."

"When we were inside the house—oh, how huge and splendid it was! We couldn't stop staring at the fine furnishings. He bade us sit and went away. Servants brought water and washed our feet."

Benji took up the story excitedly, "And when he came back, Father, he had Simeon with him. I don't know whether he was happier to see us or we him. We all hugged him and wept. Then he asked if you were well, and how you finally had agreed to let me come with my brothers."

Judah went on, "The steward now said we were to dine with the governor and went away. We talked among ourselves at the strange turn of events. We made ready your present for the governor when he should come at noon. We were still so fearful, trembling when he came. We gave him the present and bowed ourselves to the earth. His dream was fulfilled again! He seemed pleased with the gift. He smiled and said, 'Rise!' We did so and he continued, 'Is all well with you? Your father, the old man of whom you spoke, is he yet alive? Is he well?' It was Reuben who answered him. 'We are well; our father is truly alive and in good health.' We all bowed our heads and made obeisance at the governor's gracious manner. He looked around, on us all, and then his eyes rested on Benji. 'Is this your younger brother you spoke to me of?' As we nodded, he smiled and said to him, 'God be gracious to you, my son.' Then his face changed, as if he would weep, and he left us immediately. The interpreter made us welcome and soon the steward came and led us to another large room, with tables. We were seated at a long one, on the far side of the room. There were Egyptians seated at an even-longer table on the other side, laughing and talking among themselves. After a while, the governor came and sat by himself at a huge table in the center, where the steward waited. He spoke and the steward went out and servants then began to bring in food, which they set on his table.

"As he looked upon us, he called the interpreter, and they both came to our table. When the governor spoke, the interpreter bade us stand, then move as he directed. The governor pointed to Reuben and the interpreter put him at the head of the table. Then Simeon was put next to him, then Levi and me, and on down to Benji, according to our ages, so that we marveled greatly. Then the governor returned to his table and sent messes of the food to us."

Benji spoke excitedly, "And, Father, he sent me five times as much food as the others!"

"Did he, indeed?" asked Jacob, smiling broadly.

Judah resumed, "When we were all served, he sent food to all the Egyptians, and more servants brought in wine for all. The governor talked with us through his interpreter all during the meal, and we were all merry together, enjoying more food than we had ever seen before. When we had eaten as much as we could, the governor bade us have a safe journey home. Then he left us in the charge of the interpreter and the steward. They led us back to the other room and had us rest until it was cool enough to explore the city. So we rested and walked through parts of the beautiful house and surrounding grounds. Then the interpreter gave us more wine and showed us around the city. Oh, such wonders as we never imagined! But more of that later. We stayed at the governor's house that night, after being assured our animals were cared for. Again there was much food, but not in the same room where we ate before, and the governor we did not see.

"When it was day, we were given more food and sent away with our animals, loaded with grain. We had not gone far out of the city, not even to the inn, when the steward and the interpreter and some officers overtook us. The interpreter said, 'Our lord's silver cup is missing— the one whereby he does divination. Have you so rewarded evil for good that you have taken it from him?'

"We were filled with consternation and fear. Simeon spoke up first. 'Why would you accuse us? God forbid that we should do this to the governor who has been gracious to us!' Levi continued, 'We brought again unto you the money we found in our sacks; why then should we steal either silver or gold from your lord's house?'

"Then I said, 'Search us and our sacks. If the cup is found with one of us, let him die and we will be the governor's bondmen.'

"The steward answered, 'So shall it be, except that he with whom it is found only shall be kept as a bondman, and the others shall be free.'

"Then we each took down our sacks from our animals, and he searched them. There in each sack was our money again, but no cup—until he came to the last, Benjamin's. There it was!"

Judah paused and Benji said, "Father, you know I did not take the cup!" Jacob nodded and he went on, "I was so frightened, I began to tremble and could not speak."

Judah continued, "We all were. We cried out and tore our clothes; then we put all the sacks back on our animals and returned to the city with the steward and officers. We went straight to the governor's house. He had not yet gone to the selling floor. We fell before him on our faces, protesting our innocence. He spoke sternly, 'What have you done? Do not you know certainly that I can divine?' I said to him, 'What can we say to you? How can we clear ourselves? God has found out our iniquity; behold, we are your servants, both we and him with whom the cup is found.' But he answered, 'God forbid. Just the man in whose hand the cup is found, he shall be my servant. You others go in peace to your father.'

"But I came near unto him again and bowed. I asked him to let me speak again to him and that he not be angry with me. 'For,' said I, 'You are as Pharaoh.' He gave me leave to speak. Then I reminded him that he had asked us when we first came if we had a father and another brother. 'We told you that we did, my lord,' I told him. 'Our father is old, he had a child of his old age, a young man. His brother is dead, and he alone is left of his mother, and our father loves him dearly. Sir, you told us to bring him down to you that you might see him. We told you that if he left his father, his father would die. Then you said to us that except we brought him down with us, we would see your face no more.'

"Father, I then told him what a hard time we had convincing you to let us take Benji with us, that you would not consent until all our grain was gone. I also told him that I had become surety for my brother unto you, that if I did not bring him back to you, I should bear the blame to you forever. Then I cried out to him with tears, 'If I go back to my father without the young man, my father will die, for his life is bound up in his son's life. Thus we will bring down our father's gray hairs with sorrow to the grave.' Then I begged. 'Oh, sir, let me stay as a bondman to you instead of my brother, and let him go back to his father with the others. I cannot go back to my father without the lad, for I know what will happen to my father if I do.'

"When I said this, the governor cried out and everyone but us left him immediately. I was still bowed before him. He lifted me to my feet and suddenly began to weep aloud. Then he said, in our language, 'I am Joseph. Oh, tell me, does my father truly yet live?'

"We were very troubled and more afraid than ever and we moved away from him. Then he said, 'Come near to me, I beg of you.' He was weeping still, so we came near. Again he said, 'I am Joseph, your brother, whom you sold into Egypt. Now do not be grieved nor angry with yourselves, for it was God who sent me here to preserve life. Already the famine has been two years in the land, and there are yet five more years when there shall be no harvest. So, you see, God sent me before you to preserve you a posterity in the land, and to save your lives by a great deliverance. It was not you that sent me here, but God—our God, Jehovah. And He has made me a father to Pharaoh and lord of his house and a ruler throughout all the land of Egypt, as you see.'

"We were still so amazed and frightened we could not speak. He continued, 'Hurry now and go up to my father and tell him, your son Joseph is yet alive and God has made him lord of all Egypt; come down to me, do not wait. You and all our family shall live in the land of Goshen, near me. Bring your flocks and herds and all you have, and I will surely take care of you, lest you and all your family come to starvation, for there are yet five years of famine.' Then he said, 'Behold, you, and even my brother Benjamin, see me with your own eyes, you know I am Joseph. Tell my father of all my glory in Egypt and of all you have seen, then hurry and bring my father to me.' " Judah paused for breath.

"My father," declared Benji, "the governor is truly Joseph. He told me and we wept together. Then he kissed me and all of the others and wept with them. Then we all talked a long time together. And afterwards, Joseph called his steward and bade him go to Pharaoh's house and tell him that his brothers had come. When the man returned, there was an officer of Pharaoh with him who spoke our language.

He told Joseph how pleased Pharaoh was, along with all his house."

Judah took up the story. "He even told Joseph to have us hurry back and invite you to bring all your households down to him. And he promised to give us the good of the land of Egypt. His very words were, 'You shall eat of the fat of the land. Now I command you to take wagons out of Egypt for your wives and your children and bring your father, and come. Don't regard your possessions, for the good of the land of Egypt is yours.' And Joseph gave us the wagons, as Pharaoh had commanded, and filled them with the good things you have seen. And he gave us ten extra donkeys loaded with good food for you to eat now, and ten more with grain and bread and food that will not spoil for the trip back to Egypt.

"So we departed and came as fast as we could. Father, you have seen it all; you know we speak the truth. You will go, won't you?"

Jacob's eyes were radiant with joy and wonder. It was again Israel, prince of God, who spoke, forcefully and decisively, "It is enough. Joseph my son is yet alive. I will go and see him before I die."

Epilogue

And Israel took his journey with all that he had, and came to Beersheba, and offered sacrifices unto the God of his father Isaac.

And God spake unto Israel in the visions of the night, and said, Jacob, Jacob. And he said, Here am I.

And he said, I am God, the God of thy father: fear not to go down into Egypt; for I will there make of thee a great nation:

I will go down with thee into Egypt; and I will also surely bring thee up again: and Joseph shall put his hand upon thine eyes.

And Jacob rose up from Beersheba: and the sons of Israel carried Jacob their father, and their little ones, and their wives, in the wagons which Pharaoh had sent to carry him.

And they took their cattle, and their goods, which they had gotten in the land of Canaan, and came into Egypt, Jacob, and all his seed with him . . .

(Genesis 46:1-6)

Other Books by Helen Wood:

Prince of God
(prequel to *Jacob of Canaan*)
paperback/$8.00

A Brief Summary of the Bible
paperback/$4.00

Obtain both for $10.00

To purchase these titles or to correspond, please send to:

Helen Wood
Rte. 2, Box 354
Georgiana, AL 36033